The Adventures of Miss Wiseman

The untold story of an Australian actress

Published by Libby Cameron / Lulu Press

Design: Libby Cameron
Front cover image: Frances Jane Wiseman c. 1864-65. Reproduced courtesy of the Australian Performing Arts Collection, Arts Centre Melbourne.

ISBN 978-1-7635786-2-3 (Paperback)
ISBN 978-1-7635786-3-0 (ebook)

A catalogue record for this book is available from the National Library of Australia.

This story is based on true events.

Acknowledgement of Country

I live in Turramurra, Sydney, New South Wales, Australia, home to the Terramattagal people of the Eora Nation.

This story is about Miss Frances Jane Wiseman, who lived and worked in many parts of the world, but predominantly in Victoria, Australia.

I acknowledge the traditional owners of the land on which I live, and in which Miss Wiseman and many people in this story lived.

I pay my respects to Elders past, present and emerging.

Always was and always will be Aboriginal land.

Cultural Advice

There may be some terms or views in the book that were historically acceptable to some sections of the community, but these views are not appropriate now.

There is no intention to cause offence of any kind.

Thanks

To all the volunteers who have donated their time transcribing records for the Trove website (the Australian online library database). With the click of the mouse, I was able to undertake extensive research from my home office.

To my Aunty-in-law, Nicola Cameron, for her guidance and advice.

To my husband, Daylan, for listening to all my ideas and discoveries, and for his unwavering support and love.

To all my family and friends who encouraged me.

Contents

Acknowledgement of Country		
Cultural Advice		
Chapter 1	The interview	1
Chapter 2	Melbourne, Victoria	15
Chapter 3	Gold	37
Chapter 4	Back Creek, Victoria	47
Chapter 5	Lamplough, Victoria	55
Chapter 6	Bendigo and Ballarat, Victoria	59
Chapter 7	New Zealand	69
Chapter 8	Adelaide, South Australia	79
Chapter 9	Mrs Hall and Mrs South	93
Interlude		115
Chapter 10	Calcutta, the winter capital of India	117
Chapter 11	Simla, the summer capital of India	127
Chapter 12	Death on the trains	135
Chapter 13	My darling son	149
Chapter 14	England	157
Chapter 15	Back to Australia	169
Chapter 16	Topsy	179
Chapter 17	Touring with *The Cabin*	195
Chapter 18	The Firm	205
Chapter 19	Sydney, New South Wales	213
Chapter 20	Wedding anniversary	223
Chapter 21	Changing times	239
Chapter 22	Skating on thin ice	251
Chapter 23	Old love, new love	257
Interlude		273

Chapter 24 The courthouse 275
Chapter 25 Two more daughters 291
Chapter 26 A new century 301
Chapter 27 The war to end all wars 317
Chapter 28 The last act 333
Interlude 339
Epilogue 341
Author's note
Timeline of events
Family tree
Photographs
Endnotes

To my family, who inspire me every day.

Chapter One – The interview

I'd been ready for hours.

I heard the familiar knock on my door, followed by my nurse Mary Catherine, entering my room.

'Excuse me Miss Wiseman, your young man from *The Herald* is downstairs,' she said with her Irish accent and a big smile.

'Thank you Sister Kitty, I'll be there in a minute.' Everyone called her Kitty; it was the name given to her when she was young.

Sister Kitty shared my excitement. It's not every day a journalist interviews you for the newspaper. Mr Robinson telephoned me a few weeks ago to ask if I was interested in 'telling my story' in a three-part weekly series in his newspaper. The answer was of course, 'yes.' I am an actress after all!

As I entered the parlour, I could see a tall, slim young man. He was wearing a suit, and his white shirt had the modern soft collar.

'Good morning Mr Robinson,' I offered my hand for him to shake.

'Hello Miss Wiseman, I'm so pleased to meet you. I hope you're feeling well today.'

'Yes, extremely well for an 81 year old. I don't mind telling you how old I am. After our interview, you'll know a lot more about me than just my age.'

I think I saw a slight blush on the young man's cheeks. I hadn't expected that, but I guess he'd already done some research about my life.

'Thank you Miss Wiseman. Shall we sit down here? Are you comfortable?'

I nodded yes.

He had indicated the red plush couch where I loved to sit in the morning, it was the perfect spot to feel the warmth of the rising sun.

He took a fountain pen and paper from his leather satchel and sat down on the straight-backed wooden chair near the small wooden table. He was perched on the edge of his seat. I hope he's comfortable, I thought to myself, as we may be here awhile.

Mr Robinson tilted his head to the left and looked over his spectacles. I could see he had an inquisitive look, a passion to ask questions, listen and learn. I had lived through some remarkable times in Australia, travelled the world, and had worked with the best actors that had 'trod the boards.' It was 1927, and I wondered if current day Australians would be interested in my life, the things I'd seen and the things I'd done. Things were so different now compared to when I was young.

Mr Robinson then asked me, 'Please tell me what you remember of your life, start as far back as you like.'

I closed my eyes.

What do I remember? Memories extending over the allotted span of life are many and varied, and oh, I have such a host from which to choose. Memories drab and bright, memories sad and happy, but thankfully, the latter predominate.

I opened my eyes.

'Mr Robinson, let us begin at the beginning, as they say in the story books, and for me the beginning was in London.'

And so, my story begins.

*

I was born on the 20th September 1846 and was christened Frances Jane Wiseman. My father, Richard, was a master tailor and an outfitter to several large theatrical companies in the North of London. He would often be called urgently at night to the theatre to help with costume malfunctions.

He was welcomed backstage by flamboyant and extravagant characters, and he fell in love with the excitement of the stage. His love of the theatre rubbed off on me and my sisters and brother.

My mother, Mary Ann, was the kindest soul you could ever meet. She and father shared a love of the theatre and were always attending the first night of any new production.

My sister Emily was two years older than me. Our parents took us to the theatre twice while we lived in London. The first time, we went to Sadler's Wells Theatre in Islington, to see Mr Samuel Phelps in Shakespeare's *Henry IV*. The second time we went to see Mr William Hoskins perform as Dr Ollapod in Coleman's *The Poor Gentleman*.

When I was four years old, the great Mr Ira Aldridge, the African-American actor, came to see my father about some costumes. My sister Emily and I were at the top of the stairs, out of sight but within listening distance to any visitor entering the house. We could hear Mr Aldridge talking. His accent was so unusual and so lovely. We edged down the stairs a little and could just see Mr Aldridge from our vantage point. He was sitting in the parlour, listening intently to what father was saying.

I had heard father talking to mother about Mr Aldridge only that morning. Father described him as a 'gentleman of colour' who was receiving great acclaim as an actor. He had the lead roles in several Shakespearean plays in London. Apparently, he had moved to London to escape discrimination. At the time, I didn't understand what the word 'discrimination' meant. When I was a little older, the meaning of the word and the awful ramifications became very clear.

My father called my name, and I raced down the stairs. He picked me up and stood me on the small footstool and asked me to recite a poem.

I said, 'Good morning sir,' and curtsied.

Mr Aldridge bowed and said, 'How do you do Miss Wiseman, it's a pleasure to make your acquaintance.'

I smiled and started to recite one of my favourite poems, *A Red Red Rose* by Robert Burns,

O my Luve is like a red, red rose
That's newly sprung in June;
O my Luve is like the melody
That's sweetly played in tune.

So fair art thou, my bonnie lass,
So deep in luve am I;
And I will luve thee still, my dear,
Till a' the seas gang dry.

Till a' the seas gang dry, my dear,
And the rocks melt wi' the sun;
I will love thee still, my dear,
While the sands o' life shall run.

And fare thee weel, my only luve!
And fare thee weel awhile!
And I will come again, my luve,
Though it were ten thousand mile.

Mr Aldridge was so impressed, he told my father that I ought to go on the stage.

The seed had been sown.

*

We lived at 1 Wilsted Street, Somers Town, in St Pancras, North London, in a two-storey terrace. Emily and I loved watching the comings and goings of our parents. They were busy with the tailor shop and would often leave us with Helen. Helen lived a few streets away with her large family; she was one of 11 children. She was only 10 years older than me, but seemed very much like an adult. She'd help mother with my little brother Richard, who was two years old, and sister Alice, who was just a baby. She'd also help Emily and me in the morning, with combing our hair and getting us dressed.

Mother knew Helen's family was struggling, and she would give her a few shillings every week. She told Emily and me that a few shillings would help keep Helen out of the workhouse.

Helen always seemed like she was in a hurry, which would vex Emily and me, but just when things would be reaching boiling point, she'd give us a wink and say,

'You know girls, I love ye like me own little sisters, now stop dawdling.'

Emily and I would often be outside playing with the neighbourhood children. We were very fond of Mr James and Sarah Appleby's children, Thomas and Ann. Mrs Appleby would happily hand over little Ann, who was two years old, to Emily, who would expertly carry her on her hip, as she'd seen mother do with Richard and Alice. Thomas was four years old and would follow me around like a little puppy.

As a treat, sometimes Mr Appleby would give us a small cup of coffee with sugar. He was the coffee housekeeper of The Somers Town Coffee House, which we thought was very exotic. We'd often see well-dressed gentlemen in the coffee house – either in quiet and serious discussions or loudly talking and gesticulating with their hands.

I thought life was wonderful exactly as it was, and I didn't want anything to change. But life has a funny way of surprising us with the unexpected.

We were returning home after attending Sunday mass in St Pancras Church. My little brother Richard was walking slowly, holding Helen's hand and pointing at all the different houses and telling Helen who lived in them. Helen listened and nodded every time Richard looked up at her.

Mother was pushing the perambulator, and now and then she'd look down at little Alice to make sure she hadn't woken up.

As we turned the corner from Chapel Path into our street, we could see a commotion of people, smoke and fire. Father started running in the direction of our home. Mother stopped walking and stood as still as a statue. She was looking directly at our house, and I could see that her eyes were full of tears. Alice woke up and started crying, adding to the distress we were all feeling.

Our neighbours, the Appleby's were standing on the street with their little Thomas and Ann. They were frightened their house would also catch fire. When they saw mother, they hurried over and stood next to her, consoling her and offering their deepest sympathies.

I can still feel the heat from the roaring fire and the sound of people rushing back and forth with buckets of water. In those days, when a fire took hold, there was almost nothing anyone could do to stop it. Our house and all our belongings were destroyed. The Appleby's house was saved, and for that we were all grateful.

This became a real turning point for my family.

Our uncle and auntie took us into their home while we were recovering from the shock of the fire. Then one night after our evening meal, father asked us to join him in the sitting room, as he wanted to speak to the whole family. He announced that we would be leaving England to try our luck in the Dominions. He said there were lots of people emigrating to Australia, mostly to Sydney and Melbourne, and that's where we'd be going. The climate was better, employment was more constant, wages were higher, and gold had been discovered.

He said, 'Life will be better.'

Emily and I looked at each other. I think we were both stunned. My little brother and sister were too young to understand. I was seven years old, and even I didn't really understand.

My imagination started running wild. We were going to a strange place on the other side of the world.

I was excited. But no one told me how much I would miss my grandparents, my aunties and uncles and my adorable little cousins. No one told me how long the journey would take or what to expect when we arrived. And I suppose even if they had told me, it could not have prepared me.

*

We boarded the *Saldanha*, one of the Black Ball Line sailing ships, on the 18th March 1854. The wooden clipper had only been built the previous year. It sailed from the port of Liverpool, so we had left my hometown a few days earlier, as the distance from St Pancras to Liverpool was over 200 miles. It was a cold and windy day, which seemed to mirror my emotions. I took Emily's hand in mine, and as always, we were united in our feelings.

The bells were rung, and visitors were ordered ashore. We heard one of the sailors call out, 'cast off,' and our adventure began. Emily and I, still holding each other's hands firmly, smiled at each other as we left England.

There were 676 passengers onboard the *Saldanha.* Father had paid for our second-class tickets, so we had a cabin below the poop deck. We'd brought some clothing, utensils, extra provisions and bedding to fit out our berth.

Life on board the ship quickly fell into a routine. Emily and I would help mother with breakfast and prepare Richard and Alice for the day. We were then sent off to school, which we didn't mind at all. We enjoyed seeing all the other children who were of a similar age to us. We would return to our cabin just before 1:00 pm to have a meal, and then the afternoons were our own. Emily and I were allowed to go to the poop deck and some other areas on the ship unaccompanied, as long as we stayed together. My little brother Richard was five years old and Alice only four, so they had to stay with mother and father.

We were keenly aware of places we could not go on the ship, and the command deck was one such area. We had seen Captain Finlay from a distance. He had dark hair and a kind-looking face. He always walked with purpose, and he had a loud, booming, commanding voice. We knew to keep our distance from him as he had serious work to do.

Emily and I quickly discovered the joy of observing and interacting with people from all walks of life. We were, I suppose, precocious children. I was like Emily's shadow, and wherever she went, I was sure to follow.

The ship became our playground, and we would often walk from bow to stern, singing and laughing. We would imagine we were princesses travelling to foreign lands, who were then shipwrecked and befriended by mermaids. Or we were swashbuckling pirates, mean and nasty, growling at each other and having pretend sword fights.

We would call out to people we knew.

'Good morning, Mrs O'Malley.'

'Good morning, Miss McGreal.'

They, in turn, would nod their heads, smile or give us a wave. Miss McGreal was our favourite. She was tall and elegant. She had lovely auburn hair and translucent pale skin. Her eyes were emerald green, and we imagined they were the same colour as the green hills of Ireland, her homeland. She told us that she was travelling to Melbourne to work in The Royal Melbourne Hospital. She was a nurse, just like our grandmother. We thought she was the prettiest lady on board, other than our mother, of course. She was travelling with her brother, Mr Finnian McGreal. He walked with a limp and used a walking stick. We heard the reason for his limp was due to a terrible accident. He and his sister had been walking along a road in Dublin, Ireland, when a horse pulling a carriage reared up suddenly. The horse lost its balance and was going to fall on top of Miss McGreal, but her brother quickly pushed her aside, out of harm's way. The horse fell on him instead.

He was never far from his sister's side.

We would often watch the sun set over the ocean and marvel at the colours in the sky.

There was always something happening on board the ship. Sometimes there were dances, or passengers would get together and put on a theatrical or musical performance. But the more mundane things still had to be done. We would help clean our bedding once a week, but that only happened if we had fine weather, as we had to carry the bedding onto the deck and shake it out and air it. We also had to regularly wash down the cabin with soap and water.

Our parents would read to us every night. Our favourite book at the time was *A Wonder-Book for Boys and Girls* by Nathaniel Hawthorne. The book had stories about King Midas and his 'Golden Touch,' and other Greek myths. Our parents were trying to lull us to sleep, and it certainly worked for Richard and Alice. Emily and I were enthralled with the stories. Rather than sleep, we were wide-eyed and excited.

Everyone on board celebrated when we crossed the equator. The captain even dressed up like Father Neptune with a crown on his head and a trident in his hand.

Our halfway stop was at the Cape of Good Hope, the southernmost point of Africa. The ship took on supplies, and some people stretched their legs onshore. Then we were back to our journey, travelling to Australia.

I had heard mother and father whispering at night, about the vast ocean we were on, and their fears of drowning. Two people had died on board the ship, but I didn't know the cause.

For most of our voyage, we had fine weather and moderate winds; however, at times, Emily and I were scared. We experienced strong winds and rough swells from the 'roaring forties' in the Southern Ocean – our ship laboured under the strain and the decks were awash with seawater. Inside our cabin, we would roll from side to side, and cooking utensils, books and clothing were tossed around between our bunks. At these times, our mother would hold onto Richard and Alice and silently pray. Our father would hold onto Emily and me, reassuring us that the bad weather would pass. We knew our safe passage to Australia depended on Captain Finlay's ability to steer the ship through the rough seas.

When we finally saw the coastline of Australia, we were told that it would still be several weeks until we would be putting down anchor in Port Phillip Bay, Melbourne, in the colony of Victoria.

Finally, on Friday, 16th June 1854, we stepped off the ship and onto Station Pier. We had been at sea for three months.

Dozens of porters and touts were gathered to greet the passengers. They were eager to earn a few pence carrying luggage. I looked up at my mother and father and could see their resolve to find somewhere for us to live. They called for a porter, and off we went.

Chapter Two – Melbourne, Victoria

Back then, South Melbourne, down near the banks of the Yarra Yarra, was called 'canvas town' on account of the vast tents that had been erected to house all the emigrants. Accommodation was very difficult to procure and very rough when procured. We spent a few nights in 'canvas town,' but thankfully, we were very lucky to find a small place in town.

Mr and Mrs Charles Young lived next door to us. Mr Young was the sole lessee and manager of the Queen's Theatre Royal, and he and his wife, Eliza, were actors.

Our family friendship with Mr and Mrs Young was to become another turning point in all our lives.

Mother had suffered badly during the journey from England. I thought it was just seasickness, but it was morning sickness. My baby brother Arthur was born soon after we arrived in Melbourne. But he was very sickly and never had a real chance at life.

Mr and Mrs Young were very kind and helped mother and father through the difficult time of caring for baby Arthur and adjusting to a new country and way of life.

*

Gold had been discovered in several towns close to Melbourne, and it seemed to me that everyone benefited, not just the gold fossickers. I remember asking mother and father why there were so many men in town in rough working clothes. They told me that very important buildings were being constructed. They mentioned the Melbourne Museum, University of Melbourne, the Melbourne Library, and Flinders Street railway station.

All these buildings are landmarks today, but back in 1854, they were just dusty and noisy construction sites.

I suppose I was a very observant child. To be honest, I was fascinated by people – how they walked, how they talked, and their eccentricities.

One Sunday after a family picnic in the Botanical Gardens, I was walking with my mother, holding her hand as we traversed the streets of the city. We stopped suddenly when we came to Collins Street, and I felt my mother's grasp tighten. There was a stream of men walking in single file down the street. They were holding wooden poles over their shoulders with a bundle attached to the end of the pole.

Their clothing was unusual, and their hair was not cut short in the usual style but was one single long plait at the back of their head. I was fascinated and asked mother who they were. She became less tense and explained to me that these men were from China. They were hoping to find gold, like so many others. Father also said that there were many people from America, Germany, South Africa and even Scandinavia, and they were all hoping to find a way out of poverty and become rich. He said the men were walking to the goldfields of Ballarat, Beechworth, and Bendigo. I wondered if any town that started with a 'B' had gold!

Father and mother both read the morning newspaper every day, and sometimes they would read the evening newspaper as well. They would share the most important things with us. They always encouraged us to read different parts of the paper too.

Sometime in October 1854, my father came home holding a newspaper. There was something different about his walk. He saw me in the sitting room. I had been reading a poetry book, which I put down when he sat next to me. He opened the newspaper and told me it was called *The Age*, and he said it was a significant day. It was the first edition.

He announced in a very theatrical voice, '*The Age* – a Journal of politics, commerce and philanthropy. Dedicated to the record of great movements and the advancement of Man.'

I looked at him with interest, but he could see I did not understand. He explained that a new newspaper meant that Melbourne was growing, and that there would be many opportunities for us. He felt vindicated that the decision to immigrate to Australia had been the right decision. I did not know at the time, but my father had been very troubled by the move to Australia and by my mother's health.

It was early November 1854 when our neighbour, Mr Charles Young, knocked on our door, asking to speak to father. Emily and I had been in the kitchen. We stayed out of sight but listened intently. We strained our ears to hear what they were saying. We heard Mr Young say to our father,

'Mr Wiseman, I am producing the Christmas panto *Cherry and Fairstar* at the Queen's, and I need two young ladies to play the role of the fairies. I think your daughters, Emily and Fanny, would be very good in these roles. They are the perfect age, as I believe Emily is 10 and Fanny is eight years old.' Silence followed Mr Young's request. We knew our father was thinking. He was not the type to blurt out a response until he had considered the implications of his words.

Father responded with a simple 'no' and then proceeded to put forward the reasons for his response. Mr Young was quiet and attentive as he listened to father. When father had finished speaking, Mr Young promised that his wife, Eliza, would always be with Emily and me, supervising and helping us with our performance. He promised that at any point, if Emily or I wished to stop, then it would be so.

Eventually, after much discussion, father agreed. Father had, of course, worked with actors and actresses in London. He loved the theatre. We realised years later that father's initial refusal had more to do with concern for our future lives, rather than just this one pantomime. He knew once we were on the stage, it would be very hard to get us off!

The first time I stepped backstage, my eyes darted everywhere. There were ropes hanging from the stage ceiling, and there was banging and shouting as men were moving large wooden frames. Several rostrums, which looked like giant's tables, were in one corner of the stage. Down by the footlights, a few feeble gas jets shone on a group of ladies and gentlemen rehearsing their lines. One gentleman was sitting at a little table holding the prompt book. I could hear the orchestra rehearsing.

We attended every rehearsal with Mrs Eliza Young and listened carefully to her instructions. We watched Mr Young direct the stagehands with all the props and ropes. He had nautical training and knew a lot about tying ropes and the dangers backstage. Mr and Mrs Young were also starring in the panto. Mr Young played the role of the clown, and his natural wit and appreciation of the ludicrous made him a huge success. Emily and I enjoyed every second; it was just like playing make-believe on board the ship.

While we were enjoying ourselves, we were unaware of the impending tragedy that was unfolding.

Our little brother Arthur, despite all our mother's efforts to keep him alive, died on the 19th December 1854. He was buried in the Melbourne General Cemetery, and I will never forget the sadness that was etched on the faces of my mother and father.

My mother's grief was palpable, and we were all so worried about her. Her health had been badly affected. Emily and I told our mother we didn't want to perform in the pantomime anymore, we wanted to stay at home and look after her. But she told us that she was looking forward to seeing us perform onstage, and so we carried on.

Cherry and Fairstar opened at the Queen's Theatre Royal in Queen Street, on Boxing Day, 26th December 1854. Our fairy dresses were very pretty. They were made of white book-muslin and strewn with silver paper stars. The pink rose wreaths we wore on our heads were beautiful. The orchestra lifted us to heavenly heights.

I instantly fell in love with performing onstage.

The pantomime played for about four weeks, and we had a full house every night. Emily and I thought at the time how devastated we would be when it all finished.

Well, we didn't have time to be devastated.

Mr and Mrs Young asked my father again if he would allow us to join them in the next theatre production called *Sea of Ice,* a melodrama adapted from a French play by d'Ennery and Dugué. I would be cast in the child part of Marie, which sounded good to me because I was still a child.

My father agreed.

He could see that Emily and I loved being onstage, and it gave our mother great joy to see us so happy.

Sea of Ice was a long play, just over three and a half hours. There's a scene where mutineers of a ship strand the captain and his family on a sea of ice, which then breaks up. I had a very spectacular entrance involving a block of ice. We had been rehearsing for weeks, and I felt confident that everything would work as planned.

On opening night, something went wrong with the mechanism of the block of ice to which I was fastened. The ice stuck fast when I was making my entrance. I was so terrified that real tears were streaming down my face. The audience was delighted with my 'natural' acting, and they cheered again and again.

The next production at The Queen's Theatre was *A Woman's Love,* and again Mr and Mrs Young took Emily and me under their wings. I played the part of Lady Jessie. Mrs Young promised me a beautiful doll if I played the part well. Let's just say the doll was mine within days. One of my lines was 'I am Lady Jessie, and I am six years old.' I thought how strange to say these lines onstage, when in truth, I had only recently arrived at that very mature age.

Emily and I didn't know it at the time, how could we, we were still children, but the theatre was to become the backbone for our entire family.

In February 1855, I met the famous Mr Gustavus Vaughan Brooke, the great Irish actor. He had been brought out to tour the colonies by theatre manager and actor, Mr George Selth Coppin. Mr GV Brooke brought with him an entourage that included Miss Fanny Cathcart, who was Mr Brooke's leading lady, and Mr Richard Younge, who was the stage manager. Mr GV Brooke was producing several shows in Melbourne. He and his wife, Marianne, or Polly as she was called, sought out mother and father and asked if the three Wiseman girls, Emily, Alice and me, would appear in some of the shows. Thankfully, our parents agreed.

The first thing I noticed about Mr GV Brooke was his expressive eyes. He seemed to 'say' a lot without ever speaking. But when he did speak, he could switch between his native Dublin brogue to Shakespearean English in a heartbeat. Mr GV Brooke could whisper but make himself heard in the remotest recess of the theatre and could then trill the listener as effectively as a trumpet. He was a true gentleman, generous to a fault, and he looked after us like his own.

To start Mr Brooke's tour, he opened with Shakespeare's *Othello* on Monday, 26th February 1855. Mr Brooke played the main part, and Mr Richard Younge played Iago. Mr Robert Heir played Cassio and Miss Fanny Cathcart played the role of Desdemona. Mr Robert Heir and Miss Fanny Cathcart were engaged to be married, and every time they were onstage together, you could see their affection for each other. Mrs Eliza Young (our neighbour) played the role of Emilia.

The play was a huge success, and the Melbourne audiences were thrilled to have Mr Brooke in the colony. The newspapers were enthralled with Mr Brooke's talent, especially a well-known critic by the name of Dr Neild. He wrote about Mr Brooke's generous character and said he was a king onstage, but a 'hail-fellow-well-met' offstage.

Shakespeare's *Macbeth* was next on the playbill, with Mr GV Brooke in the title role. Mr Brooke was tall and had a commanding figure and a deep voice. He could play any of the lead Shakespearean roles with mastery. I was cast as one of the apparitions, and in the cauldron scene, I was supposed to enter the stage through the trap-door. In the scene, Macbeth says,

> 'What is this, that rises like the issue of a king,
> and wears upon his baby-brow
> the round and top of sovereignty.'

Unfortunately, when my head appeared through the trap-door my crown was set most rakishly askew. I had knocked my head as the trap-door opened, and the crown most *definitely* was not on my 'baby-brow.' But as they say, the show must go on.

The next production was *Rent Day* a play by Mr Douglas Jerrold. Mr Brooke played the character of Martin Heywood, alongside his leading lady, Miss Fanny Cathcart, who played his wife, Rachel. Miss Cathcart was very young and beautiful and had a careful and meticulous manner.

In one scene, my sisters and I were on the stage with Mr Brooke, and his character Martin Heywood, is reproaching his wife in a fit of jealous fury. My sister Alice, aged only four, looked up into Mr Brooke's face, then into Miss Cathcart's, and seeing the latter crying, she decided that it was real, and she too burst into tears.

Alice had no handkerchief, so she lifted up the skirt of her little frock to wipe her eyes. Her sobs were heartrending. When the curtain fell at the end of the act, Mr Brooke went to comfort Alice, endeavouring to still the tempest. He tried to lift her in his arms, but she would have nothing to do with him and said indignantly, 'Naughty man, scold pretty lady.'

Miss Fanny Cathcart came to the rescue. She leaned down to Alice and hushed her crying with a little lullaby. This was the remedy that was needed. Miss Cathcart told Alice that Mr Brooke had been 'playing make-believe'. She said he was a very good actor, and that Alice should remember that he was also a very kind man. Miss Cathcart told Alice that Mr Brooke was her guardian as they travelled across the ocean from England to Australia and had brought her safely to Melbourne. At this point, Alice peeked over her handkerchief-dress and looked long and hard at Miss Cathcart and Mr Brooke. Mr Brooke gave her a wink, and with that, I think Alice realised it was all just 'make-believe.' She never again burst into tears in that particular scene.

Our performances were held on Monday to Friday evenings, and Saturdays were spent rehearsing.

After *Rent Day* had played for a few weeks, the stock company, which included our neighbours Mr and Mrs Young, took possession of the Queen's Theatre, and the regular season of drama resumed.

I was to learn the rhythm of the theatre world very quickly. Essentially, the mainstay theatre companies were called the 'stock company.' The stock company would perform plays almost every night, but never on a Sunday. The stock actors were well-versed in acting. They were expected to have word-perfect knowledge of all the parts and therefore be able to play all the roles at short notice. They were reliable and steady. The stock actors were paid a low wage, the juvenile actors even less, but they had consistent work for weeks and months at a time.

Then there were 'star' performers like Mr GV Brooke, who would perform with the stock company and would sometimes bring their own leading ladies and other actors with them. The star performers were very well-known, and they would often go on tours throughout the colonies. They would be paid very well, as they were a draw-card to bring the audiences in. There was fierce competition between theatre houses and between theatre managers, so if a manager could entice a star to come to Australia, it was a real achievement.

It was common practice at the time to provide several different types of entertainment on the same playbill. There could be a scene from Shakespeare's *Macbeth*, followed by a comedy, and then a singing or dancing act. There was something for everyone, and most people enjoyed going to the theatre. Ticket prices varied. For the 'well-healed' theatre goer, they could purchase seats in the Boxes at around 8 shillings; these were private seating areas. The Pit was the least expensive at around 5 shillings; this often meant only standing space near the stage. The Gallery was at the back of the theatre and provided tiered seating above the Pit and offered a range of views and prices. For the very savvy or hard-up individual, they could come at interval and pay half price.

The Christmas pantomime season was my favourite time of the year. The pantos were often based on fairy tales and were very popular with everyone.

*

Mr Charles Young and his wife, Eliza, were regular visitors to our home. I remember on one occasion they were very excited and told mother and father that Mr George Selth Coppin was in Melbourne and would be managing and starring in a revival of the play *Sea of Ice*. Well, you can imagine my ears pricked up when I heard that, and I prayed that I would be asked to perform in the play again.

They said Mr Coppin was a great friend of Mr GV Brooke. Apparently, when they were both in London the previous year, in 1854, Mr Coppin engaged Mr Brooke for the Australian and New Zealand tour. He offered Mr Brooke a fixed fee of £10,000 for 200 performances, but this was later renegotiated to £25 for each performance and half of the net receipts[i]. Theirs was a real partnership, as the deal ensured that both parties wanted each other to succeed.

A short while later, I found out that Mr Coppin had requested that Emily and I join the company for the *Sea of Ice*. I guess he had heard of my 'realistic' acting. But this time, I prayed the mechanism for the block of ice would actually work!

The first time I met Mr Coppin, I was very nervous. I need not have worried, as he made me and everyone else feel completely at ease.

He gathered the company together and introduced himself. He was dressed in a traditional dark coloured knee-length frock-coat with a lavender coloured silk waistcoat and immaculate grey striped trousers pressed with a perfect crease. He wore lovely shiny black boots.

He said that he had literally been born on the stage as his parents were strollers in England. I had heard the term 'strollers' before, so I knew that Mr Coppin had been well versed in every aspect of putting on a performance. The strollers were usually a small group of actors that walked from town to town performing – they would do everything from organising the printing of the playbill, to setting up the chairs and constructing the stage.

Mr Coppin told us he had two rules that he would not compromise on.

The first rule was no smoking in any part of the theatre. He said,

'The officers of the establishment have strict orders to suppress it. Ladies could not be expected to endure a small hall polluted with fumes of hand-cut hunk or coarse home-grown tobacco.'[ii]

The second rule was that of punctuality, which was not only for rehearsals but also for performances. He said that if the performance was to start at 7.30 pm, then that's the time the curtain would rise.

In the *Sea of Ice,* Mr Coppin played a comedy character by the name of Barabbas. In my part, I had to ride on his back, pull his nose, and say, 'Bark, Barabbas, Bark.' Years later, Mr Coppin declared that *I* had pulled his nose out of shape! He used to make me laugh so much.

Mr Coppin had a very solemn face, and he was very round in the middle. He used these physical characteristics extremely well for playing comedy. He was a very skilled actor and very amiable.

Mr Coppin would often ask Emily and me how we were liking the stage. I heard some of the older lady actresses talking and saying how valued they felt, which was not always the case with other managers. His buoyant spirits lifted everyone.

On the closing night of *Sea of Ice*, a late-night party was held on the stage after the final curtain had fallen. Mother and father allowed Emily and me to attend. It was during that night that I heard Mr Coppin tell the story of how he and his wife Maria had left England and ended up in Australia and not America. It was due to the toss of a coin!

Heads meant America, and tails meant Australia. Mr Coppin told us that he had flicked a halfpenny in the air, it fell on its edge, rolled, and settled flat. Mr Coppin and his wife bent over it, and she burst into tears when she saw the coin had landed with the tails pointing skywards. She was originally from America and had been praying the coin would go her way. But Mrs Coppin was true to her word when she said she was willing to go wherever the coin decided. When they sailed into Sydney Harbour, Mrs Coppin exclaimed that she had never seen anything more beautiful.

I heard later from one of the older lady actresses that Maria, Mr Coppin's wife, had died in 1848, and he had been heartbroken. He had thrown himself into work ever since.

Mr Coppin always had something on the go. He told us that his next venture was the construction of a new theatre in Melbourne. So, it wasn't long after *Sea of Ice* had finished that on 18th April 1855, the foundation stone was laid by Mr GV Brooke for Mr Coppin's Olympic Theatre. The theatre was located on the corner of Lonsdale Street and Exhibition Street. What an ingenious construction, a prefabricated iron building built in Manchester, England and shipped out to Melbourne. It apparently cost £4,000.

It was a great building, but unfortunately, very hot during summer, and so it was nicknamed the Iron Pot. The theatre was very popular with Melbournians. But after a few years, there was too much competition from The Princess Theatre, and so the Olympic was turned into the first Turkish Baths in Melbourne. That was a long time ago, and I believe there is recent talk about the Comedy Theatre residing in the same location.

I would often hear mother and father talking about the goings-on in Melbourne. Mr Coppin and Mr Brooke (George and Gus) became like brothers; they were seldom seen apart. They went to the races together, went fishing together, they dined and wined together. I also learned that Mr Coppin married Mr Brooke's sister-in-law in 1855. So, George and Gus weren't 'like' brothers, they actually 'were' brothers-in-law.

Mr George Selth Coppin was a remarkable man and greatly admired by everyone who met him. When I was an adult, I had the honour to call him my friend.

*

It was at the Olympic Theatre that Madame Anna Bishop, along with Madame Carandini, Mr Conlon and Mr Laglaise, appeared in Bellini's opera *Norma*. Madame Bishop was one of the sweetest-tempered women I have ever met, although some people have said the opposite. But during the time Emily and I worked with her, she was the most amiable person we knew. Madame Bishop was a soprano, and she wore the most beautiful costumes and jewellery. She played the character of Norma, and Madame Marie Carandini played Anelgisa. Mr Conlon played Pollio, and Mr Laglaise played the Archdruid. Emily and I were cast as the children. It was a remarkable time. The music is still fresh in my memory as though I had been fortunate enough to hear it only last night.

Two of my uncles, Mr Thomas King and Mr Edward King, played in the orchestra. I'll explain how they came to be my uncle's later in the story.

I think everyone who was involved with that production of *Norma* has now passed.

It was around this time, when Emily and I were at the Olympic Theatre, that we first met Miss Julia Mathews. Her family emigrated from England to Australia in the same year as my own family, 1854. You may recognise Julia's name as she was a great singer, but she also had a connection with the Burke and Wills Expedition.

Julia's voice was wonderful even back then when she was just 13 years old. She was bright, happy, and had the rosiest cheeks I've ever seen.

We spent a lot of time together as we would often be at the theatre rehearsing for various shows. Her father hailed from Scotland, or as he used to say, 'the land o' cakes, ye ken'. I didn't really know what he meant, so one day I asked Julia.

She smiled and told me, 'land o' cakes' comes from a Robbie Burns poem.

'Oh yes,' I said, for I knew some of Robbie Burns' poems, but I must have had a quizzical look on my face. Julia laughed at me and continued,

'When the Scots were warring with the English, they didn't carry much food with them, but they carried oats and a broad piece of metal which they used to make thin biscuits or cake[iii]. So that's why some Scots call their homeland the "land o' cakes." And of course you know, "ye ken" just means "you know."'

I would sometimes practice my Scottish accent with Julia. I tried to sound just like her father. Julia would close her eyes and just listen to me, and then open her eyes quickly, which would send her into fits of laughter. She said it was the funniest thing to hear her father's voice coming from a young woman. We would both end up laughing, so much so that we would have tears rolling down our cheeks.

I can remember on one occasion Miss Julia wanted some white satin ribbon for her ballet shoes, so she asked her father for the money and was told, 'What do ye want to tie them on for, canna ye sew them to your stockings.' Entreaties were of no avail, the 'bawdees' were not forthcoming, and poor Julia did not get the ribbon. She had to sew her shoes on!

Old Mrs Hickey, our dresser and the sweetest of ladies, often tried to shame him into purchasing what was needful, but all to no purpose. As long as he had his snuff and a glass of toddy, he hadn't a care.

It was funny to see them walking home from the theatre at night. The old gentleman would strut on ahead. Miss Julia followed after him and her mother, dear old Mrs Mathews, bringing up the rear. Tiny woman she was. I can see her now. Hair done up in a knob at the back and a bunch of curls down each side of her face. Her daughter was the light of her life.

*

In 1856, at the Olympic Theatre, Mr Brooke produced both tragedy and comedy shows. After his season ended, Mr Young produced Jerrold's *Mutiny at the Nore* in which I was to play a 'breeches' part. At first, I didn't cotton on to what that actually meant. But it finally dawned on me that I was playing a boy part, that of young Jack Adams. And of course, this meant wearing trousers or breeches. I remember how strange it felt the first time I wore men's clothing, but also how comfortable they were.

While we were rehearsing the piece in early October 1856, who should come onstage, but Mr William Hoskins and his wife, Miss Julia Harland (she was one of the Wallacks of America). They had just come out to the colonies. I kept rehearsing, trying not to appear nervous. Mr Hoskins sat at the side of the stage and listened intently to the speech I was delivering. When I had finished, he walked across the stage to me. But before he had a chance to speak, I said,

'Oh, I know you.'

He was surprised and said, 'Oh, do you indeed. And where have I had the pleasure of meeting you?'

'We have never *met* sir,' I replied, 'but I saw you about four years ago in England at Sadler's Wells Theatre. You played Dr Ollapod in *The Poor Gentleman*, and in that play one of your lines was, "Thank you, kind sir. I owe you one."

Needless to say, he was astonished, so his remark back to me, 'You're a wonder' was quite natural.

But in the next breath, I almost destroyed the good impression I had made, for I replied,

'I've got a good memory, and no one who once saw you could ever forget you. The way you swing your right leg is enough to make anyone remember you.'

The very audacity of the remark, which I made in all innocence, must have appealed to his sense of humour, for he started to laugh. He never bore me any ill-will.

I would have the honour of playing leading parts in his company in future years and of calling him 'Billy' as all his friends did. He was a great man, and I was to learn many of my acting skills under his tutelage.

While he was still laughing about my comment about his leg, he reached into his coat pocket and pulled out 10 shillings and said,

'Well Miss Wiseman, I'm very impressed. Now go and buy yourself some lollies.'

*

Emily and I felt like we were on a playground see-saw. When one play ended, we had a few days of downtime to rest, then we would be offered another play, and we would be up at all hours with rehearsals and then performances. We simply loved it.

Our next performance was in November 1856, and it was the ballet of *Cinderella* at the old Princess Theatre. In those days, the Princess Theatre did not really look like a proper theatre; it was more like a large wooden barn.

Emily and I played alongside Mr William Hoskin's wife, Miss Julia Harland. She was a very fine singer and had a charming personality. There must have been thirty of us children, and we were drilled in rehearsals by Mr Powell to move this way, then that way. The *Melbourne Herald* critiqued *Cinderella*, saying:

> 'It was delightful to witness the performances of these Lilliputians, but it was surprising to think of the great care which must have been taken to train these children to such perfect discipline, to make them dance so well, and to cause them to exhibit so much conformity and grace in all their movements.'

It was no surprise to us, because we had been rehearsing the steps endlessly for weeks.

Mr Tom Lee and his wife, Miss Emma, had staged the show. They were seasoned performers and were well-known at the time as rider and rope dancers. At the conclusion of the opening night performance, they stepped out onto the stage and received the most tremendous applause. Emily and I had cardinal parts playing the Proud Sisters, so we followed Mr and Mrs Lee onstage and were given just as much applause.

I remember looking over at my sister whilst taking our bows and thinking how happy I was.

My smile stretched from ear to ear.

Chapter Three – Gold

In early 1857, our family moved from Melbourne to Specimen Hill in Ballarat. Our journey was made in a Cobb and Co. coach, which bumped up and down on the very rough roads. At one point, I flew up in the air and came down on an irritable Englishman's knee. I was so embarrassed, as was my mother. She held me very tight after that.

Gold had been discovered at Specimen Hill, and a lot of people had rushed there in the hope that they would also get lucky. It was big business. Fortunes were won with great fanfare and then lost almost as quickly. For some who found gold and managed to hold on to the money, it launched them into a future they could only imagine, and no doubt, even now, their descendants have benefited greatly.

The gold discoveries near small towns would result in that town quadrupling in size almost overnight. And with all the extra people came the demand for extra entertainment. That is what motivated our father to take us to Ballarat.

Our family became well known in the area, not just because Emily and I appeared regularly at the Montezuma Theatre and the Charlie Napier Theatre, but because father was a skilled tailor and poet. He seemed to know everyone, or everyone seemed to know him. My mother was also well-known for her skills as a healer. She had learnt her skills from my grandmother Mary, who was a nurse in London.

Mr John Rodger Greville[iv] was the stage manager at the Charlie Napier Theatre, and he made sure that Emily and I were always looked after. We were billed as the Misses Wiseman's, minor entertainment, but we were still a draw-card. Having juveniles on the stage was very popular, and audiences would love it when Emily and I sang or danced.

We would often perform the Scottish Triple Highland Fling, which was a very demanding dance that required strength, stamina and good technique[v]. Every time I performed it, I thought fervently of Mr Charles Powell. He had been our ballet master at the Princess Theatre in Melbourne. For hours and hours every day, Mr Powell had 'tortured' us, he had us turned out, twisted and twirled. The teaching was thorough, but oh, my poor little toes had been black and blue. I was a spitfire back then, and if I could not learn a step as quickly as I thought, I would talk to myself sternly. Poor Mr Powell, he often had his patience sorely tested with me. But looking back on that time, I am incredibly grateful for his attentiveness. He 'joined the great majority' long before I was in my teens.

We got to know Mr JR Greville and his wife, Miss Charlotte, very well. He was quite dashing with a trustworthy face, and she was beautiful and elegant. He would often tell us stories about growing up in Dublin, Ireland. He emigrated to Australia in 1852 with the belief that he had only to touch the Australian shore, and Midas-like, the gold would be his. He had no funds to make his way out to the gold diggings, so he thought he'd raise a little money by taking on a theatrical engagement in Melbourne. He applied at the old Queen's Theatre, but the manager sent him packing. A kind musician named Mr Joseph Megson, who'd overheard his audition, offered him the chance to sing with the musicians at one of the Saturday night concerts at the theatre. He said the manager would not notice another singer in the group. So, he made his Melbourne stage debut at the Queen's Theatre just like Emily and I had.

He was a natural comedian and would have us clutching our stomachs in pain from the laughter when he told us stories about his gold-digging days. He said he spent days sinking holes 15 feet deep, but he wasn't good at throwing up the washdirt. For every spadeful he threw up brought two spadesful down. His mates thought he'd be better at the puddling tub, but that proved to be more disastrous than sinking holes. He said, 'he'd made a muddle of that puddle' and consequently had to try his luck back on the stage.

He'd been in Ballarat in December 1854 during the Eureka Rebellion and had been arrested for sedition but later released. He'd apparently indulged in a few jokes at the expense of the government of the day, and as a consequence of this, he had been arrested.

Interestingly, he never bothered to assume a character onstage, he played every part as himself, and the audiences loved him for it.

He would often say,

'I am the luckiest man alive as I'm married to the beautiful Charlotte.'

In 1855, when he was 21 years old, he had set his mind to marrying her. She was part of a very famous theatrical family and quite accomplished in her own right, having played alongside Mr GV Brooke.

He would also say,

'I am the luckiest man alive and I'm going fishing.'

After we'd heard him say that numerous times, Emily and I coined a nickname for him. Instead of JRG for John Rodger Greville, it became GFG for Gone Fishing Greville.

*

We met the Edouin family while we were living in Ballarat. Their family was remarkably similar to ours, although they did not use their real surname, which was Bryer, for their stage performances. We, on the other hand, were always known as The Wiseman Family or The Misses Wiseman's.

Sometimes there would be fierce competition between my family and the Edouin family. Emily and I would be performing at the Charlie Napier Theatre on the Main Road, while the Edouin family would be performing at the Montezuma Theatre, located around the corner.

In those goldrush days, Ballarat probably had more loose easy money in its pocket than any town in Australia, and the theatre companies played week after week to fine business.

We learnt that the Edouin's had emigrated from England to Melbourne in 1857. Mrs Sarah Elizabeth Bryer was the head of the family and was always in charge. She was a courteous little lady, and the family were as homely as a kindly mother could make them. I never asked where Mr Bryer was. There were six children; the eldest boy was Edwin, but he was always called Charlie. Then came Johnnie, Eliza, Rose, Willie, and Julia.

Charlie, Johnnie, Eliza and Rose were all older than me by several years. Willie was the same age as me, and Julia was three years younger.

The Edouin's were great entertainers and were in Ballarat for several months.

My mother always chaperoned us when we needed to go into town. Mother might be buying some groceries from Lucas & Co., or fruit from Clayton's fruit store or meat from the butcher Mr Edward Cantor. Sometimes we'd visit the post office that Mr George Heath operated. Mrs Bryer would chaperone her children as well. Quite often, we would all be in town together – the Wiseman and the Edouin families.

After a while, we became very friendly with the three Edouin girls, Eliza, Rose and Julia. We'd often see them in Raphael Brothers, the clothiers, or Turner & Hoey the drapery store. We would talk about our shows, the audiences, who forgot their lines, and who got the most applause. We would always laugh when we asked about the applause. We were all just having fun and always wished the other family the best of luck when we parted.

After a few months, the Edouin family left Ballarat and started travelling through all the mining and agricultural towns in rural Victoria. All the towns were eager to have the best actors and actresses visit them. For many of the townspeople, it was the only evening entertainment available.

We eventually followed the Edouin family by going on tour, often performing in the same rural towns as them. And it was while we were travelling that we heard the devastating news of poor Eliza Edouin. The Edouin's had been in Daylesford for a show, but Eliza had been told to stay in bed because she was very unwell with inflammation of the lungs. No one knew how unwell she was. When the family returned from the show to the Mount Alexander

Hotel, they were shocked to find she had died. She died on the 2nd October 1857.

My mother seemed the most shocked when she heard the news. She took even greater care to ensure we were all well-dressed for the cold and that we rested when we were unwell. She did her best, but there were times when we just had to perform regardless of how we were feeling.

We did remarkably well while we were travelling and performing at various towns; however, at times we got stuck, yes, literally stuck in the quagmire of mud. Actually, we didn't call it mud, for it was more like glue.

When we were travelling from Smythesdale to Carisbrook for a performance, a distance of 45 miles, our horses jibbed and refused to go an inch further. The wheels of our carriage were sinking deeper and deeper in the quagmire. Fortunately for us, my father saw a man coming along with a wagon and team of bullocks. The wagon was empty, and so father offered a small sum to transfer us and our belongings to the wagon and to take us the rest of the way. When we arrived at Carisbrook at about 7:00 pm, we were cold, wet and hungry[vi].

I remember my mother was not happy. We had no time to have a proper meal as the manager told us there was a large crowd in the hall, or should I say long dining room, and they were waiting for us to perform.

There were no dressing rooms, so we had to dress in the hotel. Because of this, we had to walk through the audience to get to the 'stage.' I say 'stage' with a liberal laugh, because it was really only two large tables put together.

My brother Richard, who was only nine years old at the time, didn't mind in the least; in fact, he rather enjoyed it. But Emily and I were simply disgusted. To think we could not take our entrance in the orthodox manner, but had to step on the tables. This is not what we were used to, and we considered it a little below us. You must remember we were used to performing in large theatres.

We were unaware back then how hard life was for our parents and how grateful they were that we had been engaged to perform, even in a small hall.

*

After our first tour through the goldmining towns, we returned to our home in Specimen Hill, Ballarat.

The town was 'a buzz' with people talking about the Great Nugget Lottery. This was a big event, and lots of people had bought tickets to win the large nugget of gold. Emily and I were asked to assist with the event by drawing the tickets onstage.

The event was held on Thursday 4th February 1858, at the Charlie Napier Theatre, and thankfully it was large enough to hold the hundreds of people who came. Mr Samson, the promoter of the lottery, had gone to great lengths to ensure it was fair and honest. He had enlisted Mr Fitzpatrick, Esquire, who was a Justice of the Peace, and Mr Warden

Daly, to supervise the proceedings. I had never seen such an event before. There were 2,600 tickets, and all had been numbered and carefully counted by Mr Daly. Two ticket boxes were set up on the stage. One box held the numbered cards 1-2,600, and the other box held blank cards, all except one card with the word 'Prize' written on it.

Emily stood next to one ticket box, while I stood next to the other, and simultaneously we drew out a ticket from our boxes. Mr Fitzpatrick read Emily's numbered ticket, while Mr Daly examined the counter-cards I had drawn, to see whether the wished-for inscription of 'Prize' was there.

The excitement of everyone in the room was intense. For about three hours, the drawing continued with only the production of blank cards. About half the numbers had been drawn, and then Emily drew out card number 1,730, and my corresponding ticket had the word 'Prize' on it. I held my ticket up for everyone to see, and Mr Daly called out the magic word 'Prize.'

An explosion of applause erupted from the room when a young man stood up with the winning ticket number, 1,730. His name was Mr Evans, and he immediately offered to 'shout' forty pounds worth of drinks. But many voices were heard saying, 'Give it to the hospital, not the pub.' Mr Evans immediately agreed that the hospital was in far greater need.

Mr Daly complimented Emily and me for assisting, and thanked Mr Samson for running an honest and fair lottery.

We were given a hearty and loud applause by everyone in the theatre. I never found out how much the tickets cost, but I think Mr Samson did well out of the enterprise and of course, Mr Evans, who won the great gold nugget.

Chapter Four – Back Creek, Victoria

In mid-1859, my parents received a letter from Mr JR Greville. He and his wife, Miss Charlotte, had left Ballarat and were now in Back Creek. He was offering Emily and me an acting engagement. It was a great opportunity. Father decided to let our house in Ballarat and with my mother and five children (for our family had grown by another daughter, her name was Laura), we travelled to Back Creek. The journey was around 93 miles and took us two days.

Gold had been discovered in Back Creek and had attracted many people there. We lived in a tent that had four rooms, and it was surprisingly very comfortable. There were only a few houses back then, and the only substantial buildings were a few shops, the bank, the hotel and the theatre, which had been erected by Mr John Bennett, a blacksmith from Ballarat.

We were excited to be working with Mr Greville again and wondered if there was good fishing in the area. It seemed like no time had passed since we had last seen him.

Mr Greville had taken over the management of The Theatre Royal in Back Creek and was also acting in many of the plays – this was a very common thing for managers to do.

Mr Greville asked me to take the role of Topsy in *Uncle Tom's Cabin*. You may have heard of this play, or the novel of the same name, but at the time, I had not. Mrs Harriet Beecher Stowe, who was an American, had written *Uncle Tom's Cabin* in 1852. The novel was about anti-slavery and social justice, and it had become extremely popular. Mr Greville told me that I would have to blacken my face because Topsy was an African slave. I didn't really know what he meant because I had never had to do this, so I sought guidance from the older actors. They showed me how to use burnt cork to blacken my face.

On Wednesday, 26th October 1859, I performed in the Theatre Royal in Back Creek as Topsy. The next day, the newspaper said:

> 'The Theatre Royal was remarkably well attended last evening to witness *Uncle Tom's Cabin*. Miss Fanny Wiseman, although but 10 years of age, played the part of Topsy with astonishing ability. At the close of the performance, she was loudly called before the

> curtain and received such heart-sprung applause that must have produced most gratifying feelings to her youthful mind.'

The newspaper had one thing wrong and one thing right. I was actually 13 years old, not 10, and I *was* most definitely gratified.

We were living in Back Creek when gas was piped into the town. The streets and hotels were lighted with this amazing new power. One of the spirited promoters of the gas work, Mr Moody of the United States Hotel, oversaw the pipes being laid throughout Scandinavian Crescent. I remember hearing people talk of Mr Moody, praising his entrepreneurship and comparing Back Creek with Ballarat, which was still waiting to get the gas.

⁕

Back Creek was a town of highs and lows, depending on how well the gold mining affairs went. When things were going well, there was no scarcity of money. The silk mercer's shop was well attended. The wives of the miners could be seen in the very best silk and satin dresses, with bonnets that looked like flower gardens. It was said that when the mining was good, one could not distinguish between a magistrate's wife and that of one of the fossickers; they were all dressed in the same finery!

We loved living in Back Creek, and there was always something happening. We were often involved in fundraising events, like so many other actors and actresses.

In early November 1859, Emily and I were asked to support an event to raise money for the Amherst Hospital. It was a benefit for one night only, and we would have the pleasure of working with Mr William Hoskins again.

When Mr Hoskins saw Emily and me, he greeted us like long-lost daughters. In reality, it had only been three years since we last saw him in Melbourne.

We were chuffed he remembered us so well. I admit that I blushed when he mentioned how taken aback he was when I had mentioned his swinging leg when we had first met – then he grinned from ear to ear and laughed.

Mr Hoskins was known for his fastidious interpretation of all his characters, but especially his Shakespearean roles. Whenever the meaning of a passage or the delineation of a character was in question, he would help us understand.

The *Maryborough and Dunolly Advertiser* newspaper announced on Wednesday, 9th November 1859:

> 'The Amateur Dramatic Society have fixed upon Friday evening for their performance for the Benefit of the Amherst Hospital and has issued large and handsome bills announcing their intended appearance on that night in the well-known, beautiful domestic drama, *Rent Day*. The characters in this piece are to be sustained by a number of the most generally well-known inhabitants of Back Creek, who have, for this charitable object, consented 'for the night only' to

> tread the stage and face the glare of the footlights. There will be prologue and epilogue to usher in and conclude the play, both written expressly for the occasion by members of the Amateur Company. A ballad by Mr Chas Smith, and a dance by the Misses Wiseman are promised between the play and afterpiece, and the performance is to conclude with the laughable *Yankee Farce*, the principal character in which is to be sustained by Mr Hoskins.'

On the night of the performance, it was an extremely good house, as most people wanted to support the charity event for the hospital, but they also wanted to see Mr Hoskins perform onstage. Not a single seat was vacant, and the ladies who attended late had to stand upon their fairy toes in order to catch a glimpse of the performance.

Emily and I enjoyed the performance so much, and it brought back happy memories of when we had performed *Rent Day* with Mr GV Brooke back in Melbourne in 1855.

Mr Hoskins wasn't in Back Creek for long. When he left, he told Emily and me that he was returning to Ballarat and he hoped to see us soon.

We continued acting at Back Creek under the management of Mr Greville.

Our family were given a benefit on Friday, 25th November 1859, at the Theatre Royal. Having a 'benefit' was a very important event to financially sustain an actor's income. We were told by Mr Greville that a percentage of the takings from the night would be given to us, on top of our usual weekly pay.

Benefits were usually held at the end of the season, and audiences knew how important these events were and would do their best to fill the entire theatre. As part of the benefit, my little brother Richard and sister Alice made their first appearance before the Back Creek audience. They were billed as 'Master Richard and La Petite Alice.'

We started the show with Schiller's *William Tell*, and Richard sang a comic song that went down a treat. Richard was 11 years old, and Alice was nine. It was a great success.

*

The *Tarrangower Times and Maldon District Advertiser* newspaper wrote a good review of a performance we held on Wednesday, 28th December 1859. The entire Wiseman family were onstage at the Kangaroo Theatre for this performance.

The first piece was *Betsy Baker*, a comedy written by Mr Morton, and the parts of Betsy and Mr Monser were sustained by Emily and me. The newspaper said we acted in a style that would have done credit to first-class full-grown actors, and Master Dick and Miss Alice made the most of the small parts of Mr Crummy and Mrs Moaser.

In the interlude, a song from my little brother was vociferously encored, and the jockey hornpipe folk dance executed by me brought down a perfect storm of applause and demand for repetition. Emily then sang the beautiful song *Ever of Thee,* written by Mr George Linley, in a sweet manner, and the burst of applause that followed the conclusion of the song was well deserved.

We all read the review the following day, which said:

> 'There was a large attendance at the Theatre last evening, for the benefit of the Wiseman Family. The main characters are sustained by the two young ladies, Miss Emily and Miss Fanny, who have played here so long, who have long been the 'pets of the public', and a little boy and girl, named Richard and Alice. They are no doubt very clever for their age.'

Chapter Five – Lamplough, Victoria

When the Back Creek rush for gold slowed to a dawdle, Mr Bennett opened another theatre called the Theatre Royal at Lamplough. He was a talented man, not only a blacksmith, a theatre manager, but also a musical director. The entire company left Back Creek and went along with him to Lamplough.

This, of course, meant another move for my family, but this time we only had to travel 22 miles.

It was late January 1860, and the weather was all anyone could talk about in Lamplough. There had been a drought, and what little water was available for drinking was very doubtful in its quality. Horses and cattle had been in it, and one day I even saw a large frog in it. The only comfort people had in drinking the water was something I heard an old man say,

'What the eye does not see, the heart will not loathe.'

However, I had seen what had been in the water!

I heard people saying that unless we had rain immediately, water would have to be carted from Bet Bet Creek, a distance of four miles. There were scores of families without a shilling to buy a bucketful of water. How were they going to afford water carted from Bet Bet? It was a very scary time.

Mother and father told us that robberies of every description were taking place regularly. Father said,

'When the gold rush broke out in Back Creek, there was a lot of crime, but I think that Lamplough will eclipse Back Creek in crime of every class.'

We were all on our guard whenever we left the house.

Despite all these hardships and dangers, Emily and I enjoyed living in Lamplough and being onstage learning our craft. We also loved how we felt part of the theatre community. When we said goodbye to one of the actors or musicians, we knew it would not be long before we saw them again, perhaps in another town, but still onstage or performing in the orchestra.

Mr Bennett, our manager, had come by the theatre one afternoon after our rehearsals were finishing, with some exciting news. He announced to the company that the following week, we would have the honour of performing with Mr GV Brooke and Miss Avonia Jones. Emily and I were thrilled with the thought of seeing Mr Brooke again.

The next week arrived, and our reunion with Mr Brooke was as heartfelt as it had been with Mr Hoskins. Our performances with Mr GV Brooke were wonderful, and the house was always full. Mr Brooke could attract a crowd even if he was 'opening an envelope.'

Miss Avonia Jones was an accomplished American actress who was widely acclaimed. There was no doubt she was talented, and she quickly became a favourite with Australian audiences. She had attentive dark eyes, was quick-witted, and always ready with a smile. She was Mr Brooke's leading lady.

⁕

Thursday, 9th February 1860, is etched into my memory for the seriousness of the event that occurred. Emily and I were late leaving the house for the Theatre Royal. We knew exactly how long it took to walk from our house to the theatre and exactly what time we were due onstage. We were old enough to walk to the theatre unchaperoned, as long as we stayed together. I was 13 years old, and Emily was 15.

We had just crossed Amherst Street and could see the theatre ahead. But then I heard a blood-curdling scream, and everything went black. I was later told, the scream had come from me when I fell down a disused mining shaft. The shaft was twenty-two feet deep!

Mr Bennett lived close to Amherst Street and, upon hearing the scream, had rushed out of his house to see what had happened. There were many people who came to my rescue. As you can imagine, it was a difficult task getting me out of the mine shaft.

My poor mother. I can see her face, even now. She must have thought I was dead when she saw two men carrying me in a blanket. I saw the worry on her face. I, however, wasn't worrying about what had happened to me, but who went onstage for me. God love my sister Emily, for she had to carry on with the show without me. She was the brave one, as the entire time she was onstage that night, singing and dancing, she did not know if I was dead or alive.

I was very lucky. There were no broken bones, but my arms and legs had been badly injured.

During my recovery, both my sister's Emily and Alice, had to take on extra work. I was out of action for three months. At the time of my accident, I was 4 feet 8 inches tall. My body had been shocked so badly that I never grew another inch from that day!

When I had finally recovered and reappeared onstage, I was so heartily welcomed that for a moment I could not speak my lines. Mr Bennett gave me a complimentary benefit, and I think every man, woman and child in the district was there.

We left Lamplough soon after the benefit and returned to our home in Specimen Hill, Ballarat.

Chapter Six – Bendigo and Ballarat, Victoria

Emily and I had the pleasure of performing again with Mr William Hoskins in Ballarat. He was the manager of the Theatre Royal and was also performing in many plays. The Theatre Royal was a fine building and was equipped with the latest mechanisms – a fly system and trap-doors. The theatre held 1,500 people, and dogs and babies were allowed in too, which meant that sometimes we had to compete with them in volume!

I was having the time of my life.

We travelled to Melbourne for a short engagement at the Princess Theatre to perform in Byron's famous burlesque *Aladdin*. The best part of this engagement was that we were with our old friend Miss Julia Mathews. She played the part of Aladdin, Emily was the Slave of the Lamp, and I was the Genie of the Ring.

Mr Hoskins was in Ballarat only for a short time and then moved on to Sandhurst, or Bendigo, as it is now known. A few months after he left, he sent mother and father a letter and asked if Emily and I could join his company for a three-month season at Abbott's Lyceum Theatre in Bendigo. Mother and father accepted the engagement, they let our house again, and in June 1860, we all moved to Bendigo.

When we started our rehearsals at the Lyceum, we found the dressing rooms were anything but clean, and consequently, we had to get dressed in our rooms in the Metropolitan Hotel. The hotel had a back door which opened into a passage leading to the stage entrance, so we were able to access the theatre and return to the hotel without anyone being the wiser.

After our engagement at Abbott's Lyceum ended, we were asked to perform at the Shamrock Hotel's Concert Hall, which was only a few streets away. The proprietors were Mr William Heffernan, who was energetic and enterprising, and his brother-in-law, Mr John Crowley.

What characters both men were – they both came from Ireland, had travelled through America and were lured to Victoria in search of gold. They owned the Shamrock Hotel and the Concert Hall, which was next door.

Mr Heffernan and Mr Crowley provided entertainment free of charge – they employed a regular company of performers and an orchestra, and they paid everyone quite well. There would be a mix of acts featuring singers, comedians, dancers, actors and sometimes acrobats or magicians. Some diggers would walk several miles to see us perform and then indulge in the liquors in the hotel next door.

If the performances were not over before 10:30 pm, Mr Heffernan would send round an order to the stage manager to drop the curtain.

Mr Heffernan was a shrewd middle-aged businessman, and he knew the 'theatre time' was eating into the 'drinking time.'

One night, I overheard the stage manager plead with Mr Heffernan, he said,

'Mr Heffernan, we only need 10 more minutes to close the show.'

Mr Heffernan replied in his Tipperary Irish accent,

'Sure, it's not out of the actors I be making me money. It's from the fools that drink at me bar that I find the wherewith to be paying ye.'

There was no arguing with him. He was the owner, and when he said to drop the curtain, the stage manager had to follow orders.

Emily and I at first thought he was a hard man, and we said as much to our father. Father chuckled when he heard Emily and me express our consternation about Mr Heffernan, and then he told us a little more about him, which opened our eyes to his honesty and good nature.

Our father said, 'Only the other night, I saw a lucky miner, Mr Hardy, who had made a rise of a hundred pounds, and on the strength of it imbibed too freely in intoxicants. Mr Heffernan saw the state of the man and knew by morning he would have drunk away, given away or had the money stolen away from his pocket. Mr Heffernan asked one of his employees to tell Mr Hardy they would keep his money in the hotel safe overnight. Mr Hardy was far too drunk to even know if he was 'Arthur or Martha,' he just nodded his head. Mr Heffernan and his employee counted the money in front of Mr Hardy and signed a paper stating the amount. The money was then placed in the safe.

The next morning, Mr Hardy came to his sober senses and, having no recollection of what had become of his money, went to the landlord to beg a glass of beer, as he hadn't a shilling left.

Mr Heffernan was called and gave Mr Hardy a lecture on the foolishness of overindulgence. Then, to the surprise and intense delight of Mr Hardy, Mr Heffernan produced from the safe his money from the previous night.'

Father smiled at us, 'So, you see my darlings, sometimes things are not what they seem. This is just one example that I saw with my own eyes and heard with my own ears. I have heard of many more stories of his good nature.'

It was a reminder to Emily and me to never make assumptions about people.

While we were performing at the Shamrock Concert Hall, the great actors Mr Clarance Holt and his wife, Marie, joined us. They opened in a piece called *Twelve Axe and Crown,* a very fine melodrama written by Mr Tom Taylor, and a favourite play of the Holt's. Afterwards, they produced *Louis XI,* an adaptation of the play by Irish playwright Mr Dion Boucicault. I was cast as Dauphin, and Mr Holt, of course, played the lead role of Louis.

Mr and Mrs Holt had been acting together for 20 years. Mr Holt would often be heard saying 'Good-bye, God bless you, dear boy,' whenever he parted from rehearsals. He was skilled at telling anecdotes and kept us all amused when we were in rehearsals or after a performance.

*

After our engagement at the Shamrock Hotel Concert Hall, with Mr William Heffernan and Mr John Crowley ended, my family left Bendigo and returned to our home in Ballarat.

Our time in Back Creek, Lamplough and Bendigo theatres had been excellent from every point of view, not the least being the experience it gave Emily and me, in all types of productions. Emily and I played everything in those days – burlesque, comedy, farce, tragedy, and melodrama.

Burlesque was the most popular form of stage entertainment during the 1850s and 1860s. Burlesque in those days was a form of parody of serious plays, nothing like how it was transformed in America into more of a 'strip-tease' performance.

*

It wasn't long until Emily and I were engaged to perform with Miss Avonia Jones at the Theatre Royal in Ballarat, in the play *Camille,* by Mr Alexandre Dumas. Emily played the role of Olympe, I played the role of Nanine, and in the title role of Camille was Miss Avonia Jones. She was so elegant, and her stage presence was wonderful.

I was a great mimic in those days, and after seeing some of the actors perform, I was able to impersonate all their peculiarities to perfection. I think I developed the skill of mimicry during our long journey from England to Melbourne, when Emily and I had so much time to observe people.

In August 1860, Emily and I were in our dressing room, getting ready for a performance. As usual, we were laughing and talking about what had happened during the day and anticipating what would happen onstage. I was talking about Miss Avonia Jones. I was in awe of her, and I was pretending to be her, imitating the beautiful way she would pronounce her words. But I got the fright of my life when Miss Avonia's mother, Mrs Melinda Jones, came into the room. She had been walking past our dressing room and had heard 'the imitation' and wanted to know who the culprit was. I was so frightened, for she was a big woman and not very amiable. I gathered my courage and said,

'It was I, Mrs Jones.'

She responded in a booming voice,

'Well, come into Avonia's room and do it again.'

I knew everything was alright because she had a big smile on her face. I was alright then. Emily burst into laughter as soon as Mrs Jones left our dressing room, as she had seen the initial panic on my face.

The next day, an announcement was made to the effect that I would be going onstage and giving imitations of Miss Jones in several of her well-known characters.

On Tuesday, 4th September 1860, the local newspaper said:

> 'The chief attraction of the evening was the imitations of Miss Jones by Fanny Wiseman; she has added two or three more to her previous role, and she last night succeeded in taking off the tragedienne so successfully, that had she been concealed from the audience, it would have been difficult to pronounce as to which was speaking, the actress or her imitator. She was as happy in her gestures as in the intonation of her voice. Her acting of the part of Helen O'Hara, in the *Wild Irish Girl*, was first-rate, the brogue she assumed being as rich and unctuous as the veriest daughter of Erin could desire.'

The critics loved it.

*

I received a letter from my friend Miss Julia Matthews in September 1860. She told me that Mr Robert O'Hara Burke had recently left on the Victorian Exploring Expedition. The expedition involved the first white men to cross Australia from south to north. I had never met Mr Burke, but Julia had told me about him, and I had read about him and the expedition he was leading in the newspapers. There was a lot of excitement about the expedition, and even our dear old friend Mr George Coppin had some involvement in it. Earlier in the year, he bought camels from Karachi for his Cremorne Zoo in Melbourne. He sold several of the camels to the expedition for £50 apiece, and the turbaned Afghans looked after them. These desert animals were far better than horses for travelling through the sandy outback.

Julia first met Mr Burke in 1858 when she toured to Beechworth. Mr Burke was a police inspector there. Julia told me that Mr Burke had attended all her performances and sat in the first few rows every night and just beamed at her. He was quite infatuated.

Julia told me that he had proposed to her twice, but she had refused him both times. The first time was soon after the Beechworth performances, and the second was when Julia was performing at the Princess Theatre in Melbourne. He had attended only a few of these performances as he was preparing for the expedition. She told me that he had requested a personal and confidential interview with her after one of her performances – it was on the eve of his expedition, so that would have been on the 19th August 1860.

Mr Burke gave her a miniature portrait of himself and told her that he had made her his sole beneficiary in the event of his death. He had pleaded with her to marry him before his great adventure commenced, or at least to become engaged. She had told him to ask her again on his return, and the answer might be more favourable. She said in the meantime, no other man would have her love. She gave him a lock of her beautiful hair as a keepsake. I cannot say if I knew why she refused his marriage proposals. He was 21 years her senior in age, but this was not an uncommon situation, and he had a good name. Perhaps Julia's mother or father did not approve of the union.

Julia knew it would be some time before she heard from Mr Burke after he left on the expedition, possibly more than one year.

I read later in the newspaper that over 15,000 people turned out to see The Burke and Wills Expedition set off from the Royal Park in Melbourne.

*

Julia and I wrote to each other very often. She knew she had to keep herself busy.

She told me in November 1860 that she was just about to start rehearsals for the pantomime *Jack the Giant Killer,* and she would be performing alongside my old friend Miss Rose Edouin. They were performing at the Pantheon Theatre at Cremorne Gardens in Melbourne.

Julia was a very popular performer and had regular performances. Although she was busy, I knew she was thinking of Mr Burke and longing for his return.

Chapter Seven – New Zealand

We had heard about the gold found at the Dunstan Diggings in New Zealand, so it wasn't a surprise to hear that many actors and actresses were going there. My father would often say,

'There is more money to be made by performing in the goldfields than by working in the diggings.'

We had been home in Ballarat for a little while when we received an invitation for a six-month engagement with Mr Shadrach Jones of the Princess Theatre in Dunedin, New Zealand. The engagement was for Emily and me.

Our mother and father were not able to travel with us. If we accepted, we would have to travel alone. My parents wrote to Mr Shadrach Jones, and he offered to act as our guardian while we were there. After much discussion and agreement to write home every week, our parents agreed we could accept the invitation.

My mother impressed upon Emily and me that when we were off the stage, we must behave modestly and avoid any attachment to men. She said that people would recognise us and that we'd be under constant scrutiny.

She said, 'You must remember your public and private lives are inseparable.'

I listened attentively to my mother. I always trusted her advice. Emily and I did not know at that time that in many people's minds they associated the occupation of 'actress' with the occupation of 'women of the night!'

Emily and I left for New Zealand on the *Nor'Wester*, with Captain Almey. He was a thorough Yankee and a real good fellow. The other passengers whom Mr Shadrach Jones had engaged were Mr George Fawcett, who was easily angered but great company, Mr John Dunn, who was always good humoured, Mr George Loder and his wife Miss Emma Neville, and Mr Johnnie Hall. Mr Hall was a slight young fellow who had not made a name for himself, yet.

The *Nor'Wester* was a sailing vessel, and as such, we had to get used to its lilting ways, which often meant having soup in our laps! For the most part, our voyage to New Zealand was a very pleasant one. There were the occasional outbursts from Mr Fawcett, but after Emily and I had seen one or two of these incidents, we realised he was just hot-tempered, and he'd cool down and apologise to everyone almost immediately. Emily and I had seen Mr Fawcett at the Princess Theatre in Melbourne. He was a very good actor, director and scenic artist, a skill he learned from his father. He was also a great storyteller. In the evenings, on still nights, he would regale all of us with anecdotes from the goldfields or from his hometown in Exeter, Devon in Southwest England. On other nights, Mr Loder and his wife Emma would sing or play the flute.

It seemed that all the members of our group had travelled and performed through the goldfields of Victoria and performed in the theatres in Melbourne. During our trip, Mr Dunn told us about his family and mentioned his daughter Rosa, who'd performed with him many times. He said that she'd been a leading lady for Mr George Coppin when he opened at the Cremorne Gardens, Melbourne in 1856 and had shared the stage with Miss Julia Matthews and Miss Rose Edouin. It really was a small world.

When we arrived in Dunedin, we put on so many plays – dramas and comedies – you name it, we did it. Emily played opposite Mr Johnnie Hall in many of the plays. We were also honoured to perform with Madame Marie Carandini again. She remembered us fondly from when we performed with her in *Norma* in 1855.

The streets of Dunedin were often muddy, but that didn't stop the hustle and bustle of life – there were innumerable hotels, pubs, and churches. Mr Shadrach Jones had told us that the place had seemed gloomy before entertainment such as ours had arrived. He was an entrepreneurial man and had taken over the Provincial Hotel with his business partner, Mr Charles Bird.

Mr Jones had a ruddy face, was about 5 feet 5 inches tall, and was rather stout. He had large side whiskers and curly, dark hair. He was well recognised by everyone as he always wore a chequerboard waistcoat and smoked a fat cigar. He seemed to always have his bulldog following at his heels. Thankfully, it was a friendly dog and wagged its little tail whenever it saw Emily or me. Mr Jones had a big personality, was gregarious and generous, and lived life to the full.

There were many Scottish people living in Dunedin, and on every corner, we'd hear 'Hoo's a' we' ye the noo?' I often thought of my friend Julia Matthews and her father when I heard the Scottish accent.

We learnt that when the English came to Dunedin, they bought land from the Māori people, but it was not a fair trade.

Mr and Mrs Clarence Holt were in Dunedin at the same time as us, but they were in a rival company, performing at the Theatre Royal, which was some distance out of town. We were at the Princess Theatre, which was in town. Our shows were very popular, so much so that the Holt's play *Walter of Leith,* written by William Dail, had to close up. It could not compete with our show. But it all ended well, as Mr Shadrach Jones was able to engage Mr and Mrs Holt at the Princess Theatre, and they opened with *Belphegor the Mountebank,* written by Mr d'Ennery and Fournier.

Emily and I would often visit the post office on the corner of Jetty and Princes Streets. We had to 'apply' for our letters through an opening about two feet by one and a half. Outside this opening, a barrier was erected about two feet from the window. We had to slide up to the window like sheep going through a race. We'd tap at the window, and then a man with a strong Aberdeen accent would say,

'Well, what do you want?'

Emily and I would say, 'Are there any letters for us, Emily and Fanny Wiseman?'

Then would come the 'Where do you come frae?',

'Ballarat, Victoria,' we'd reply.

The Aberdeen man would then hand over the letters from our family, and we'd read them over and over. Sometimes the news from home would make us laugh, and sometimes it made us cry from being homesick.

At the end of our engagement, Mr Jones wanted us to stay for another six months. Mother decided otherwise, so Emily and I returned home to Ballarat.

Mr Johnnie Hall had established himself as a firm favourite with the Dunedin public, and he remained in New Zealand. We left with sadness in our hearts, as we had enjoyed the entire season. My sister seemed sadder than I had expected. I didn't realise that she and Johnnie had formed a strong friendship.

Over the next four years, their friendship would blossom into a love story.

✻

At the beginning of 1861, Emily and I were engaged to act with Mr Fred Younge and his wife, Miss Emma Corri, at the Duchess of Kent Theatre, on Main Street, Ballarat. The theatre was owned by Mrs Scorer.

The Duchess was one of only a few buildings that had escaped a terrible fire on 11th January 1861. Emily and I had been away in New Zealand during the fire, but our parents had written to us describing the terrible event. The Montezuma and Charlie Napier Hotel, along with 60 or so houses, had been destroyed. It was said that the flames were first seen issuing from the roof of the Montezuma Theatre, which, being entirely made of wood, was soon in a blaze from top to bottom. It was understood that the fire originated in the small tobacconist shop, located alongside the theatre.

Almost immediately after the fire, the townspeople started talking about rebuilding. Mr Symons, of the ill-fated 'Old Charlie', had stated that 'like a Phoenix, another building shall arise from the ashes of the former one.'

The long line of dark and desolate ruins that had marked the site of the great fire of January was almost entirely changed into a series of handsome and substantial shops, offices, and dwellings.

Our time performing with Mr Fred Younge at the Duchess of Kent was extremely good. Mr Younge had a careful manner in which he played all his parts, many of them taken at a day's notice. He was an actor with more ability than half of the great stars who would 'parade' themselves onstage.

After a few months, Mr Younge made up his mind to form a small touring company. My parents agreed to allow Emily and me to join the company, and so we travelled with Mr and Mrs Younge to many towns in rural Victoria. I remember camping out alongside roaring creeks, and the rain would be pouring down on the tent of the wagon. At times, we felt we would be washed away.

Mr Younge was a good-tempered man with a sunny disposition, with no thought of the morrow. He taxed his wife's patience severely. I used to wonder why Miss Emma was so cross with him, but I can look back now, with experience as a wife and mother, and I can completely understand her frustration.

✳

In May 1861, we heard that Mr Brooke's tour through the Victorian goldfields had come to an end, and he held his last performance on 23rd May 1861 at the Theatre Royal in Bourke Street, Melbourne. The newspapers reported that when the curtain fell, he made a valedictory speech and his last words from the stage were,

> 'The moment has arrived when I must speak the word which I literally dread to utter, for who shall lift up the dark veil which shrouds the future? Who shall dare to look so far for words and to presume so confidently upon the "hatch and brood of time" as to predict that we shall meet again in this place at any distant day? Not one of us.'

We were all so sad to see him leave Australia and return to England.

We found out sometime later that he and Miss Avonia Jones had fallen in love during their time together on tour. This was obviously not good news for Mrs Brooke!

It was Miss Avonia Jones and her mother, Mrs Melinda Jones, who travelled to England with Mr Brooke on the *SS Great Britain* on 31st May 1861. Mrs Brooke had been left behind in Melbourne.

*

In July 1861, Emily and I were asked to assist with a benefit for Mr W Irwin, whose property, The Star Hotel in Ballarat, had been destroyed by fire. Emily and I wanted to help. The memory of our own home being destroyed came to mind immediately. The Ballarat townspeople had also recently gone through the January fire, so everyone wanted to help.

The benefit was held at the Mechanics' Institute on Tuesday, 9th July 1861. The large hall was pretty well filled with about 1,000 people. The entertainment was divided into two parts, each commencing with an overture by the

Rifle Corps Band. The other portions of the concert consisted of solos, duets, and trios by members of the Philharmonic Society. Miss Julia Harland (Mr William Hoskin's wife) also sang two solos.

Mr Thomas King played the accompaniment. This was well received with enthusiastic encores. Emily and I first met Mr Thomas King in 1855, when we were in the opera *Norma*. It would be several years in the future when he would become my uncle by marriage.

Part of my performance involved the imitation of Miss Avonia Jones. I imitated her gait, gestures, and peculiar style of vocalisation with so much accuracy – I had everyone in fits of laughter.

The benefit was a gratifying success. We were informed that the receipts amounted to about £80, a handsome amount for poor Mr Irwin.

⁕

In September 1861, Julia Mathews sent me a letter. She was in a state of panic. She was expecting Mr Burke to have returned from his expedition. He had been gone for 13 months, and she didn't know what to do. She felt a great uneasiness. She could not just sit and wait, which is what everyone had told her to do. Her letter described in detail her perplexed state of mind. She defiantly expressed her objection to the advice she was receiving to 'just wait.'

I wrote back to her and encouraged her to follow her heart and do as much as she could to generate support for a search party.

Chapter Eight – Adelaide, South Australia

At the beginning of 1862, mother and father received the post, and there was a letter from our old friend Mr JR Greville, or as Emily and I called him, GFG (Gone Fishing Greville). He was offering Emily and me positions with his stock company.

Mr and Mrs Greville had left Ballarat a few months back, and Mr Greville had taken the management of the Victoria Theatre in Adelaide, in the colony of South Australia. He was inviting us to join his company for twelve months.

Our parents were not able to move the entire family again. After several hours of talking through the do's and don'ts, mother and father agreed we could go as long as Mr and Mrs Greville agreed to be our guardians. I was now 15 years old, and Emily was 17.

Mother took Emily and me aside and spoke quietly but sternly to us. She said we must 'guard our reputations carefully'. We understood mother's concern. We were older now, and we would be attracting more male attention. We had to be careful, for slurs to our names could have serious and damaging ramifications to our careers and our family name.

The last time Emily and I had travelled alone was to New Zealand in 1860-61, and although our mother had delivered a very similar message to us then, her words had greater meaning now.

Emily and I left for Adelaide aboard the old *Aldinga* with Captain John McLean. Our fellow actors aboard the ship were Mr and Mrs Greville, Mr and Mrs Chapman, Mr Ted Melville and his wife Mary Ann, Miss Emma James, Mr Willie Shute, Mr and Mrs Rae, Mr and Mrs Robert MacGown, and a very handsome young man by the name of Mr William Thomas King South.

When I first saw Mr South, it was from afar. Emily and I had boarded the *Aldinga* and were walking the deck, our arms locked together, as usual. I could see a young man at the stern of the ship, leaning over the edge and looking down into the water. We were approaching the stern and coming closer and closer to where Mr South was standing.

He was still staring down into the water, and then in a split second, he turned towards us and his eyes met mine. There seemed to be a magnet between us as I could not look away. It really was not the polite thing to do; I should have looked away and continued walking, but I could not. Emily felt the change in my body and tugged at my arm, indicating she wished to continue walking. But I could not move.

Mr South tipped his hat towards us and introduced himself. All the while, I was speechless, which is very unlike me. I felt butterflies in my stomach, my heart was beating like a drum, and my cheeks felt hot as the blood rushed to them. I had no clue what was happening to me; I only knew I could not control it. Thankfully, Emily took charge of the situation and said sensible and polite words.

We were to spend a lot of time with Mr South aboard the ship and then later, onstage with him. I did eventually find my words and talk with him, but I don't think the butterflies ever left.

We quickly realised how many connections we shared. Mr South's uncles, Mr Thomas King and Mr Edward King, had been in the orchestra for *Norma* in 1855, and we'd also performed with Mr Thomas King in Ballarat in July 1861 for Mr Irwin's fundraiser. Mr South had just finished a three-month season with Mr Greville at the Victoria Theatre in Adelaide. He had been acting alongside the Edouin family, Miss Susan Wooldridge, Mr Willie Shute and Mr Chapman. The business had done so well that Mr Greville had re-engaged him and many of the others, along with Emily and me, for a longer period of time.

Our time in Adelaide, as part of the stock company, was one of the happiest times of my life. We were there for more than the original 12 months (it was actually more like two years), but that was just fine with me. I enjoyed all the different roles I was entrusted with. Acting alongside Emily and Mr South was so much fun.

During this time, several notable stars visited the 'City of Churches', as Adelaide was known, and played under Mr Greville's management. The first stars to visit us were Mr Charles Dillon Snr, and his wife, Clara.

Mr Greville always had rehearsals finished by 1.00 pm and would not wait for anyone. He liked his dinner in the middle of the day, and woe betide any member of the company who happened to be late for rehearsals.

We were to learn that Mr and Mrs Dillon weren't familiar with Mr Greville's rehearsal schedule. On the day that rehearsal was called for Shakespeare's *Richard the Third,* we assembled at 10:00 am sharp and waited until midday, but there was no appearance of the stars. Mr Greville dismissed us.

I heard later that at 12:30 pm, Mr and Mrs Dillon arrived for rehearsal and asked the stage manager, 'Where are the people?'

The manager replied, 'Gone home, sir. The call was made for 10:00 am.'

I'm glad to say that Mr and Mrs Dillon never kept Mr Greville waiting again.

Their opening piece was Shakespeare's *King Lear,* and I played The Fool. I was very nervous, as it was a difficult part, but I suppose I got on all right, for Mr Dillon was very pleased with me.

It struck me at the time that Mrs Clara Dillon was a particularly clever lady. She was a skilled actress and seemed to know how to manage all the ins and outs that went on during rehearsals. But she was often sidelined. I had thought the stage was an equal medium for men and women, but I started to become more aware of the inequalities. At the time, I wasn't even aware that the leading ladies were paid much less than the leading men despite sharing the stage equally.

Mr Joseph Jefferson from America was another star who joined us in July 1862. He came from a long history of actors and was first onstage at four years of age. He was tall, slender and wiry. He had a grace about himself and was a great conversationalist.

He was one of the finest stars to play in Australia. During his stay with us, Mr Jefferson produced *Our American Cousin* by Tom Taylor, *The Octoroon* and *Rip Van Winkle* by Dion Boucicault, *Cricket on the Hearth* and *Nicholas Nickleby* by Charles Dickens. We played so many pieces, and with the rapidity with which they were being produced, well, rehearsals were called every day.

On the morning following the initial performance of *The Octaroon,* one of the actors, Mr Ted Melville, could not be found. His wife, Mary Ann, was beside herself with worry.

Everyone who was available had gone out looking for him. To this day, he is still missing.

A change of parts had to be made quickly, and Mr William South was put in Ted Melville's part of McClosky.

It had been a good opportunity for Mr South to show what he could do, and afterwards Mr Jefferson shook his hand and said,

'Young man, if you like, you have a great future before you.'

I was fortunate enough to be cast in every one of the pieces and acted alongside Mr Jefferson. I appreciated the honour, for it was an honour of the highest to be associated with him. His season was a most successful one in every way. When Mr Jefferson left Adelaide, we all felt we were parting with one of the best and kindest of men. There was no doubt about it, he was loved and admired by all who came in contact with him.

Emily and I were very happy in Adelaide. Mr John and Mrs Charlotte Greville made us feel part of their family. I think I've already mentioned that Mr Greville was a very funny man. I'd seen him many times in a railway station or carriage, meeting people for the first time. He would have them roaring with laughter before they had travelled far together.

The Adelaide community had come to know us well. The theatre stagehands and stage doorkeeper, Mr Peddlestone, also knew us well. They saw us just about every day. Gifts were occasionally left for Emily and me with Mr Peddlestone. He was an old crusty fellow, '100 years in the shade' we used to say.

He had previously worked in a looking glass factory where he absorbed too much mercury into his system, which caused a sort of St Vitus' dance of his hands. His hands would jump about, and he could not control them. When we asked politely for our gifts, Mr Peddlestone would say in a thick Cockney accent,

'No, I'll give 'em to your mother when she comes down. I'll have none of 'ose stage door Johnnies 'anging around waitin' to see ye.'

He was only obeying orders, for mother was very strict with us. Mother had no objection to us receiving flowers, but nothing else. We learnt sometime later that the term 'stage-door Johnnies' referred to men who 'followed' female actresses and were waiting at the stage door after their performances. They were waiting to be let in to visit the actresses in their rooms!

Emily and I had performed in front of many audiences and in many towns. We were often dressed in tightly fitted clothing or showing our legs in stockings for 'breeches' parts. We kept our 'wits about us', but there was certainly a lot that we did not know back then.

During these years, Emily and I learnt our stage-craft through blood, sweat and tears. There were no theatre schools back then. It was the same for all the actors. We all learnt by performing onstage, listening to the audience's reactions and being coached by our fellow actors.

At the end of the first season in Adelaide, most of the company returned with Mr and Mrs Greville to Victoria to open at the old Geelong Theatre. We were joined by Mr Joseph Jefferson, and how thrilling it was to see him again.

We played the regular round of pieces, and Mr Jefferson appeared, for the first time, I think, as an Irish character, Barney O'Toole in the *Peep O'Day Boys.* I was cast as Biddy Farrell, and while dancing an Irish Jig, I had the misfortune to break a blood vessel in my throat, so I was out of action for the rest of the season.

In late 1862, the stock company with Mr Jefferson left for Hobart. I had not recovered, so I could not go with them. I returned to my family in Ballarat. I missed my mother and father. Emily was allowed to go with the company under the care of Mr and Mrs Greville, and they were gone for 10 weeks.

Emily wrote to me several times to give me updates on the season and how everyone was doing. I must admit I missed everyone in the company, especially Mr William South. Emily said they played all the stock standards, *Rip Van Winkle, Octoroon, American Cousin, Nicholas Nickleby,* and *Cricket on the Hearth.*

Mr South retained his part as McClosky in the *Octoroon*, gaining valuable experience in this role.

Finally, the 10-week tour came to an end and the company returned to Adelaide for a second season. I joined them once again, thrilled to be back.

We finished 1862 with a Christmas pantomime called *Cinderella and Harlequin Prince Pretty Pet*. We all enjoyed ourselves immensely.

⁕

In 1863, the company travelled up to Port Adelaide for a fortnight whilst the old Victoria Theatre was closed for a fortnight for repairs. We travelled in horse-drawn carriages with all our luggage strapped together on the roof. It wasn't a long journey, only 12 miles.

All who knew Mr Greville knew he loved fishing. Mr Greville took the opportunity, whilst he was in close proximity to the harbour in Port Adelaide, to indulge in his passion, which almost caused his demise.

He had gone out early in the morning, expecting to return by the afternoon to prepare for opening night. Mrs Greville hadn't seen him, but she knew her husband and wasn't surprised at his absence. She thought that he'd gone early to the theatre and had stayed to manage the set, or to see to the costumes. But when she realised no one had seen him and the stage curtain was due to rise in only two hours, the word was sent out. We all thought of Mr Ted Melville, who had gone missing and was never found, and we started to panic.

The curtain was kept down as long as the audience would endure it. We were all dressed in our costumes and makeup, waiting backstage, hoping for a miracle. Then, to our great relief, in walked the bold fisherman. There was not a single fish to show, and Mr Greville was dripping with water from head to toe. He had to walk onstage as he was and deliver his lines. Only after the first act could he change out of his wet clothes. He told us that he had lost his fishing lines, and when trying to recover them, the boat capsized. I do not think he lost his passion for fishing, but I believe he learnt to be a little more careful in boats!

*

I had been reading in the newspaper about the Burke and Wills Expedition. They were supposed to be on the southward return journey to Melbourne. My dear friend Julia Mathews was urging a search party to be set up to look for them.

She had gone to see Mr Watts, the editor of the *Melbourne Argus*, and asked him to use his power and influence to arouse public opinion to the gravity of the situation. Unfortunately, we found out later, it was all too late. Mr Robert Burke, Mr William Wills and Mr Charles Gray had died at Cooper Creek in South Australia. The only survivor was Mr John King. He told the Royal Society of Victoria, which had organised the expedition, that the party had originally been suspicious of the Aboriginal people, but he only survived because of their help. He owed his life to the Aboriginal people who had given him shelter, food and water. If only the rest of the party had accepted the help that was offered by the Aboriginal people and not been so fearful, then the story might have had a different ending.

A funeral procession was held in Melbourne on 21st January 1863 for Mr Robert O'Hara Burke and Mr William John Wills. They had generated so much interest and support from Melbournians that 40,000 people attended the funeral procession. It felt like the entire colony grieved the loss of the explorers and what they stood for – courage and a willingness to venture into the unknown. My childhood friend and Mr Burke's true love, Miss Julia Matthews was asked to sing Rule Britannia in a memorial held in Castlemaine, Victoria.

I think she grieved the most. She had lost Mr Burke and had lost a future life with him. I truly believe she was going to say 'yes' when he returned and asked her, for the third time, to be his wife. Julia was 'lost at sea' with no set course. She was completely heartbroken.

Later that year, I heard Julia left Melbourne for a singing engagement in New Zealand, and the next year she married her manager, Mr William Mumford. Her fate, sadly, was sealed when she married that man.

⁕

Emily and I continued acting with Mr Greville's company at the Victoria Theatre in Adelaide, South Australia, for several more months.

*

Later in July 1864, we heard that Mr Coppin had left Sydney bound for San Francisco, America. His mission was to bring Shakespeare to Broadway. He travelled over with Mr and Mrs Charles Kean – they were English theatre royalty. I thought Mr Coppin was incredibly brave as the American Civil War was still raging.

President Abraham Lincoln had proclaimed a naval blockade of the Confederate states, and I just hoped that Mr Coppin would be safe and that all the slaves would be set free. At the time, I didn't know very much about slavery, other than the information that Mrs Harriet Beecher Stowe had written in her novel and play, *Uncle Tom's Cabin*. I knew there was often harsh and inhumane treatment of slaves at the hands of their 'owners.' Only a few years later, I would meet the most gracious man who would tell me firsthand what it was like to be a slave.

*

Our second season with Mr Greville was very successful, but our engagement finally came to an end. Mother had arrived in Adelaide for the last few weeks of our engagement and brought my sisters, Alice and Laura.

My mother was very fond of Mr and Mrs Greville, and I often saw them talking together. I didn't know it at the time, but the Greville's were informing mother of what they felt was a blossoming friendship between me and Mr William

South. I found out later that they told mother he came from a good family and was a hard worker. I think over the past two years, the Greville's had become like parents to me and Emily, and they felt it was their responsibility to tell mother everything. Thankfully, mother kept this to herself, for I surely would have died from embarrassment if she had raised the subject of Mr South with me.

We boarded the steamship *Rangatira* in Adelaide on the 14th October 1864, bound for Melbourne. Mother had booked a cabin which was much smaller than we expected and was badly ventilated. We were accustomed to sharing small spaces, but even so, it was a little too cramped for all of us. I decided to spend as much time as possible on deck. Mr William South travelled in steerage, which was located on the lower deck, and his conditions were a lot worse than ours. He also preferred to be on deck.

I was 17 years old and felt very worldly at the time. My sisters, Alice and Laura, were 14 and six years old, respectively. I loved them dearly, and we spent the time onboard the ship sharing stories.

After four days at sea, we sailed into Port Phillip Bay on Monday, 17th October 1864.

Chapter Nine – Mrs Hall and Mrs South

As one door closes, another opens.

When we returned to Melbourne, we were planning on staying for a few days before heading back to Ballarat. My father and brother met us in Melbourne, eager to see us and have the family reunited. After our long engagement in Adelaide, Emily and I were thrilled to be back with the family.

Just before we were to leave for Ballarat, we received a letter from New Zealand. It was an offer for a six-month engagement from Mr Johnnie Hall, who was managing a theatre in Christchurch. When my sister Emily heard the offer, she beamed with joy. Emily and Johnnie had formed a special friendship when we were last in New Zealand under the management of Mr Shadrach Jones of the Princess Theatre in Dunedin. They had been writing to each other, and their friendship and love had grown over the years.

And so, we didn't end up going back to Ballarat. In late October 1864, my mother, Emily, Alice, Laura, and I travelled on the *Albion* across the Tasman Sea to New Zealand. Mr William South and his younger brother, Mr James 'Jimmy' South, had also been engaged by Mr Johnnie Hall and were onboard the *Albion* too. We were excited to be joining a new company and starting a new season, but we also reminisced on the season just ended, and how wonderful that had been with Mr Greville's company.

My father and brother travelled over later and joined us in Christchurch. I didn't know it at the time, but Mr Johnnie Hall had written to my parents and had asked for Emily's hand in marriage.

During that season in New Zealand, Emily's fate, and mine, was decided.

My sister Emily Louisa Mary Ann Wiseman married Mr John Laurence Stephen Steele Woolloxall and became Mrs Hall on Wednesday, 21st December 1864. It was the happiest of days. Emily told me later that it had been love at first sight for her and Johnnie.

My parents decided to stay in Christchurch for a while and open a boarding house. My brother Richard and sisters Alice and Laura were thrilled. They were just happy that we were all together again, as a family.

Mr William South and I performed onstage in various roles. The butterflies were always in my stomach every time he looked at me. When we came into close contact, I felt the electricity between us. There was no doubt in my mind that he felt the same way.

When we were engaged with a company, it was always busy. We were either rehearsing, performing or resting. The company became one big extended family, and we were in and out of each other's dressing rooms.

It was a strange feeling knowing that things had changed between my sister and me. Of course, I was happy for her; in fact, I was over the moon. But at the same time, I felt a little lost. Those feelings must have been obvious to everyone in the company and to my family.

After a Saturday matinee show, Mr South, whom I now called William, called out to me as we were leaving the theatre. He asked me if I would like to walk down to the pier and have an ice cream. My spirits lifted, and with a smile, he knew my answer was yes.

When we reached the pier, William took my hands in his. I looked up and fell deeply into his blue eyes, as I always did. But this time, his eyes seemed to express a nervousness. I thought at the time he was going to tell me he was leaving the company. He had seemed tense for a few weeks, and I had seen him talking most earnestly with his brother James. But instead of telling me he was leaving, he told me how much he admired me, and then he said,

'Frances Jane Wiseman, you are the most amazing woman I have ever met, and I've fallen head over heels in love with you.' My heart stopped, and the world stood still.

I felt a rush of emotions. All my worries and doubts disappeared and were replaced with excitement and hope. William's hands tenderly reached around my waist, and he brought my whole body close to his in an embrace, and then he kissed me. A gentle kiss, at first, then a more passionate kiss.

I knew then that my life would never be the same. I was excited to start a new chapter with my beloved William.

I now knew how my sister Emily felt about her Johnnie. I could not wait to see William, to spend time with him, to be onstage with him. We kept our relationship secret, but looking back, I realise we fooled no one. The company all just played along, and I'm sure they all shared secret smiles and giggles with each other when our backs were turned. It was becoming impossible to hide our true feelings.

Then one night, after we'd just finished a performance, almost as soon as the curtain had fallen, William fell onto his knee and took my hand in his. Everyone who was still onstage stopped what they were doing.

'Fanny, I have loved you from the first moment I saw you. Would you do me the greatest honour and marry me?'

I was so excited, the words rushed out of me, 'Yes, yes, of course, the answer is yes.'

We embraced and kissed, and everyone onstage applauded.

My parents were thrilled when William and I told them of our engagement. Thankfully, they weren't upset that William hadn't initially asked my father for my hand in marriage.

On Saturday, 7th January 1865, I married William Thomas King South in the Anglican Cathedral in Christchurch. It was one of the happiest days of my life.

We could only take a few days to go on our honeymoon, as there were many work commitments. Those few days of being alone together as husband and wife are such sweet memories. I can close my eyes and remember the tenderness and love we both felt for each other.

After our six-month work engagement in Christchurch came to an end, William and I returned to Melbourne. My family decided to stay in New Zealand. It was so hard saying goodbye to everyone, especially Emily. We were best friends and each other's confidants. Our bond was unbreakable. But now we were married women, sharing our lives with our husbands, we had to go our separate ways.

*

When William and I returned to Melbourne, we received a letter of offer from Mr Henry D Wilton, who was Lady Don's manager. Lady Don was an outstanding singer and actor from England, and she was very popular with Australian audiences. She was elegant, dashing and made a striking figure. She had returned to Australia for her second tour. But the second tour was tainted with sadness as Lady Don was travelling without her husband. Sir William, a Scottish baronet, had died on their first tour when they were in Tasmania.

Many businesses rode on the coat-tails of successful performers. The sweet shops in Melbourne had started to manufacture immense sticks of rainbow-colour 'rock' with the words 'Lady Don' in red letters deeply embedded in the recesses of the confection. The sweets were very popular and certainly added to the excitement of Lady Don.

Mr Wilton was regarded in the industry as 'the Napoleon of agents' as he was a skilled strategist with scrupulous attention to detail. Luckily, he was also good-humoured, which made our transactions with him very memorable. He managed many actors, including Mr GV Brooke.

Mr Wilton informed us that Lady Don was performing at The Theatre Royal in Ballarat, and she wanted to engage William and me as principal members of her company. We happily accepted the offer.

Meeting and performing alongside Lady Don was an honour. I greatly admired her. She was 16 years older than me, and I knew I would learn a lot from her. One of the things she said to me early on was to retain my maiden name, which was also my stage name, and not be tempted to change it to my married name of Mrs South. Whilst she did change her name, it was obviously advantageous to be known as Lady Don rather than by her real name, which was Miss Emily Sanders. She often gave me advice, which I took eagerly.

After several of the performances, she would send the manager to my dressing room. He would knock loudly on the door and say,

'Excuse me Miss Wiseman, Lady Don wishes to speak with you.'

I came to understand that when she called for me, she wanted to impart some of her knowledge and experiences with me.

I remember her saying, 'Fanny, you must look after your health, for without it you won't be able to play challenging roles and perform long hours on the stage and during tours.'

On one of these evenings, she told me about her first night performance in The Royal Haymarket Theatre in Melbourne in August 1864. She had just arrived after the long sea journey from London.

'Fanny, I have to tell you about when I had a breakdown. I want to tell you, as it can happen to anyone. You have not experienced such grief that it can consume you. And I hope you never will.'

She paused, and I could see she was upset with the memories.

'I was excessively nervous, and the memories of my husband and daughter were overwhelming. My husband had died, and I had to leave my daughter in Scotland with her grandmother. I was emotionally fragile. When I was onstage that first night, I was a mess. After that disastrous start, I managed to centre myself and start afresh. The experience shook me to the core, and I vowed to myself to be more aware of my emotional state.'

I felt honoured that Lady Don had shared such personal information with me.

It was an extremely successful season, and I definitely learnt a lot from Lady Don. It was wonderful to be back in Ballarat. William's parents, uncles and aunties lived there, so we spent as much time as we could with them.

Lady Don's next engagement was in New Zealand in February 1866, and then she planned to tour in America. She wanted William and me to go with her to New Zealand; however, we decided not to travel with her. It was so tempting as my parents were still living in Christchurch.

Lady Don was an exceptional actress. She was also very friendly and charming. Her success, I think, was in part due to her business sense and in part due to her personality.

After our last show together, the manager asked me to go to Lady Don's dressing room.

I knocked on her door and she welcomed me into her dressing room and asked me to sit down.

She said, 'My dearest, you have done so well, and the audiences love you.'

She beamed at me and continued, 'I have seen how you approach each performance and the respect you show to our profession.'

I nodded and felt there was a 'but' coming.

'But you need more challenging roles to extend yourself. After the New Zealand tour, I want to take you with me on an 18-month tour to America. I know you and your husband William have declined the New Zealand tour, but I want you to think carefully about my offer for an American tour.'

My first reaction was pure excitement. I had heard so much about the American theatre business. She told me they would be starting the tour in California in July 1866 and would only be touring in the Northern States. But there was a catch. Lady Don did not need William in the company. She explained to me that the company already had plenty of male actors who were more experienced than William.

It was a wonderful chance for me, and I had wanted to go to America for some time. I knew of many married couples that were separated for short periods of time as they undertook work. I thought, perhaps William would see this opportunity as my 'big break.' Perhaps he will be supportive and excited for me.

I rushed back to my dressing room to talk with William. My excitement was obviously visible, and William asked immediately what had happened. I told him of Lady Don's offer. My excitement turned quickly to disappointment.

He said, 'Absolutely no.'

He wasn't going to be separated from me.

'It's too dangerous to travel to America,' he said.

'How can you even consider Lady Don's offer?' He seemed hurt, like I was 'leaving' him. My goodness, we had only been married for a few months, and I was completely in love with him.

I started to feel guilty. Had the prospect of travelling to America for fame and fortune appeal to me more than having a happy marriage?

Couldn't I have both?

At the time, I accepted my husband's decision without questioning his motives; it was how things were done back then. I was an obedient wife, but, oh, I was an angry one.

*

William and I took several engagements at The Royal Theatre in Ballarat and worked with many actors and actresses. We were constantly working. Our lives fell into a rhythm of rehearsals and performances.

April 1865 was a month of extreme highs and lows. We had heard that the American Civil War effectively ended when Confederate General Robert E Lee surrendered his troops to Union General Ulysses S Grant in April. But then we heard of the assassination of President Abraham Lincoln. The President was enjoying the performance of *Our American Cousin* at Ford's Theatre in Washington on 14th April, when Mr John Wilkes Booth, an actor, shot the President during the play. President Abraham Lincoln was a great man, and all the theatre folk felt a deep sadness, especially as the one who committed this heinous act was one of our own. Mr John Wilkes Booth was on the run for several days until he was shot by a soldier

I would later hear first-hand from Mr George Coppin, who was in Washington at the same time as the President's assassination, how it affected the American people. The assassination had occurred during the Easter weekend. This was usually a very prosperous time for the theatre business as everyone was out enjoying themselves. The nation went into mourning, and all the theatres were closed for four days. Mr Coppin told me that it almost broke him financially.

Mr Coppin said he saw the funeral procession in New York when the President's coffin was carried into the City Hall. The nation experienced a great sadness, but also a great patriotic pride shone through.

*

My sister and her husband, Johnnie, had lived in New Zealand since their marriage in December 1864.

Emily had given birth to a baby boy in September 1865. I was so happy for her.

She wrote to me with the news that they were returning to Melbourne in November 1865 on the *Alhambra*. I couldn't wait to meet baby Asa Hoyt Leander Holgate Hall Woolloxall. It was a big name for a little person to live up to!

Although Emily and I wrote to each other often when she returned to Australia, it was hard to visit each other, either in Ballarat or Melbourne. Work commitments made things difficult, so we had to be happy with writing letters.

⁕

In mid-March 1866, there was another tragedy that shocked the theatre family. I still remember where I was when I heard the devastating news of Mr GV Brooke's death. I was walking with William to the Theatre Royal in Ballarat for a performance. We had turned the corner into the main street where the paperboys were calling out the 'news of the day.' The young boy was saying,

'Mr Brooke, the great Irish actor, is dead.'

I almost collapsed with the shock.

We knew that Mr George Coppin had re-engaged Mr Brooke for a two-year tour through Australia and New Zealand. Mr Coppin had returned to Australia from America and had been expecting Mr Brooke to arrive from England any day.

The newspapers said that Mr Brooke and his sister Frances were returning to Melbourne aboard the steamer *SS London*. The ship sank on 11th January 1866 off the coast of Spain in the Bay of Biscay. It was reported by the 19 survivors that mountainous seas had pounded the vessel for several days.

The survivors said that Mr Brooke had worked at the pumps incessantly in an effort to save the ship. Captain

John Bohun Martin, who was an Australian, told all the passengers to be prepared as the ship was sinking. The lifeboats had been launched, but they immediately filled with water. They made a final attempt to launch the last lifeboat, and this time it was launched successfully and didn't fill with water. But passengers didn't want to get in it. They were too frightened. They feared certain death if they were in a tiny boat amongst the overwhelming waves.

Mr Brooke helped people into the lifeboat but stayed onboard the ship with his sister. The newspaper also reported that when the lifeboat rowed away, he called out, 'If you succeed in saving yourself, give my kind farewell to the people of Melbourne.'

The ship sank soon after, and 250 people died.

I will always remember Mr Brooke as one of the greatest actors, but more importantly as a kind and generous man. My heart just ached for Polly, his first wife and my old friend Avonia Jones, who had become Mr Brooke's second wife.

On 21st April 1866, the Brooke Memorial Fund was held at the Princess Theatre in Melbourne. My friends, Rose and Julia Edouin and their sister-in-law, Miss Lizzie Naylor, who was married to Mr John Edouin, delivered the eulogies.

⁎

My parents, brother and little sisters left New Zealand and returned to Australia in April 1866 aboard the *South*

Australian. We were eventually reunited when they returned to Ballarat.

William and I had been living and working in Ballarat for quite a while. I had been feeling a little unwell and just thought it was exhaustion. But when my tummy started to get a little bigger, I realised I must be 'with child'. That was around May 1866. William was thrilled, but I had my worries. I had seen how the women who had children managed when they were acting and touring. It was a challenge.

My sister Emily and Johnnie were busy with her little boy, Asa, in Melbourne. Emily took on work when opportunities arose. She wrote to me often, which was a great comfort when I had doubts about how I was going to manage. But tragedy struck when little Asa was only 10 months old. He had been unwell with a cold, which suddenly got worse. It was winter, and many people had died from influenza.

Our beautiful little Asa died on 22nd August 1866. He was buried in Melbourne General Cemetery. Emily, Johnnie and my parents were at the funeral. It brought back memories of our little brother Arthur, who had also died before he could celebrate his 1st birthday. He was buried in the same cemetery. We were all so devastated.

*

My mother knew my time to give birth was soon approaching. The local granny had come to see me and had listened to my baby's heartbeat. I was getting nervous. It was not uncommon for women to die during childbirth. But I was not worried about myself; I was worried that my little baby would not survive. Granny Watts reassured me and said she would help me birth my baby. She had helped many women.

She kept saying, 'Don't be worrying, now, the baby knows what to do, and your body knows what to do. Trust in yourself.'

When the time came, Granny Watts was called for, and with her and my mother's help, my baby was born on the 14th November 1866. He was a healthy little boy, and we named him William Wiseman South.

I could not have imagined the love I would feel for my little boy. He was my everything. When I became a mother, everything changed for me. My purpose in life, my love for my parents, family and husband. It seemed to grow bigger and deeper.

*

In early 1867, when little William was about three months old, we left Ballarat and returned to Melbourne and set up house at 3 Brunswick Street, Collingwood. The rest of the family soon joined us in Melbourne, as Emily and Johnnie had put together a company and needed all the Wiseman girls to perform.

The company was made up of Johnnie Hall, my husband, and my sisters Emily, Alice and Laura, and of course, myself. We also had Mr Olly Deering, Mr William Bain Gill and several members of the Edouin family.

I was thrilled to be working with John and Julia Edouin again, and Miss Tilly Earl, John's wife. And thank goodness I was surrounded by my own family. With a newborn baby came a lot of new responsibilities, and I needed all the help I could get.

I had told William many stories of the competition between the Edouin family and the Wiseman family when both families were travelling through the Victorian goldfields. The Edouin's were a talented family and could do anything from farce, comedy and burlesque.

We opened at the Princess Theatre, with *Ixion,* a burlesque written by Mr Frank Burnand. It was met with a full house almost every night. After several weeks, Johnnie decided to take the company on tour.

My sister Emily was pregnant with her second child, and while we were on tour, she gave birth to a boy on 3rd April 1867. They named him John Laurence Samuel Wiseman Woolloxall. We were all so happy for her, but we were also sad thinking of her other little boy, Asa, who had died only the year before. I knew Emily so well and could see she was worried that baby John would have a similar fate to Asa. I did what I could to give her support and comfort.

My baby was with me wherever I went. I could not bear to be parted from him, and like other actresses with babies, William slept in a cot in my dressing room when I was performing. My parents toured with us, so I was never without the support of my family.

My brother Richard was in charge of the business arrangements. He was 19 years old and had been around the stage most of his life.

We taunted him by saying that taking on the manager role came naturally to him as he loved bossing his sister's around, especially Laura, who was only 10 years old. But it was all in good humour. We were grateful to have him in charge – we trusted him with the performance takings and looking after all our belongings. In all truth, he worked very hard. His role as manager involved organising the printing of the playbills, arranging the ticketing and collecting the sales at the end of the night. He had to pay the printer, the theatre manager and make sure everyone was paid their wages. He was careful and courteous and made many friends in all the towns we visited.

Mr William Bain Gill was a great help to my brother. He was like a big brother to Richard. He was very observant and eloquent. He never ruffled anyone's feathers; he was a true diplomat.

We were a happy, loud and energetic group. At times, one could not hear oneself think. Mr Olly Deering was always making jokes, and you'd think he was a 'relaxed' performer. However, that was far from the truth. His father was Mr Henry Deering, and he'd performed alongside Mr George Coppin in the early days when Mr Coppin had first arrived in Sydney. Olly, I was told, was very similar to his father. He was meticulous with his preparation and would practice his lines and his stage positions during rehearsals until we all begged him to finish so we could go home or back to the hotel.

John Edouin and his wife, Tilly Earl, would gently convince Olly that he had perfected his lines, and it was time to go to bed.

After many months of touring with *Ixion*, William and I received a letter from Mr George Benjamin William Lewis and his wife Miss Rose Edouin. They were putting together a new company called The Burlesque and Dramatic Company and were planning on going to Calcutta in India. They wanted actors who were steady, well-trained and successful and were inviting William and me to join the company.

Julia told us she was joining her sister Rose and said most of the Edouin family was also excited to be going. Mr Olly Deering had been invited to join the company as well.

Mr WB Gill encouraged us all to go. He had travelled with Mr Lewis' company in 1864 and 1865 to Shanghai, Hong Kong, Japan and India. He said it had been a very profitable enterprise, and it had been a wonderful experience. He said Mr GBW Lewis' company was the first theatrical group to perform a pantomime in China!

My childhood friend Rose Edouin had married Mr GBW Lewis a few years back, but the last time I had seen Rose was on the goldfields of Ballarat and Bendigo.

Throughout the year, I had been performing with Rose's sister and brother, Julia and Johnnie, so I felt very familiar with the family. The thought of working with Rose and the rest of the Edouin family was very enticing.

The letter from Mr GBW Lewis and Rose included some details about the travel plans and an offer from Rose to meet and discuss how the children would be cared for while we were on tour.

I knew Rose had two children. I was grateful for the chance to talk with her. So, I quickly sharpened my quill and wrote back to set up the meeting.

*

We arranged to meet at the Menzies Hotel on the corner of Bourke and William Street in Melbourne. I arrived early and sat patiently watching the colour and movement of Melbourne all around me. When I saw Rose enter the room, I was not the only one. She was wearing the most splendid silk dress, the colour of deep red with black velvet trims. Her bodice was in the new style with a V-neck, which was beautifully complemented with a black velvet choker and a shiny black oval jet pendant. Her hat was tilted slightly and tied with red ribbons. She was a well-recognised personality in Melbourne, and I could see the heads turn when she glided past the other patrons.

We embraced as old friends. She was thrilled that William and I were considering the offer to go to India. She said there was no question that my little William should come. Rose told me that she was taking George, who was two years old, and Lucy May, who was only three months old. All the children would be part of the 'travelling family'.

I did not want to leave my baby, but I was worried about taking him to an unknown country. Rose had her husband, her mother and her sister and her brothers to help her.

Although I knew they would help me as well, it would be a lot harder. Rose told me about Calcutta and how wonderful the trip would be. We reminisced about our childhood and touring through the goldfields, and we both shed a tear when we spoke of her older sister, Eliza, who had died so young.

Rose told me about her husband and how he saw Asia as a new and untapped market for British theatre. Mr GBW Lewis had engaged the Edouin family a few years earlier, in August 1864, and had a very successful tour through China and India. Whilst on that tour, Rose and Mr GBW Lewis had fallen in love and were married in Shanghai Church of the Holy Trinity on 19th November 1864. There was 26 years difference between them, Rose being the younger. It was not uncommon to have a big age difference between a man and a woman. Mr GBW Lewis had worked hard for many years and had become very successful and wealthy.

Before we finished, I thanked Rose for her time and patience, and I said that she would have our answer by the following day. We walked out together, Rose turning right, and I left.

William and I talked about the Lewis' offer long into the night. This was a great opportunity for us, and we could earn a lot of money, but I was apprehensive about taking my baby to India. I knew my parents would willingly look after him if we did go, but I just did not want to leave baby William behind.

The deal was sealed when William said,

'If we go for a season or two, we could make enough money to buy a little house in Ballarat for us and William.'

I loved travelling to new places and meeting all different types of people. But since having my little baby, I seemed to long for more stability, a place to call my own.

With a deep sigh, I said,

'I'll ask my parents to look after William, and we'll go for a season and save as much money as we can.'

I wasn't quite ready to commit to more than one season. We embraced, and William kissed me all over my face. With a huge smile on his face, he said he'd inform Mr and Mrs Lewis of our decision in the morning and would then start making the preparations. William was very excited, but I didn't feel the same way; I just felt anxious.

Not for the first time, I started to prepare for a long sea journey. Travelling from England to Australia when I was seven years old was wonderful. Perhaps going to India would be the same.

My parents happily agreed to look after William while we were away, and my brother Richard and sisters Alice and Laura were going to help as well.

When it came time to leave, we made our way to Melbourne Pier. All my family came to see us off. When I said farewell to my little boy, I honestly felt sick. I had to 'wear' a brave face. I knew if I let my true feelings show, it would only upset my little William. I kissed and hugged him. I could not let him go. It felt like my heart was breaking in two.

My husband gently took my baby from my arms and handed him to my mother. We all embraced and promised to write often. Then William and I walked towards the ship and up the gangway. When I was at the top of the gangway, I turned to wave and saw my family, standing in the same spot as we had left them. I could see my baby was upset and squirming in my mother's arms. Alice and Laura were fussing over him and trying to comfort him. He didn't see me.

I had a deep sense of foreboding.

Interlude

'Mr Robinson, I fear I have become very tired.'

'Oh Miss Wiseman, of course, we can take a break.'

'Actually, I think it's best if we resume our interview in the morning.'

Mr Robinson could not imagine how it felt to be 81 years old; he looked like he was in his mid-twenties. After a lifetime of living, the body becomes tired even if the mind still feels young and active.

I had been talking for a few hours, remembering the early days. My family and friends from those days were all gone. I missed them. I could remember the happy and challenging times, but a sadness crept in.

Mr Robinson put his pen and papers back into his satchel. He stood up and straightened his jacket. He stretched out his hand and offered to assist me.

I took his hand. I felt the strength and tenderness as he assisted me from the couch.

He offered to walk me to my room.

'Thank you Mr Robinson. I can manage from here.'

'Yes, of course. Will I meet you at the same time tomorrow?'

'That would be perfect.'

As I left the parlour, Sister Kitty walked me to my room. She knew me so well. She made me a cup of tea in my favourite Royal Doulton teacup. The saucer had a little crack in it, but it was still so special to me. It reminded me of a time in my life, long ago.

I had only touched on the 'tip of the iceberg' of my life.

Mr Robinson had obviously done his research, but there was a lot that had happened in my life that I had never spoken about.

As an actress, you are always curating your life so that the public sees a specific image of you. They don't see your heartbreak, your struggles, your sadness. They also don't see your joys. But these were the things I was going to tell Mr Robinson.

Tomorrow.

Chapter Ten – Calcutta, the winter capital of India

I was waiting for Mr Robinson in the parlour. He arrived right on time.

He greeted me warmly, and we sat down on the same couch and chair as the previous day.

After arranging his papers and pen, and settling in, he said, 'I'm ready when you are Miss Wiseman. Please tell me more about your life.'

And so, I began again.

*

We left Melbourne on the 20th July 1867 aboard the *SS Underley*, an iron clipper ship. Our Captain was John Brown. He was a grand old fellow, full of fun and teased us all when he had a chance.

Aboard the ship was the rest of the company. Mr GBW Lewis, his wife Rose Edouin and their two children, George and baby Lucy May. My dear friend Julia Edouin and her mother Mrs Sarah Elizabeth Bryer, Mr and Mrs Henry

Chapman, Mr Olly Deering and his sister Miss Waddy Deering, Miss Lizzie Melville, Mr Harry Richardson, Mr John H Allen (an American), Mr Henry Birch, Mr Compton, who played the piano beautifully, Mr ED Haygarth, Mr Harry Stoneham, Mr Edward Hunter, Mr Kenneth Douglas, our musical conductor, me and my husband.

Julia Edouin and I were already life-long friends, as we'd spent so much time together performing and touring with *Ixion*.

On the journey over to India, I spent a lot of time with Julia, Rose, Waddy and Lizzie. We were all of a similar age. We shared tips on how to navigate the theatre business and how to keep ourselves healthy while we were onboard the ship.

Rose told us the continuous exposure to sea air was detrimental to our voices, and gargling with cold water was a good remedy for a sore throat. She said her old tutor recommended, when overexertion causes the voice to fail, to drink an egg beaten into a glass of madeira or sherry, or three spoonsful of the compound tincture of cinnamon in water. I liked the idea of the madeira or cinnamon; however, neither of those was available onboard the ship.

One evening, we were all talking about how we started in the theatre business. Many of us had been child actors.

Rose told us how the stage name Edouin was given to her family by their French dancing teacher when they were growing up in London. It was a derivative of their father's given name of Edwin. She said her first acting mentor in London was the world-renowned Mr Samuel Phelps. He had taught her all her stage skills.

Her first performance was at age six with Mr GV Brooke at the Marylebone Theatre in London in May 1850. Oh, just hearing Mr Brooke's name. The entire company felt in that moment a collective sadness. I held back the tears as I thought about how poor Mr GV Brooke's life had ended only the year before. He was a great man and tried valiantly to save the sinking ship. He had saved many people, but he and his sister had gone down with the ship to a watery grave.

Then we started talking about our old friend Mr George Coppin. Captain Brown, who had decided to dine with us that evening, piped up and said Mr Coppin was also his old friend. At that point, we all burst out laughing. Of course, Mr Coppin knew everyone, and we had no doubt he and Captain Brown were firm friends.

Mr GBW Lewis was a very tall man, I think he was 6 feet 4 inches, and he had a big presence when entering any room. He had a steely focus when confronted with a problem or a task. Nothing could stop him from achieving his goals; he just forged ahead and got the job done. I felt William and I were in safe hands, even though we were going to a foreign country. Mr GBW Lewis told us many stories about his previous visits to India and China. Only 10 years earlier, the British had taken control of India, and it was now part of the British Empire, and Queen Victoria was the ruling sovereign.

I wondered why one country would 'take' another country? I came to learn that this happened frequently, and I felt a little guilty that I had never really thought that was what the British had done in Australia. I had seen Aboriginal people on the outskirts of Melbourne and in the gold-mining towns. But at the time, my thoughts were on learning my lines and arriving at the theatre on time. As I grew older, I saw many injustices towards Aboriginal people. People in power could be unfair, unkind and unjust and just say 'that's how the world works.' It made my blood boil when I heard those attitudes.

⁂

The journey from Melbourne to Calcutta took about five weeks, and we arrived in early September 1867. When we arrived, all my senses went into overdrive. The sounds, the sights, the smells, and the heat. Indian women wore beautiful saris, and the men wore white turbans on their heads. I felt like I was staring, which was a little rude of me, but I couldn't help it. I loved the colour and all the differences.

We were taken to the Great Eastern Hotel in Calcutta, nicknamed the Jewel of the East. It was a three-storey hotel, well-constructed, and it had lovely little white shutters on the windows. William and I were given a room on the second floor. When we walked in, we could see through the window, which opened onto the main street. We fell onto the bed, exhausted and exhilarated at the same time.

There were lots of Britons living in Calcutta, and many of them were in official positions supporting the government. We learned that they were called 'super-bureaucrats' or 'Pukka Sahibs.' Most of them were very aloof from the local Indian people. There were private clubs and well-guarded British military cantonments, which were constructed beyond the walls of the old, crowded city.

The Britons and Indian upper classes loved the theatre, which was a good thing for us. Mr GBW Lewis told us that theatre was often performed in the private homes of the wealthy zamindars and bhadralok classes (land-holders and tax collectors for the British)[vii], and we would be well supported with their patronage. But we were also going to perform in front of the general Calcutta public, and our audiences would be comprised of mostly British and European members of the civil and military services, their families and educated Bengalis.

*

We were not the first foreign entertainers to visit Calcutta. Many entertainers stopped there on their way to or from tours in British colonies. But there had never been a permanent English theatre in Calcutta because of government restrictions.

The Lewis' had acquired rent-free land on the Maidan. The Maiden was a park-like space between Chowringhee

Road and the Hooghly River. The area also contained Fort William, a major British defence structure, and Eden Gardens, the botanical pleasure park.

I was to find out that Mr GBW Lewis was highly respected by the people of Calcutta. When he first arrived in Calcutta in 1859, he often held special charity performances to raise money for the Calcutta Alms Houses and the Orphan Free School.

It didn't take long for Mr Lewis to organise the construction of a large theatre on the Maidan, which they called the Royal Lyceum Theatre. The theatre roof was made from sheets of corrugated iron, and the building itself was also made from prefabricated corrugated iron and bamboo. It could seat 800 people. The stage was imposing, and there was beautiful gilt plaster ornamentation and plush red velvet seats.

Opening night at the Royal Lyceum Theatre was on 17th September 1867. Our opening pieces were Tobin's comedy *The Honeymoon* and the farce *The Quiet Family* by Samuel French.

The Honeymoon is a piece well calculated to test the power of the actors. Miss Rose Edouin played the character of Juliana and presented the character from the first to the last scene with exceptional acting.

In *The Quiet Family,* Miss Julia Edouin played the meek Mrs Benjamin Bibbs, and Miss Lizzie Melville played the fiery Mrs Barnaby Bibbs. I played the character of Snarly, and William was Mr Grumpy. We were a complete little picture and performed with much spirit.

We had good audiences despite the ticket prices being a little high for the time, two to five rupees, and we had a few seats under the gallery for one rupee. But a few nights we had some rough and bad behaviour from those who had the cheaper seats, so Mr Lewis closed that section off.

We only gave three performances a week – Mondays, Wednesdays and Saturdays. The business was excellent. There was no other competition there at the time. Mr Lewis was a businessman at heart, and this venture was certainly paying off.

We usually went to bed about 2:00 am, and only a few hours later, at about 5:30 am, we would be roused by a hotel attendant, who would exclaim while waking us, 'Tea sahib.' Of course, we were grateful and, having thanked the fellow, we would turn over and go back to sleep again. The attendant, whether you bless or curse him (not that I ever cursed him), was thankful for our patronage at the hotel.

Unquestionably, the theatre was frequented by British and Europeans living away from their homeland. They were nostalgic and wanted to experience familiar art and culture. Our repertoire involved more of the crowd-pleasing and fashionable dramas, burlesques, and extravaganzas, the latest from Drury Lane. Shakespearean plays were also included because they were very popular.

*

The cooler months in Calcutta are from October all the way through to March, similar to what I remember in London. Our hotel attendant had told us that in the winter, you can sometimes lie with a blanket over you, but I think that must be a stretch of the imagination. The weather did start to get a little cooler, but I thought it was quite warm.

We still had the punkahs going, which is a fan made from cane operated using a rope and pulled by one of the hotel attendants. We used the mosquito curtains as well. We would not last long without those curtains, as the mosquitoes were like monster bloodsuckers.

Talking of size, you should have seen the prawns they had in Calcutta. Without exaggeration, I saw some as large as small lobsters. The Indian chefs make a delicious curry with them. But there were no vegetables except potatoes, and they were so small and scarce that we generally only received one each at dinner. We quickly learnt that everything good to eat and drink was either unobtainable or very expensive.

*

On the 1st November 1867, after we had only been playing at the Lyceum for four weeks, we were visited by a most powerful and dangerous cyclone. It started about 9:00 pm and did not abate in its violence and destruction until 11:00 am the next day. We were dreadfully scared and began to think the world had come to an end. It caused a great deal of damage. The theatre was completely flattened. The piano was smashed into small fragments, but strangely, the double bass was spared any damage. Fortunately, neither of the two men left in charge of the building was hurt; their escape from injury was a miracle.

After the cyclone, Mr GBW Lewis immediately set about rebuilding the theatre, and we kept rehearsing in the hotel. Mr Lewis was very determined, and after only eight days, he had erected another theatre. On our re-opening, the theatre was packed to the rafters.

We continued on and played everything from Shakespeare to Byron. Rose Edouin shone in pantomime, burlesque and comedy, but saying that, she was extremely versatile and could undertake melodrama and tragedy equally well. We played to appreciative audiences until the end of the season in March 1868.

After our first season came to an end, Mr Lewis brought the company together and said,

'I have always endeavoured to bring the best available talent to the people of Calcutta. And I'm very proud of the season we've had. I feel it is my duty to bring a respectable company, respectability is equal to talent.' He paused for a moment and then said, 'We continue to provide great entertainment to our fellow men and women and bring them Shakespeare and modern plays.'

We all applauded. It had been a tremendous time.

The theatre had to be dismantled at the end of the season. At the time, the government did not allow a permanent structure. One of those odd Calcutta municipal authority requirements. [viii]

When the rainy season commenced, Mr Lewis said we needed to leave Calcutta and head towards 'the hills.' I was to learn that 'the hills' meant a place called Simla, near the foothills of the Himalayas.

Chapter Eleven – Simla, the summer capital of India

Calcutta and Simla were the winter and summer capitals of India. Calcutta was extremely hot in summer, so the British government would pack up all their government records and personal belongings in spring and travel to the cooler climes of Simla. As winter approached, Simla would become too cold and damp, so the British government would again pack up everything in autumn and return to Calcutta, where the winter weather was pleasant.

This bi-annual mass migration from plains to hills and hills to plains had been taking place for decades. When I was there, the migration involved the Viceroy of India, Lord John Lawrence, and all the government administration, including judges, bureaucrats, politicians, and military attachés. I was told that nearly 5,000 staff, wives, children and servants participated in the migration.

Simla's reputation for beauty and comfort had become well known across the British dominions. Simla was not just a government retreat from the heat of Calcutta, but also a centre of British high society, where officers and their families lived lavishly. We didn't know it at the time, but Simla's reputation for beauty was equally matched by a reputation for British 'steamy' social life.

The trip from Calcutta to Simla was no holiday jaunt. The government migration would take five or more arduous days, but for us, it took weeks.

We went on a gruelling tour through northern India and stopped at many military station towns. I had no idea how hot it would be travelling through the plains. Rose and I were both pregnant and suffered terribly in the heat.

We travelled by train to the military stations and towns and stayed for a week or two. We performed twelve pieces in each town. Then we were back on the train. Sometimes the train journey would be very long, 300 miles without a stop, a twelve-hour ride before you could thoroughly stretch your legs. The heat was over 100 °F. We went to Dinapore, Patna, Benares, Jamalpore, Allahabad, Lucknow, Cawnpore, Elbhi, Imballa, Lahore, Kalka, Kussoli, Delhi, and our final stop was Simla. We travelled a distance of 2,000 miles.

I remember when we stopped at Dinapore. The hotel was six miles from the railway station and three miles from the theatre. We rehearsed every day, and it was rather tiring travelling to and fro. We played two pieces every night except Sunday. The performances generally began about

9:00 pm, finished at midnight, and then we rode back to the hotel for supper. We certainly were not idle.

We were welcomed at every stop, and the business was first-rate all the way. But tragedy struck after we'd left Benares, and we were at Jamalpore. Rose's baby, Lucy May, who was 10 months old, died from teething problems and convulsions. The wee little girl was buried in Mooltan. It was a devastating time. Rose's little boy, George, who was now three years old, was her light during this dark time, and he was the one who kept her going. And we *had* to keep going. Simla was our final destination, and it was where we could all take some respite and recover.

We travelled across the plains of India, across rivers and a bone-rattling journey by train, horse, elephant, bullock cart and sedan chair. I must admit I felt uncomfortable riding in the sedan chair, as it involved two Indian men carrying me in an 'Egyptian' style cabin on two poles. Mr Lewis told me that it was the only work these men could find, and they would be grateful for the rupees they earned.

Slowly, we made our way up steeply winding slopes to a place that I had heard people describe as 'heaven on earth'. As we travelled skywards up the winding roads, we could see the mists rising from the mountain floor. The skies above us were piercing blue. There was a wonderful change in the air after the stifling heat of the plains.

We spent two months in Simla, from April to June 1868. Simla was the most wonderful place. I had never seen such natural beauty. The mountains seemed to stretch on forever, and we felt we were on top of the highest point in the world.

There are two high points in Simla. The first is where the vice-regal lodge is located, a very impressive Tudor-style building. The other point is Jakko, and on this summit live Hindus, Indian devotees, with yellow and white pigment on their faces, and a tribe of monkeys.

William and I and the entire company stayed in the Cecil Hotel, which had only recently been built. We had all the luxuries we could want, and our lives quickly fell into a routine of performing three nights during the week and the rest of the time was our own. Although I should say we weren't on our own very often.

We would be invited to three or four dinner parties per week, and the same with luncheon parties. It was a whirlwind of entertainment, interspersed with some quite gorgeous ceremony and pomp. The three-wheeled rickshaws were operated by Indian workers dressed in special uniforms, often bearing the family crest of the rich British family that they were serving. They would shuttle their masters and mistresses around to very ostentatious occasions.

There was a very flat area just off the main street, called Annandale. It became the public playground. We went there many times to watch cricket matches, polo games, tennis competitions, horse racing, football, archery, rifle-shooting, golf, and croquet. And did I forget to mention dog shows! We even attended a moonlight gymkhana.

The altitude can take its toll on those who move too quickly on the steep hillsides. So, walking in Simla is by necessity a leisurely affair. About 6:00 pm every evening, you see Simla residents turn out, some attending the service in the church with the pale lemon façade overlooking the town, while others would promenade along the Mall Road. The Mall Road was an elegant shopping street, designed for leisurely walks. William and I enjoyed the evening air and the sunsets. We would often stroll along the Ridge away from the church, past the British army bandstand and the town hall and walk towards Scandal Point, where the Ridge meets the Mall.

Scandal Point was a social gathering spot and was rumoured to have been named after an elopement scandal involving a British woman and an Indian Maharaja. It became a place for British residents to meet and gossip.

Near the bandstand, there was a small Indian operated food stall called Goofa, which means 'cave' in Hindi, where coffee, tea and light snacks could be purchased. I fell in love with pakora, a deep-fried puff pastry stuffed with vegetables or cheese. Sometimes they also sold samosas, which were the most delicious small turnovers stuffed with meat or vegetables. These delicious treats became my favourite foods.

In the mornings and evenings, the scent of wood fires and Indian spices from the hundreds of small Indian homes would waft up the hill. The sounds of Indian's and Britons were interwoven with the singing of birds.

The United Services Club was the centrepiece of social life in Simla, and it catered to British military personnel. The officers participated in many sports like polo and cricket, and it really reinforced Simla's reputation as a place for both work and leisure. Women and the local Indians were not permitted to join the Club, although guests were admitted. I went there with William as his guest, to visit the library, which was packed with books for members to enjoy. Rose, Julia, Lizzie and I would often go together and spend hours in the reading room.

From the vantage point of Cecil Hotel, we could see the aristocracy head out on hunting trips or for jaunts in their liveried rickshaws. The mountains were great hunting areas.

Simla attracted scores of young British girls in search of husbands. But they were often out of luck, as the young men seemed more attracted to the 'widows,' ladies in their 40s who still had husbands but were travelling without them. Simla became known for intense flirtation and trysts. Many years after we had left Simla and India, Mr Rudyard Kipling visited the town and wrote:

> 'The young men come, the young men go,
> Each pink and white and neat

She's older than their mothers,
but They grovel at Her feet.
They walk beside Her rickshaw-wheels
None ever walk by mine
And that's because I'm seventeen
And she is forty-nine.'

There were stark class divisions in Simla's neighbourhoods. At the top, on the Ridge with the freshest of the mountain air and views to both sides, lived the Viceroy, senior British officers and other wealthy and distinguished residents. Domiciled Britons, those who permanently resided in India, and mixed-race Anglo-Indians lived a tier below, around the Mall. Finally, down in the Lower Bazaar, which stank of the sewage runoff from above, lived the Indian workers, labourers, rickshaw pullers, maids and *dhobis* – washer women.

The people who lived in the Lower Bazaar had built Simla and kept it going.

*

At the end of our time in Simla, in early June 1868, Rose gave birth to a little boy, and they named him William. We were all so thrilled for her to have a healthy baby. Her tears of joy were tinted with the sadness of losing her baby girl, Lucy May. Life was often bittersweet.

I was not far behind Rose. But when my time came in late June, I felt things were not the same as when I'd given birth to William.

The baby was stillborn. I cried for days.

We named him Richard, after my father.

I missed my little William. I longed to hear news from home, but the letters were not frequent.

When the rainy season had ended, we packed our bags to head back to Calcutta. We played in all the different towns on our way back. The entire company helped both Rose and me.

Rose needed help with her baby.

I needed help with my grief.

I felt so weak and heartbroken.

Chapter Twelve – Death on the trains

I wanted to go home to Australia and see my little boy, but my husband convinced me to stay another season.

Mr GBW Lewis once again organised the construction of a temporary theatre at the Maiden

We opened our second season in Calcutta on Monday, 5th October 1868, in the Royal Lyceum Theatre with a play by Mr Tom Taylor, called *An Unequal Match.*

Mr William Bain Gill had joined the group, and it was wonderful to see him again. He had, of course, been with us two years earlier for our season of *Ixion* and had previously travelled with Mr GBW Lewis in India. He was a very accomplished actor and writer, and said he would be writing some articles for the Melbourne newspapers, under the name of 'Call Boy.'

We all knew that Mr WB Gill and Miss Waddy Deering had been romantically linked since 1865, when they acted together in Adelaide, South Australia. Miss Waddy was married to a Mr Smith, whom I'd never met, but Waddy had told us it was not a happy marriage.

Mr Charles Edouin and his wife, Miss Lizzie Naylor, Mr John Edouin and his wife, Miss Tilly Earl, joined the group as well. These wonderful actors were like family to me. We had all spent so much time together in so many different towns. There was a bond between all of us.

Our second season involved presenting mainly tragedies and comedies, burlesque and pantomime.

*

One day, when William and I were walking down near the Hooghly River, I saw a small boat floating downstream. When I strained my eyes to focus more directly, I could see birds on top of the boat. I tugged on William's sleeve to point it out to him. As soon as he looked at where I was pointing, he told me to look away. He said the birds were feeding upon corpses in the boat. William had seen the merchant ships in port and sailors using long bamboo poles to push the corpse boats away. I was a little shocked.

*

The Lewis' told us to anticipate a most prosperous season, as there was plenty of money about. The bulk of the aristocracy had returned from the European continent and from Simla, where they had retired when the hot season commenced, so greater patronage would be accorded to us.

Mr Richard Southwell Bourke was sworn in as Governor-General in Calcutta on the 12th January 1869. He succeeded Lord John Lawrence. Mr Bourke was the fourth Viceroy of India, and everyone referred to him as Lord Mayo. We enjoyed his patronage at the theatre. Although he often looked quite glum, he had a great sense of humour.

We had great success, and the house was consistently full. The audience was predominantly British, who enjoyed theatre, and the atmosphere of 'feeling like they were home.' But there were also plenty of Bengalis. We were told that many of the schools taught English literature, with a focus on Shakespeare, and the boys were all encouraged to see Shakespeare performed on the stage.

Rose had told us there was a young man by the name of Girishchandra 'Girish' Ghosh who was very interested in the theatre. He worked at John Atkinson & Co., the company that had been engaged to look after the Lewis' business accounts. Girish and Rose were the same age. We would often see Girish in the audience, and he would meet with many of us after a performance and ask us about the intricacies of acting and stagecraft. Occasionally, Mr Lewis, Rose and Girish would take an evening ride in their four-wheeled phaeton carriage driven by two gorgeous white horses, to discuss plays and the history of theatre both in England and India.

*

Our second season in Calcutta ended in March 1869. The theatre was dismantled again, as was the government's rule.

Even though William and I had only committed ourselves to stay for one season that turned into two, we decided to stay on for a third season.

It had been lucrative, and we were saving our money. I dreamed of the time we could return to Australia, be reunited with my little William and buy a house, maybe in Ballarat.

The company decided to divide into two. Those staying with Mr GBW Lewis and Rose were Mr Charles Edouin, leader of the band and musical director, and his wife Miss Lizzie Naylor, Mr John Edouin and his wife Miss Tilly Earl, Mr WB Gill and his mother, Miss Waddy Deering, Miss Julia Edouin, Mrs Edouin, Mr Appleton, Mr Birch, Mr Stoneham, and Mr Joe Tannett, the artist. This part of the company embarked on a five-month tour of the interior of India, mostly in the northwestern provinces.

The second group decided to join the Dave Carson Company. Mr Carson had been in India since the early 1860s. William and I, along with Mr Harry Richardson, Mr ED Haygarth, Miss Lizzie Melville and Mr Olly Deering, went with Mr Carson. Mrs Carson (and her mother, father and brother) were in the group, as well as Signor Alvberto Zelman, our musical director.

We opened in Madras playing musical comedies. Mr Carson was a very clever performer. After Madras, we went to Bengalore, Mysore, Trichinopoly, Pondicherry, Negapatam and then back to Calcutta.

The monsoon season started in June, so we packed our bags to head towards Simla. While travelling by train from Allahabad to Lucknow, our tiffin basket that contained all the food we had prepared for our luncheon had been 'lost', and when we arrived at the station, Mr Dave Carson was beside himself with worry. The station manager told him everything had been commandeered by the Burra Sahib, some senior administrator.

Our distress reached the ears of Lord Napier of Magdala, and he at once very graciously asked our party to 'tiffin' with him. We gratefully accepted the invitation. He had ensured that all our tastes were accommodated. We had all the local foods, biryani and kebabs, with rich spices of cardamom and saffron. Lord Napier was a very generous host. I can see him now, with his closely cropped snow-white hair and dear old, bronzed face with eyes as bright and keen as an eagle.

*

We rejoined the rest of the Lewis company in Simla in late June 1869. I was excited to share my news that I was pregnant again. When we reunited, I could see and feel that something had changed. William and I immediately went to Mr William Gill and Miss Waddy Deering and asked them, 'What has happened?'

They looked at us with the saddest eyes, and Waddy said, 'Charles has died.'

I gasped, 'What.... how....no....no....' I felt uneasy, like I was going to fall. Mr WB Gill reached out and held my arm and eased me into a chair. The shock of hearing something so unexpected had completely weakened me. William brought me a glass of water. Just holding the cold glass gave me focus; it was something solid to hold on to. I looked up into Mr WB Gill's face and nodded. I was ready to hear how it had happened.

He sat down next to me and said, 'We were on the train travelling between Cawnpore and Agra, about 950 miles from Calcutta. The heat had been almost intolerable; it must have been over 104 °F, so dreadful, even for India. Poor Charles. He died in the carriage at 7:00 pm on the night of 9th May 1869. He had been complaining of the heat, just like all of us. He was not suffering from any illness to speak of. Apoplexy was the cause of his death. Poor old fellow! He went off as quietly as a baby might sink to rest; he could not have suffered the least pain. Our carriage was shunted off at Etawate station, and the next morning we buried him. We are hardly able yet to realise the fact of his death.'

'Oh, poor Lizzie,' is all I could say. I knew Lizzie would be heartbroken. Charles was her everything. They had been married for six years and were deeply in love.

Mr WB Gill then lowered his head and took a deep breath. I could see the pain and sorrow on his face. His body was shaking as he tried to hold himself together. But it was pointless. Soon, the tears were streaming down both our faces.

It was a very distressing time, which I think brought my baby on. Surprisingly, I gave birth to twin boys in June 1869 whilst we were in Simla. We named them James after William's father and Arthur after my little brother. They were very small and very beautiful. I had to have bed rest for several weeks. It was during this time that my beautiful boys were exposed to the plague, and they just weren't strong enough to battle the terrible disease. The pain and anguish I felt when my boys died was almost unbearable. I almost died as well. William tried to be stoic, but he was just as heartbroken as me.

And then another tragedy, on 25th June, Rose's little boy William, only 12 months old, died from bronchitis. Rose was seven months pregnant with another baby at the time. Thankfully, Rose found solace with her husband and the restorative nature of Simla. In August 1869, while we were still in Simla, Rose gave birth to a little girl, and they named her Victoria May.

*

The company stayed in Simla until mid-November and then returned to Calcutta. William and I, however, remained in Simla for a further four weeks. While we were there, the residents, both civilians and military, tendered me a complimentary benefit. I was so touched by the gesture and felt very honoured. The house was crowded, and I fully appreciated the compliment paid me. The piece we played was Byron's burlesque *Bluebeard.* Captain FitzGeorge, son of the Duke of Cambridge, sustained the main part. Lord Mayo played the part of Shacabar. Major Hefford's daughter played the character of Selin.

⁕

We travelled back to Calcutta in late December 1869. There were two events that William and I were excited to be celebrating: a wedding and meeting a Prince.

Miss Waddy Deering's husband, Mr Smith, had died a few months back. Whilst this was a sad event, it essentially allowed her to marry her 'sweetheart.' On the 20th December 1869, Mr William Bain Gill and Miss Waddy Deering were married at the Great Eastern Hotel in Calcutta. Our dear friends were so happy. Many of the original company members were there to celebrate the happy event.

Then, on 22nd December, Prince Alfred, Duke of Edinburgh, arrived in the *HMS Galatea*, a steam frigate, that had travelled up the Hooghly River. The *Galatea* was docked at the wharf, and they took stringent precautions against cholera. Men were employed in working parties to use long bamboos to push off the corpses that were continually floating down from the Hooghly, lest they should foul the moorings. William had seen them do this the previous year.

When the Prince arrived and came onshore, a procession was formed to conduct him to Government House. The Prince's arrival was a grand and imposing scene; large numbers of all classes were present to witness the reception. The crowd of Indian people was immense, lining the road from Prinsep's Ghaut to Government House. About 60 elephants belonging to the Indian chiefs were assembled. All the arrangements were perfect, and the only disadvantageous circumstance was the lateness of the hour, since it was almost dark when the Prince reached Government House. There was a lot of fanfare at the time, and lots of English aristocrats were in attendance.

The Prince left Calcutta on 7th January 1870 and went to Burdwan. Before he left, he had his photograph, carte de visite, taken by Thomas Alfred Rust in the Westfield and Company studio at 13 Government Place, Calcutta. I still have a copy of this photograph. All the actors in the company were given one.

*

In February 1870, William and I accepted another engagement which would take us to an area near Kurrachee, which is now called Karachi, in Pakistan. We left Calcutta full of excitement and travelled with Mr and Mrs Arthur Paget, Miss Annie Hill and Mr Harry Goldstein, who was a very clever pianist.

When we arrived in Kurrachee, we had to continue up the Indus River as far as it was possible to go, in flat-bottomed boats. We saw crocodiles from the boat, too numerous to mention. I have never been so frightened. It was the worst boat trip I have ever taken.

In early March 1870, Mr GBW Lewis announced he would not be continuing with the theatre company in India. The troupe of actors elected Mr WB Gill to take over the management and continue on.

Rose's final performance at the Lyceum was on 31st March. Friends and admirers joined the company for a supper on the stage of the theatre, and Rose was presented with a silver salver, tea and coffee services[ix].

The Lewis' left Calcutta for Melbourne the next day, and we heard later they arrived safely after a five-week trip.

Mr WB Gill took over the theatre and all its responsibilities, and later in the year, he opened the theatre under the new name of the Olympic Theatre.

*

In September 1870, Mrs Hefford, wife of Mr Major Hefford of the Royal Artillery, then stationed in Umballa, invited me to stay with her. I was pregnant again. She had heard of my previous losses, and she wanted to give me a safe and comfortable place to have my baby.

With her help and some of the other ladies, I gave birth to another boy on the 7th October. We named him Charles Ernest South. We baptised him on the 22nd October. I stayed with Mrs Hefford until early November. The weather had cooled down significantly, thank goodness. William and I, along with our baby, returned to Calcutta to enjoy the winter.

*

We settled once more in the Great Eastern Hotel and prepared for another season.

One of the mail-boats finally arrived in late December 1870 and brought the latest newspapers from home and abroad. It was then that we read of the devastating news that my dear old friend Mr Frederick Younge had died in England. On the 6th December 1870, there had been a horrific train accident. Poor Mr Younge was on the train.

Due to an error made by a railway attendant, who had been worked almost to death by long hours and short wages, a frightful collision occurred on the Sunderland and Newcastle branch of the Northeastern Railway. The train engine had mounted the hind part of a coal train.

The Times newspaper had received a letter from a passenger onboard the train. They published the letter, and it said:

> 'The day was tolerably clear, although damp, and there would be no difficulty in seeing a long way ahead. We went all right till we got to Brockley Whins station, which is the junction for trains from Newcastle, Shields, and Sunderland, and through which there appears to be a large and ceaseless traffic of coal wagons. We had got to this station when suddenly our carriage, which was the

> second from the engine, appeared to rear up like a horse, and passing upwards, seemed to crumple up with a sound like that of crushing in the palm of the hand some stiff paper, although the noise was much louder. I felt that a fearful collision had occurred and expected that we should be destroyed. Happily, for us it was not so; we were able to open the door of our compartment and escape to the embankment with little more than a serious shaking. But when we looked to the foremost first-class carriage (or what was a carriage) and the first compartment of our own carriage, we were horrified to see nothing but a mangled mass of wood splinters and dead and dying men and women. The sight was sickening. Help was at once given to the unfortunate sufferers; and the dead and wounded were extricated with as much care and speed as their difficult and horrible position would permit. One man appeared to have been crushed literally to a pulp, and every bone in his body was probably broken. Several ladies were shockingly injured, but, unless I am mistaken, their injuries were not fatal. How any of us escaped is a marvel to me.'

Four people died that day.

In Fred Younge's circle of friends, he was homely, quiet, and genial. He had a kind word for everyone, and not merely words but acts.

Mr Younge had a similar greatness as Mr Brooke and Mr Jefferson. He had enjoyed some great successes in Melbourne but always struggled under the restrictions of managers. He had an adventurous spirit and travelled to the country districts, where he experienced many hardships.

I remembered when Emily and I had travelled throughout rural Victoria with Mr Younge and his wife, Miss Emma Corri. It had been in the dead of winter, and we went from town to town. Sometimes we had to camp out alongside roaring creeks, and the rain had been pouring down on our frail cover, which was the tent of the wagon.

In his moments of deepest poverty and during his tours through the goldfield towns, he was often at a loss to know where next to secure a meal for himself and the company members. But he always had a kindly smile which seemed to emanate hopefulness.

Mr Younge never flinched from the task he set himself.

Before his death, he had been the stage manager at the Prince of Wales Theatre, London, and afterwards as manager of the Caste Company.

Mr Fred Younge's brothers, Richard and Frank, had for years been separated by huge distances. Australia, England and America have been the scenes of their respective wanderings at different times.

We heard sometime later through friends that about 10 days before the accident, for the first time in a very long period, the three brothers found themselves in England at the same time. To celebrate the occasion, it was resolved that during the Christmastide the Caste Company should be treated to a holiday, and that the brothers should hold a great family reunion, in which they might enjoy the unwonted pleasure of each other's society without let or hindrance.

Mr Younge's remains were buried at Elswick Cemetery, Newcastle-upon-Tyne, on the 9th of December. There were many people present at Central Station, Newcastle, to pay their respects. He was only 45 years old.

He will long be remembered in Australia as one of the best comedians this generation has seen and a true gentleman.

*

Our third season, under the management of Mr WB Gill, at the Olympic Theatre in Calcutta, came to a close at the end of March 1871. Another great season.

On the night of the last performance, Mr Dave Carson announced to the company that he had made up his mind to return to England. He left the following week, first stop Bombay, then London.

Chapter Thirteen – My darling son

My husband, baby Charlie and I stayed in Calcutta during the next few months. I had received some news from home that sent me into the depths of despair.

My brother Richard had written to tell me my beloved son William Wiseman South, whom I had left behind in Melbourne, had died from pneumonia. He was four years old. Richard told me that my little William died on the 18th April 1871, while they were living in Ballarat. He was buried alongside his great-grandparents, Thomas and Ann King. He said both sides of the family, the South's and the Wiseman's, were at the funeral for this special little boy.

I cried for days. I cried until there were no more tears left. I felt like it was my fault. I had left my baby when he was so young, so I could gain fame and fortune in India. My parents and William's parents had helped raise him. He was loved by all. In my mind, I made a promise to myself never to leave Charlie, if it was possible.

I felt like I couldn't go on.

My husband seemed lost as well. He lost his usual optimism. He was abrupt with me when we talked.

My mother and sisters wrote to me. Their support and words of love were powerful.

Somehow, I dragged myself from my despair. My little Charlie still needed me. I had to keep living, and I had to keep going.

⁂

Miss Rose Edouin wrote to us with the wonderful news that they were leaving Melbourne and returning to Calcutta. They told us Mr John Burdett Howe and his wife, Julia Hayward, were joining the company and would be travelling over with them. This was a great feather in Mr Lewis' hat, as Mr Howe was a renowned Shakespearean actor with great versatility. Miss Rose told us they planned to visit Simla during the summer, from April to May 1871, and then start the theatre season in Calcutta and build a new theatre house, which they planned on calling The Theatre Royal.

When we met up with the Lewis' in Calcutta, it was a joyous reunion. I had a moment alone with Rose, and I told her of the loss of my little boy, William. She embraced me, and I knew she understood my pain. She had known the loss of her own children.

Whilst Mr GBW Lewis was talking with the authorities about the new theatre construction, it was agreed that the company could perform in the Opera House on Lindsey Street.

We attended the Lewis' opening night at the Opera House, on Monday, 16th September 1871. The theatre was crowded in every part. They opened with Brougham's comedy *Faces in the Fire*. The elite of Calcutta were in attendance, including Lord Mayo, and two grandsons of the notorious and famous Tippoo Sahib, the Tiger of Mysore, India's native prince.

Before the show began, Mr Lewis made a delightful announcement to the packed house of his plan to build a permanent theatre house in Calcutta. Apparently, the previous government's rule that required theatre houses to be dismantled after the season had ended had been relaxed. The audience exploded with applause.

The following day, the Calcutta press reviewed the first appearance of Mr Howe and said:

> 'Mr Howe had not been five minutes on the stage, upon which he came with rounds of hearty welcome when we were quite satisfied that he was the right man in the right place...he would be a most valuable acquisition to our stage.'

Mr GBW Lewis, the indefatigable proprietor and an exceptionally resourceful and capable manager, did not waste a day in his pursuit of building a new theatre. Almost miraculously, he managed to buy a suitable plot of land at 16 Chowringhee Road opposite the Maidan.

The very next day, he engaged over 80 workmen, mostly Hindus. He had European foremen and architects. It took four days for the foundations to be laid. Huge iron pillars and rafters arrived by the dozen, and in less than three weeks, the roof was on. The decorations and scenery that had been painted at the Opera House, were then carted down the road to the new theatre.

The Theatre Royal accommodated 800 seats inside. It was entirely lighted by one large 'sun', consisting of gas jets about eight and a half feet in circumference.

Everything was ready to open by the fourth week.

Opening night and the inauguration of Lewis' Theatre Royal was on 21st October 1871, and they opened with the comedy *The Silver Lining* by Mr Buckingham. Mr John Burdett Howe and Miss Rose Edouin were the leads.

This new venture by Rose and Mr GBW Lewis was the beginning of six and a half years of the Lewis' Burlesque and Dramatic Company performing in the Theatre Royal in Calcutta.

Mr WB Gill and his wife, Miss Waddie, had stayed in Calcutta to see the Lewis' new theatre. But they decided to return to Australia and did so in late October 1871.

*

During the time the Lewis' were busy building the new Theatre Royal on Chowringhee Road, we were busy putting together our own little company with Mr and Mrs Charles Rogers, Mr John 'Joe' Small and Mr Alfred Singer. Mr

Rogers acted as our manager. He was originally from America and was very worldly. Mr Joe Small was a clever Irish comic singer, and I remembered him from when I was in Dunedin, New Zealand, in the early 1860s. Joe could pull the funniest faces, sending us into stitches of laughter. Mr Alfred Singer was our pianist.

We planned a trip to Hong Kong with a stopover at Singapore to perform in a small theatre house.

We boarded the *SS Arratoon Apcar*, a sail and steam merchant ship. Captain Miller, a fine fellow, made us feel very welcome. Onboard the ship was the Captain, the Chief Officer, our own gentlemen, and 500 Chinese workers from Calcutta. The captain had told me the Chinese workers were immigrants who had left their country in search of work and fortune.

We arrived in Singapore for a one-night only performance. Thankfully, we had planned only one night, as unfortunately, the receipts did not amount to much, only 1,000 Singapore dollars. The audience didn't seem to rouse and were not impressed by any of our acts.

After the ship had been loaded with coal, we were ready to depart Singapore bound for Hong Kong.

It wasn't long after we had left the safe waters of the Singapore harbour that we were caught in a typhoon, which lasted three days. Captain Miller had given up his cabin to Mrs Rogers and me and my little Charlie, owing to the saloon being flooded. The ship was stripped of everything that was loose by the fury of the storm. It was so wild, I think we all thought we'd die.

Captain Miller was washed off the bridge and broke his leg. During the typhoon, not a single man could be spared to look after him, so Mrs Rogers and I attended to him. We set the leg by making some splints out of a wooden box, and by the constant application of salt water, of which there was plenty, we kept all inflammation down. There was no one else who could have helped, so we just jumped in and did the job. I made sure that Charlie was safe during all of this. He was a great baby, and he seemed somewhat oblivious to the dangerous situation.

When we finally arrived in Hong Kong on 5th October 1871, we could see that the whole sea wall had been swept away. A doctor came onboard to check on everyone, and he could hardly believe that we women had done such a good job of setting Captain Miller's leg. The doctor complimented us on the fine work we had done in extraordinary circumstances. He was rather condescending, but Mrs Rogers and I were used to that kind of attitude.

We opened at the Lusitania Theatre in Hong Kong on the 16th October 1871, playing for four weeks to good audiences. We played three nights a week, Monday, Wednesday and Saturday.

We were fortunate to be staying on the top two floors of the Lusitania Club, and we met many people from the Portuguese community during our stay in Hong Kong. The

Lusitania Club had a large library, and when we weren't performing, I indulged in my love of reading, just like I had when I was in Simla. I would take Charlie with me, and we would find a quiet corner and curl up together with a good book to read. There were also billiard tables, and William and the other men would enjoy many games.

The Lusitania Club was a place where the Portuguese community socialised with members of other communities. They shared their experiences with us, and there were many evenings that we'd discuss local and world affairs. Many dignitaries visited us, including the Governors of both Hong Kong and Macau.

Then we travelled to Shanghai for a fortnight, and then back to Hong Kong, where we opened to a full house again.

There was a boat from America in port at that time, and Mr Rogers, our manager, being American, naturally wanted to see some of his friends. He went onboard but forgot to return – taking our money with him!

Mrs Rogers was completely distraught. For all intents and purposes, we were all stranded – Mrs Rogers, Mr Joe Small, Mr Alfred Singer, William and me and baby Charlie.

A few days later, the troopship *HMS Orontes* of the Royal Navy came into port. The Admiral became aware of our plight and was kind enough to grant us his patronage back to Calcutta.

⁂

William and I had been talking about our future, and we both decided we wanted a new start, so with our little boy Charlie, we set our sights on England.

We were both excited to be returning to our homeland.

We left Calcutta in December 1871.

On the voyage to England, I often thought of Rose and Mr GBW Lewis and their new theatre in Calcutta. Our time in India had been the most exciting, challenging and heartbreaking time. I had suffered through the death of four of my children – William, Richard, and the twins James and Arthur. But I had my Charlie, and I held him tightly.

I was grateful I had my little boy and my husband, and I was hopeful for the future.

Chapter Fourteen – England

We landed in Southampton, England, in February 1872. Memories of my childhood came flooding back to me. It must have been the crisp, cold air or the smell of burning coal emanating from the chimneys.

I missed Australia, which I considered my real home, but William and I were determined to put our best foot forward.

My grandmother, Mary, was still living in London. We stayed with her until we got set up. It was the warmest of welcomes when she opened her door. I honestly thought I would never see her again when I had left England so many years ago. She was much older now, and moved more slowly, but she hadn't lost her quick wit, laughter and inquisitiveness. Of course, she wanted to know all about my mother and father, and my sisters and brother. She was spellbound when we told her about our adventures in India. Our first night was spent in the sitting room in front of the warm fire, talking for hours.

After I'd put Charlie to bed and William had also retired, I stayed up a little longer with my grandmother. It was then that I told her about my beautiful boys who had died. She held me as I wept.

✻

When we had settled in, we called on Mr Charles Willmott, an old friend whom we had known in Australia. Mr Willmott was managing the Occidental Hotel in the Strand. He made us feel very welcome and filled us in on the theatre scene in London, and who was managing the different theatres. He seemed to know everyone, and it was a great comfort hearing all his updates. There were a few names he mentioned who were dear old friends of ours, and I was excited at the prospect of acting alongside them again.

William and I would often go to the Blackfriars' Bridge Hotel to meet up with colonials who had returned to England.

On one occasion, we met the great Irish playwright and actor, Mr Dion Boucicault. I could hardly string two words together; I was in awe of his talent.

We were also thrilled when we met Mr Willie Edouin and his wife, Miss Alice Atherton. We caught up on all the Edouin family news.

We were in regular contact with Mr Willmott, and he told us that Mr Dion Boucicault had commenced selecting his company and had engaged several male actors. He said Mr Boucicault was now looking for female character actors. My heart leapt when I heard those words. Within a few days, Mr Boucicault had offered me a position in his company. Of course, I accepted his offer. I was so excited to be in his stock company, where I was to act in some wonderful plays that he had written, *Arrah-na-Pogue, The Shaughraun* and *The Irish Diamond.*

I travelled to Dublin, to the Abbey Theatre, and other provinces playing parts in Mr Boucicault's plays. I had a similar petite figure to Mrs Boucicault and so was chosen for many of the heroine parts.

William and Charlie travelled with me. I could see that William found it difficult to 'play second fiddle', so to speak. He hadn't been offered any acting roles. It was a very competitive time for male actors.

*

William and I noticed that London theatre prices were quite high, and everything else seemed expensive too. But thankfully, the pay that actors and actresses received had also gone up. London had become a gaudy show city. All the world was coming to London to spend their money, and none seemed to go to Paris anymore. London did, however, compete with America, and many actors had travelled there to try their luck.

It seemed that no one was interested in travelling to Australia. Poor Mr Henry Harwood, who was trying to entice actors to travel to Australia, had a disheartening job before him. He had plenty of pluck and energy, and he opened his pockets wide to induce members of the profession to leave England for the antipodes.

My sister Emily and her husband, Johnnie Hall, had been in America for a few years. They had been playing to good houses and were acting alongside Miss Louise and Jenny Arnot at the Wood's Museum and Metropolitan Theatre in New York. But they had decided to come to London and had sold the greater portion of their wardrobe before crossing the Atlantic.

In February 1873, William, Charlie and I met my dear sister Emily, her husband and John Jnr, who was almost 6 years old, in London. It is one of my happiest memories. My sister and I had missed each other so much. She gave me so much comfort and support. We talked about everything that had happened since we last saw each other. We were lucky to have a few days together before work commitments separated us. I almost couldn't bear to be parted from her again. But at least we were now in the same country.

*

In April 1873, I had an engagement at the Prince Alfred Theatre, which used to be the old Marylebone. It was there whilst acting onstage, that I felt that unique feeling of being pregnant and sure enough, within a few weeks, I knew for certain.

After that engagement, I appeared with the Charlie Groves Company in a round of Dickens' characters, both girl and boy parts, as Little Nell, Oliver Twist, Smyke,

Barnaby Rudge, Little Emily, and Dot from *Cricket on the Hearth.*

By this stage, I was 'showing', but it was not something to hold actresses back. As long as I felt well, the work was there.

Later in the year, in September, my sister Emily and Johnnie played under Mr Henry and Mr Maurice De Freece's management in Liverpool at the Theatre Royal. They performed *Colleen Bawn* by Mr Dion Boucicault for a month and then left for America again. William and I, along with Charlie, travelled to Liverpool to spend a few days with them before they left. It was bittersweet, as during that time, the De Freece's offered William and me an engagement in the company.

Emily and I said our farewells. We promised to write more often. We both knew that with work and family commitments, it was a struggle, but we would try.

So, in October 1873, William and I started our six-week season with De Freece's company. I opened in *Nan The Good for Nothing* and the burlesque of *Black Eyed Susan.* During this time, I attracted the admiring attention of the well-known old actress Mrs Keeley, who was not satisfied until she had been introduced to me. When she met me, she asked where I had learnt my art. I told her of all the great actors and actresses I had the pleasure of working with. I told her stories of the goldfields and being onstage with my sister Emily and my time in India. She was enthralled by the adventures I'd had.

It was on the last night of the show that I knew my time was soon.

On the 4th November 1873, I gave birth to a beautiful boy, and we named him Tom Llewellyn South.

We were still under the engagement of the De Freece's but had an offer to do a panto at The Rotunda, Mr Dennis Grannell's Theatre. Thankfully, they kindly released us for the four weeks to perform for the Christmas season. The pantomime was *Puss in Boots,* in which I played the main part and William played the Giant. The opening was on Boxing Day, 26th December. The production was a great success.

⁂

We continued throughout 1874, with various engagements. There was plenty of work for me.

In January 1875, William and I met Father Nugent, a Catholic priest who was the most admirable man, who worked tirelessly to protect children and provide relief from poverty. I was engaged by him to assist in a series of lectures he was giving at the time. During one of these lectures, I had a very unpleasant experience. I was made up to represent one of the poor old drunken women, unfortunately, so often seen in big cities. I had dressed at home and was wearing a large cloak over my costume. I took a cab to the Hall.

As I was going up the steps to enter the side entrance that led to the stage, the man who was in charge refused my access and threatened to call the police and take me into custody. Fortunately, Father Nugent, hearing the disturbance, came to my rescue. They all told me I ought to have considered it a compliment, the doorman having mistaken me for one of those poor creatures I was representing.

✳

Later in the year, I travelled to London to see my dear old friend Julia Matthews, to say goodbye as she was leaving for America. I hadn't seen Julia for several years, and I was so excited to see her and her three children.

We had agreed to meet at Hyde Park, so our children had some space to play, and we had some space to talk.

When we met, it was like no time had passed between us. She was just as I had remembered, yet her exuberance for life was a little dimmed. Her three children were delightful and instantly connected with my boys, Charlie and Tom.

After only a few minutes, she told me about the demise of her marriage and said she had obtained a judicial separation. She said,

'Oh Fanny, I just couldn't bear it anymore. He drank and gambled our money away, and as if that wasn't bad enough, he was unfaithful. He expected me to work and earn all the money, while he managed my affairs. Well, it all just became too much for me. If only things had been different, and Mr Burke had returned to me. I still carry his letters with me.'

I comforted her the best I could. She was the sweetest soul, and it made me so angry that her husband treated her in that way. But I was also proud of my friend for taking control of her life.

When we parted, we said our heartfelt good-byes. I never saw her again. Only a year or so after she left London, I heard of her untimely death in St Louis, Missouri in May 1876. She had contracted malaria. She was so young.

*

William and I read the newspaper every day and would scan it for theatre news from Australia. The latest news at that time was about Mr JC Williamson and his wife, Miss Maggie Moore and their smash hit play called *Struck Oil,* that was playing in Melbourne. The story is set during the American Civil War, where Williamson played an old Pennsylvania Dutchman and Maggie plays his daughter, Lizzie.

Mr JC Williamson had bought the script, and after some alterations, he'd taken it to the American stage. It was a huge hit there. Mr George Coppin invited them to bring the play to Australia. That was in 1874. Mr JC Williamson and Miss Maggie Moore had become very well-known in America and Australia through that play.

*

Life was busy with plenty of work and raising a family. I was pregnant again and gave birth to a beautiful girl on 13th January 1876. We named her Minnie Frances Alice South. She was born in Liverpool.

A month later, on 16th February, I was engaged for four weeks at the Surrey Theatre in Richmond playing alongside Miss Carrie Nelson and her sister Sarah. The first week, we performed the burlesque *Aladdin.* Then, in the second week, we performed *Fair One with Golden Locks.* In the third and fourth weeks, we played comedies.

We performed four distinct shows – pantomimes, blood and thunder melodramas and comedies. The whole affair turned out to be a huge success. But I was glad when it was all over. It was hurry-scurrying the whole time.

⁕

My dear sister Alice wrote to me in February 1876 with the sad news that Miss Rose and Mr GBW Lewis' daughter, Victoria May, had died. You will remember that Victoria May was born in India and only just survived the plague-ridden time. My twin boys, James and Arthur, hadn't been so fortunate.

Poor Victoria, having survived the diseases in India, then died from scarlet fever while she was attending a boarding school in Carlisle Street, St Kilda, Melbourne. My heart ached for Rose and her husband.

My brother-in-law, Mr Henry Westley, Alice's husband, organised the death notice for the newspaper. Alice and

Henry were trusted friends of Rose and Mr GBW Lewis. Henry was a solicitor, so he arranged the burial plot at Melbourne's General Cemetery and followed Rose's instructions for the wording of the headstone inscription, which said,

> She is not dead but sleeps in the arms of Jesus
> Now like a dew-drop shrined within a crystal stone
> Thou art safe in Heaven my dove
> Safe with the source of love
> The everlasting one.

*

I was becoming a very popular identity in Britain, and the work offers for me kept coming through in a steady and consistent way. However, this wasn't the case for William. It seemed there was too much competition between male actors. I could see that William was despondent and homesick for his friends and family in Australia. I felt the same longing, but I could see we had a great future in London.

It was on my 30th birthday on the 20th September 1876 that William told me he had decided we should return to Australia. His words hit me 'like a ton of bricks.' I was taken aback as he had not discussed it with me. He made the announcement as a fait accompli. I had such mixed feelings.

I was becoming more and more successful with every passing day. I didn't want to leave. We finally had a good income, and I could see ourselves establishing a comfortable life for our family. We had three healthy children by then, Charlie, Tom and Minnie, and I certainly wanted more children.

But there was no changing William's mind. The decision to return to Australia, in hindsight, ended up being a big mistake for me professionally. Although I would go on to have great success in Australia, I believe that if we'd stayed in England, my success would have been greater.

On Saturday, 7th October 1876, William and I, along with our two boys and little girl, left England. We boarded the steamship *SS Northumberland* at Plymouth, bound for sunny Australia.

Chapter Fifteen – Back to Australia

A long sea journey is challenging at the best of times. As you can imagine, my hands were full looking after my three children and keeping them entertained and out of mischief. Charlie was five, Tom was two, and Minnie was nine months old.

I thought a lot about my mother and her three-month journey from England to Australia back in 1854, and how she had managed to keep Emily, Richard, Alice and me occupied. I seemed to remember a lot of the time Emily and I were exploring the ship and were on our own.

I turned to the things I knew, and every day I had a new story to tell my children. Of course, I used all my acting abilities to enthral them in the drama of the story. I also taught them the art of observation. We soon learned all about our fellow passengers. It's really the only thing you can do when you're onboard a ship for months on end.

When William and I talked to Captain Shinner about our acting careers, well, that's when things got a little more exciting. There was plenty of talk with the passengers as well as the crew about putting on a performance. The captain gave his blessings. Rehearsing, stage design and making the costumes would keep a lot of idle hands occupied.

William and I coached several of the ladies and gentlemen passengers in the play *The Little Treasure,* a comedy in two acts written by Mr Augustus Glossop Harris.

Dr V Cooper played the character of Sir Charles Howard, Mrs Laselles played Lady Florence Howard and Miss Gordon played Mrs Meddleton, the grandma. William played the character of Captain Walter Maydenblush, and Mr George Lauri played the part of The Honourable Mr Leicester Fluttermore – he turned out to be the best actor onboard!

I played the character of Gertrude, the Little Treasure.

Miss Cissie Gordon told me that she'd read the *Amateur's Handbook and Guide to Home or Drawing Room Theatricals*, by Mr Thomas Hailes Lacy. However, she'd never physically performed in front of an audience.

Rehearsals were a lot of fun. We took our time as we had plenty of it. My children were always close by, watching and learning. Charlie was very attentive.

Opening night was so exciting. For most of the performers, this was the first time they had ever been onstage. Their excitement and nervousness was infectious. Miss Cissie Gordon, however, did not fare well. She was a ball of nerves. I went over to her before we went onstage and took her hands in mine. Without saying a word, we stood together just breathing. My steady and measured breathing eventually overtook her shallow and rapid breathing. I felt the nervousness leave her body, and she became centred. We both smiled at each other, and I gave her a nod. She knew everything would be alright after that.

The first performance was so successful that we were asked to repeat it, which we did several times.

We arrived in Port Phillip Bay, Melbourne, on 23rd November 1876. We had been at sea for six and a half weeks.

William and I had been away from Australia for nearly 10 years, and when we stepped off the ship, I felt a sense of being home. I think what hits you, when you've been away and then return to Australia, is the sunlight, and the way people greet you – there's a very Australian way of nodding your head, and looking at you, straight in the eye, with a smile.

*

William and I made sure the theatre managers knew we had returned, and we were now very experienced actors. It didn't take long before we were receiving acting engagements.

In January 1877, we went to the Royal Princess Theatre in Bendigo to open with Miss Mary Gladstane under the management of her husband, Mr Lewis McLean Bayless. Miss Gladstane was an Irish-American actress. We were there for eight weeks and had fairly good business.

In May, we were offered an engagement with Signor Edoardo Majeroni's Dramatic Company for a tour to Adelaide in the colony of South Australia. This would be a real adventure for our children. They hadn't been on a long tour before, and they were very excited.

Opening night was 9th July 1877, and we had many elites of the city attend, including His Excellency the Acting Governor and a sprinkling of well-known clergymen of various denominations. We presented an adaptation from the Italian *Achilles Montignani*.

Signor Majeroni was received with a hearty round of applause on his first entrance and gave a powerful and refined exposition of the part of the wronged husband. In the most passionate scenes, he exhibited the highest refinement of dramatic art in that the art was entirely concealed.

Signor Majeroni's wife, Signora Giulia, had a singularly clear and distinct accent and enunciated perfectly. She was not one whit behind her husband in the splendid impersonation she gave of the tempted, foolish, but repentant wife. In the last scene, Signora Majeroni touched all our hearts by the deep pathos of her voice and manner and evoked a storm of applause.

Both Signor and Signora Majeroni were recalled at the end of the play and presented with several very handsome bouquets.

Our final piece was called *A Living Statue*. I played the old nurse in the prologue, and the little flower girl later on in the play and thankfully, the critics said, 'I was pleasant and unrestrained.' William played Father Anselmo and, in the churchyard scene, assumed a most extraordinarily sepulchral tone of voice. The critics, unfortunately, didn't have a kind word to offer on his performance.

We had been performing in a small room called The White Rooms, which was totally unsuited for our plays, and as a result, we did poorly with the audiences and the money.

However, it was wonderful to be back in South Australia. I had such wonderful memories from when I was a young girl, performing alongside my sister Emily, and under the management of Mr JR Greville. It's also where I fell in love with William. I had spent two years performing in South Australia and remembered how well we were supported by the community. The critics remembered me, too. They remembered me as 'a slender girl' who was now a 'plump, comfortable-looking little matron.' Oh, how I laughed when I read that description in the newspaper. They were right. My physical shape had changed. I had had seven children and was now 30 years old. But when I was on the stage, I acted with the same grace and spirit as I had when I was 15 years old.

We struggled for a few weeks, but then, thank goodness, Signor Majeroni pulled the plug. I hoped I'd never have to perform in the White Rooms again. Signor Majeroni told the company that we had been booked for a tour to Tasmania, starting in mid-August 1877. We all had two weeks to rest before the tour was to start.

So, William and I and our little ones went back to Melbourne for our break. This was a stroke of luck for me because my sister Emily, her husband and John Jnr, had returned from America and were staying with our youngest sister, Laura.

I had not seen Laura since the day William and I had left for India. Laura had only been eight years old, and at that age, she was a very clever child. I remembered she sang, danced and acted remarkably well. As soon as she saw me, she said,

'Well, you have not altered a bit.'

'Well, you have.' I replied.

'Of course,' was her retort, 'you didn't expect me to remain a little girl all my life, did you?'

And with that, we all laughed and hugged. We had a wonderful reunion and spent the next few days with each other. Emily and I fell back into step with each other, like no time had passed.

When the time came to rejoin the Majeroni's Company, we gave our sad farewells. Never knowing when we would meet again, my sister's embraced me, and we all shed some tears.

*

We had our passage booked for Tasmania, on the steamship *SS Tararua*. The skies looked calm, but almost as soon as we were outside Port Phillip Heads, everyone wanted to get off the ship. The seas were rough, and every member of our company except me suffered from mal de mer, better known as seasickness. Poor Signora Majeroni, she was fearfully ill, and so was the nurse she had engaged to look after her son, George.

The ship's stewardess came into my cabin the first morning we were out at sea, as she was in great trouble. She had so many ladies to look after, including Signora Majeroni and her son George.

The stewardess implored me, 'Please, Miss, if you're able, I need your help with the baby. There are so many to look after, I don't have enough hands.'

'Oh, yes of course, I'll look after him.' I said to the stewardess.

I had never experienced seasickness and felt extremely lucky when I saw how unwell just about everyone else was.

Signora brought baby George to me. She gratefully handed him over and then returned quickly to her cabin. She could barely speak. She was as pale as a ghost.

William looked after Charlie, Tom and Minnie, so I was at liberty to help with baby George. He remained with me for the rest of the voyage. When we docked, Signora Majeroni was so thankful and called me 'a perfect angel.'

In August 1877, we opened in Launceston's Theatre Royal, to a crowded house, with *The Old Corporal*. It is an emotional drama and is one of Signor Majeroni's greatest impersonations. Applause was frequent and spontaneous throughout the drama. Signora Majeroni's acting was extremely natural. I played the part of Marriette, a very amusing character, and my husband made himself detested as the Deputy Mayor.

Although I thought William had done a grand job of playing the Deputy Mayor, the critics had not been very kind in their description of his acting. I wasn't sure if he had seen the review; I hoped not.

We continued with good audiences for the entire trip.

At the close of our season, Signor Majeroni called all the company together and thanked everyone for standing by him and his wife in troublesome times. I was very sorry when our engagement ended, for the Majeroni's were delightful people to be with, true artists in every sense of the word. I was never associated with them again as far as business was concerned, though I had the pleasure of meeting them as friends, very frequently.

Our journey back to Melbourne was the polar opposite of the journey from Melbourne. The seas were calm, and the sun was shining. Our children, Charlie, Tom and Minnie enjoyed their time on tour. The company had rallied to my help whenever I needed it.

We weren't long in Melbourne when William and I were engaged in a panto in Ballarat for the Christmas season. We played for three weeks, with a full house every night.

It was wonderful to be back in Ballarat. William's family were well established there in various businesses. His mother, Sarah Ann and father James, along with aunties and uncles, were all very close. They all helped with the children while William and I were performing.

My parents had moved to New Zealand and had opened another boarding house. I missed them terribly, especially at Christmas time.

Chapter Sixteen – Topsy

We left Ballarat in May 1878 and found a nice house in Emerald, South Melbourne. William and I had been back in Australia for less than two years, and we felt we were re-establishing ourselves quite well on the Australian stage.

Raising a family was hard work. Raising a family *and* working long hours was exhausting. Often, William and I would be engaged by the same company, but sometimes not. And in those situations, it made it easier for me as the children could stay home with their father. But there was always uncertainty with work. You had to accept the work when it was offered, for you never knew when there would be a dry spell.

I was pregnant again and feeling great, but in the back of my mind was always some worry. Worry about work or worry about paying the bills. For there were always bills to be paid.

Our next engagement was with Mr John Sheridan for the production of *Uncle Tom's Cabin.* The play was the dramatic version of Mrs Harriet Beecher Stowe's celebrated anti-slavery novel of the same name. The play was familiar to me as I had played the role of Topsy when I was 13 years old. I was to play the same role, and William took the role of Tom Locker.

Mr Sheridan was an incredibly generous man, and he knew I was in the last stages of my pregnancy. For that reason, he paused the production until I had the baby. This was not the first time I had been pregnant and kept rehearsing and performing, and it wasn't to be the last. In those days, you just had to get on with it.

On 5th May 1878, I gave birth to my second daughter, and we named her Laura Charlotte Ann South. We named her Laura in honour of my little sister, whom I'd spent such little time with when I was growing up. My other children were thrilled with the new addition, especially my little Minnie, who was two years old; she felt like she had her own little dolly to play with. Charlie and Tom, who were seven and five years old, were excited to be big brothers to another little girl. They were very proud.

The lessee and theatre manager was Mr Lewis McLean Bayless. He'd extensively refitted the theatre only a year before we played *The Cabin,* and when reopening the theatre, he renamed it the 'New' Princess Theatre. It seemed he was 'flush' with cash. He wore a spectacular gold ring bearing a setting of three diamonds. Apparently, it had cost him £800! It was lovely seeing him and his wife, Miss Mary Gladstane, again – we last saw them in Bendigo the previous year.

Rehearsals were very interesting as Mr Bayless had spoken with Mr Charles Hicks, the manager of the Original Georgia Minstrels, who happened to be passing through Melbourne at the time. Mr Bayless had offered an unknown sum to engage the Minstrels to be part of the play. It had been good judgement in securing their assistance, which added a sense of realism to the play.

The Original Georgia Minstrels were incredible. Their melodies and plantation songs, and dances were very beautiful. Some of the performers in the group had been slaves in Georgia, but they were now free as a result of the American Civil War. I couldn't imagine their hardships. Through all their adversity and suffering, their voices were true and powerful.

Opening night was Saturday, 8th June 1878, at the New Princess Theatre, Spring Street, Melbourne. It had been one month since I'd given birth to Laura. What do they say? No rest for the wicked. I must have been very wicked indeed. I look back now and think to myself, 'How did I do it?' I had a newborn baby and three young children at home. Although that wasn't technically true. Our eldest son Charlie was onstage with us.

It was a good house for an opening night.

The success that followed opening night was a surprise to everyone. The following 17 weeks (109 performances) were played to a full house every night. The theatre was really not large enough to hold the crowds that came night after night.

Mr Hosea Easton played the role of Uncle Tom. Mr Easton was tall, strong and a coloured man of African descent. He was 27 years old.

Mr Edward B Russell played the villainous role of Simon Legree. Mr Harry Douglas played the role of Van Tromp, the Quaker, and Mr Martin Ford played the role of Marks, who is the slave-catcher. Little Belle Russell took on the role of Eva St Clare.

The storyline of the play is based around a Kentucky farmer, by the name of Arthur Shelby, who has to sell some of his slaves, as he's run into a lot of debt. He decides to sell Uncle Tom, a middle-aged man, and Harry, the young son of George and Eliza Harris, who are house slaves.

Eliza overhears the plans and decides to flee with her son and husband and go north to Canada for freedom. They are pursued by a party of slave hunters, assisted by a brace of bloodhounds, and are followed across the half-frozen Ohio River. They make their way to a Quaker settlement, where the Quakers agree to help transport them to safety.

Meanwhile, Uncle Tom is taken to a boat on the Mississippi to be transported to a slave market to be sold. On the boat, Tom meets an angelic little white girl named

Eva, who quickly befriends him. When Eva falls into the river, Tom dives in to save her, and Eva's father, Augustine St Clare, gratefully agrees to buy Tom. Tom travels with the St Clare's to their home in New Orleans, where Tom grows increasingly invaluable to the St Clare household, with whom he shares a devout Christianity. Tragedy strikes when young Eva dies, and St Clare is stabbed to death while trying to settle a brawl.

St Clare's cruel wife, Marie, sells Tom to a vicious plantation owner named Simon Legree. Tom and Topsy, a slave girl, are taken to rural Louisiana with a group of new slaves, including Emmeline, whom the demonic Legree has purchased to use as his mistress, replacing his previous mistress, Cassy. Legree takes a strong dislike to Tom when Tom refuses to whip a fellow slave as ordered. Uncle Tom receives a severe beating, and Legree resolves to crush his faith in God.

Uncle Tom meets Cassy and hears her story. She had a daughter, but she had been taken away from her. She became pregnant again but killed the child because she could not stand to have another child taken from her.

Uncle Tom encourages Cassy to escape. She does so, taking young Emmeline with her.

Uncle Tom refuses to tell Legree where Cassy and Emmeline have gone, so Legree orders his overseers to beat him. When Uncle Tom is near death, he forgives Legree and the overseers. Uncle Tom dies a martyr's death.

Cassy and Emmeline take a boat and escape. They meet George and Eliza Harris and travel with them to Canada. Cassy realises that Eliza Harris is her long-lost daughter. The newly reunited family travels to France and decide to move to Liberia, the African nation created for former American slaves.

Arthur Shelby, who at the beginning of the story had to sell some of his slaves, has died. His son, George Shelby, returns to the Kentucky farm and sets all the slaves free in honour of Uncle Tom's memory. He urges the freed slaves to think of Tom's sacrifice every time they look at his cabin and to lead a pious Christian life, just as Tom did.

Mr Hosea Easton's portrayal of Uncle Tom was exquisitely natural. It was all but perfect in its truthful imitation of what one may suppose would be the expression of deep feeling on the part of a religious-minded, Christian slave. In the Slave Auction Mart, his depressed and saddened manner, as he mounts the block, made a visible and marked impression on the audience.

Uncle Tom's dying scene is so intensely mournful that there was scarcely a dry eye in the house. There was such an air of reality about it.

Miss Belle Russell, who played the role of Eva, was only five years old and did a wonderful, life-like rendition. The audience detested the brutal wretch Legree, played by Mr Russell.

I was personally very proud of my little Charlie, who was only seven years old and played the part of Harry Harris. He loved it.

Mr Harry Grist was our scenic artist. The ice scene and Legree's plantation at sunrise were simply works of art. The reviews were extremely good.

It was the first long run performance in the colonies.

Mr James Stewart Butters was the Mayor of Melbourne, and from the opening night till the last, he never omitted sending beautiful flowers to me, and dear Belle Russell, who played the role of little Eva.

The Melbourne Leader likened my 'elf-like form' to being very suited to the part of Topsy. They said my 'ingenious precocity was admirable, and my singing and performances were outstanding.' Topsy is an unusual character, who was only half-civilised due to being mistreated and unloved by her 'owners.' I used to warble 'Golly I'm so wicked' and dance in an eccentric way, that rarely failed to bring forth laughter from both the audience, stage-hands, my fellow artists and even the orchestra.

Two weeks after opening night, on 19th June 1878, we put on the Vice Regal Command Night for the occasion of his Excellency Sir GF Bowen, Governor of Victoria, attending the show. Lady Bowen and the Excellency's entourage also attended. This was a very auspicious occasion. And as such, a special programme of the performance was printed. It was rectangular in shape, edged with a fine fringe and printed on cream silk, with the text in dark blue. We even had the appearance of the first prize thoroughbred bloodhounds, Leo and Juno, onstage. They were kindly lent by Dr Louis Lawrence Smith to give effect to the slave-hunt scene and realism to the tracking of the escaped slaves. Dr LL Smith was quite famous for many reasons, some good and some not so good. But he was a character and added great excitement when he was backstage with his bloodhounds.

Pit, stalls, dress circle and upper boxes were all crowded, and several hundred people were unable to find seats.

Night after night, people came to see the show. The enthusiasm and excitement was extraordinary.

A few days after the Command Night, our manager, Mr Bayless, sent Mr Easton, Miss Belle Russell and me to have photographs taken of us 'in character' to help promote the play. We went to Mr Timothy Noble and Co., on Bourke Street, East Melbourne. The photographs were going to be turned into carte de visite. These pocket-sized portraits were very popular at the time and only cost a few shillings to buy. I still had my carte de visite of Prince Alfred, Duke of Edinburgh, from when we were in Calcutta.

William had come with me. We were planning on taking a walk through the city streets after the photographs were taken. It only took a few hours, and we had some fun watching each other pose.

I had removed the greasepaint and costume and was getting ready to leave with William. Mr Hosea Easton was sitting in the foyer of the photographic studio, and when he saw us, he stood up and asked if we would like to take tea with him in Collins Street. We happily accepted. I was intrigued to know more about him and his exceptional and sensitive acting. During rehearsals, I hadn't been able to get to know him that well.

Once we were settled, and our tea had been ordered, Mr Easton looked at me and William with great seriousness. He spoke softly and said,

'Miss Wiseman and Mr South, I am enjoying my time in Melbourne. I have to say I'm so thrilled that the play has become so popular. Although I'm happy most of the time, sometimes my memories take me to a dark place. I want to explain a few things, so you know and understand.'

He then took a deep breath and told William and me the most upsetting and courageous account of his childhood.

He was born on the 18th June 1851 in Louisiana, on a sugar plantation owned by Mr Philips. Mr Philips needed to raise money quickly, so he sold several of his slaves to another sugar planter, Mr Charles Sheldon. Hosea was one of the slaves, and he was only five years old. He never saw his mother again, but sometimes in his dreams, he would catch a glimpse of her loving face.

His new owner and master took him to Norfolk, Virginia, where he was used as an errand boy and house-servant. When he grew stouter and stronger, he became a groom and a stable hand.

Mr Sheldon was a harsh man. He swore at Hosea continually and whipped him when he wanted. Hosea would be tied up by the hands to a beam in the stable adjoining the house, his toes just touching the ground, and would be severely lashed over his bare back by his master. At these times, so severe would be the beating that frequently blood was drawn and would trickle down to his heels. His flesh afterwards would be sore for many days, and his back would be scarred from the shoulders to the hips. The flagellating instrument was anything ready to hand — a riding whip, a length of rope, and once a knotted yard of new bed-cord, which he described as capable of producing pain worse than anything else he knew.

These whippings were generally inflicted by his master when he was under the influence of strong drink. His temper flared over the minutest of things. He would foam at the mouth with rage and fury. His violence when he was intoxicated almost amounted to madness. He appeared at these times to take a fiendish delight in brutally flogging any of the slave hands that he came across.

Mr Sheldon's wife was a compassionate, loving lady. In vain, she would intercede with her husband for the poor victims. Mr Sheldon never once heeded her piteous appeals to him, to spare even a single lash. Frequently, on hearing the screams of the wretched, helpless slaves, she would fall into hysterics, and sometimes faint and would lay on the ground unconscious for hours.

The cruellest whipping that Hosea ever had, the one that inspired his resolution to escape on the first opportunity that offered itself, was instigated by another planter named Mr Charles Pond. This man had lodged a complaint against Hosea for presumed impertinence. Hosea had refused Mr Pond the use of a boat belonging to Mr Sheldon, of which he had the care. Mr Pond claimed the boat was his property. The flogging was given with a couple of yards of cat-gut, nearly the thickness of the little finger, and was of such severity that poor Hosea was incapacitated in bed for nearly a month.

During that time, Hosea was attended by Mrs Sheldon. She would often tell him of her abhorrence and detestation she had of her husband. The scars resulting from this whipping remain on Hosea's back and chest to this day. He will carry them with him to his grave.

Hosea said he received four formal whippings. It was, however, common for him to be knocked down, kicked, struck once or twice across the legs and shoulders with a riding whip, for slight acts of forgetfulness.

He continued with Mr Sheldon until 1863, when he succeeded in making his escape and joined the United States Navy.

The Civil War in America started in 1861 and raged for nearly five years. The war was between the northern states (the Union) and the southern states (the Confederates).

Hosea lived in Virginia, a southern state, near a river. He had merely to cross the river and walk three miles on the beach to get to the harbour where a large United States Ship named the *USS Ozark* was anchored. The *Ozark* was a gunboat and contained Union men of war. However, the Confederate lookouts were always watching and would have shot him dead if he had been seen anywhere near the river.

On dark nights, it was not unusual for a crew from the *Ozark* to take a small boat and row silently up the river in search of a tavern where they might obtain liquor. To get a supply, they would generally require the services of a local guide. On one such occasion, Hosea happened to be in the neighbourhood of one of these adventurous groups. They approached him and asked for his help. Hosea, in return, asked for theirs. The proposition was at once agreed to.

He got them a big demi-john, four gallons of first-rate bourbon whiskey. To obtain the whiskey, Hosea asked for it as if it were for his master, Mr Sheldon, who, no doubt, was not pleased when he found this particular item in his account. Hosea had no alternative, for the money that had been given to him by the sailors was not the correct currency in Virginia. If he had tendered the money to the tavern-keeper, it would have led to the asking of very troublesome questions.

After the whiskey was obtained, the crew honoured their side of the bargain and took him on to their boat.

From the *Ozark*, Hosea was transferred to the Brooklyn Navy Yard, New York, then to the West Gulf Squadron, which was stationed at that time in the Gulf of Mexico. There, onboard the United States frigate, the USS *Potomac*, he served as cabin-boy in the officers' mess-room. He was then trained in the duties of a seaman and was drafted into the flagship, the *USS Hartford*, a sloop of war, commanded by Admiral Farragut. Onboard this vessel, working as a seaman, he took an active part in the storming and the capture of Mobile Bay on the 5th August 1864.

He was wounded twice, a bullet on each occasion passing through the fleshy part of the calf of his right leg. He continued in the navy until August 1867 – when he was in Brooklyn, New York, he claimed his discharge, two years after he was entitled to it.

When in the Navy, many of the officers and men took a kindly interest in him and taught him how to read and write.

He stayed in New York till the end of 1867, then travelled to New Haven in Connecticut, where he settled down, earning his livelihood as a porter. He worked in the Tontine Hotel, then in the Fremont Hotel.

He was passionately fond of music, and he succeeded in teaching himself to play several instruments. His fame as a musician soon extended to the surrounding districts. He received various offers to join several of the minstrel troupes that were then forming all over America. He finally accepted an engagement with the Original Georgia Minstrels and has continued to tour with them.

After Mr Easton had finished telling us about his childhood and how he came to be in Melbourne, I almost sobbed with grief. Mr Easton had been treated horrendously, yet he did not harbour feelings of revenge. He was the most extraordinary person I had ever met.

*

In early August 1878, Melbourne was visited by a thick fog, which reminded me of London. It started in the evening, about 6:00 pm, and by 7:00 pm, you could not see across the road. I was onstage that night, but not till late in the piece, and so I generally left home about 7:00 pm or a little later. The cabman who had been engaged to drive me to the theatre was late, and it was nearly 8:00 pm when he arrived. I got in and naively imagined all was well. The horse was going at a smart pace when all of a sudden, he came to a stop.

I asked the man why he didn't go on?

'I can't Miss, it's more than me life's worth to drive that there 'orse an inch further. Why I can't even see the lamps on the cab. Look yourself Miss.'

I looked in front of the cab, and he was right. I couldn't see any more than he could.

I asked the cabman, 'Where do you think we are?'

He replied, 'Well Miss, as near as I can reckon, we'd be near Prince's Bridge.'

I implored him to make a greater effort, but he would not budge. A nice plight I was in. It was no good my attempting to go on by myself. There was nothing else for it but to have a real good cry. Which I did.

Then I heard a voice say, 'What's the matter Miss?'

To be honest, I could only hear the voice; I could not see who was asking the question.

Through my tears, I told the invisible person I was late for the theatre.

'Oh, I'm walking for that point myself, so keep close to me and I'll do my best for you.'

The only way I could keep close to him was to hang on to his coat-tails, which I did and tightly too, I can assure you. We had been going along some time, when I ventured to remark, 'Do you think we are close to the theatre?'

The words were no sooner spoken than I was grabbed by the arm, and the grabber said, 'Is that you Miss Wiseman? The second act is over. You'll have to hurry up.'

I wasn't able to say a word of thanks to my pilot for steering me safely, because I was hustled into the theatre. I broke the record dressing that night. The audience was rather impatient at the unusual delay.

Mr Bayless told them, 'I'm sorry to say that Topsy had been lost in the fog.' A chorus of 'Ohs' came from the crowd.

'But I am happy to say she's found,' at which the audience applauded.

*

Our Melbourne season eventually came to an end. While there was still interest in *The Cabin,* there were many members of the company who wanted to take it on tour, to the other colonies. Some of the members were agreeable and others were not. We were in the camp of taking the play on tour.

With the aid of Mr John Liddy, who was the business manager, Mr George Collier, and my husband William, everything was fixed to our satisfaction so we could go on tour. We would have some new actors joining the tour, which was exciting.

However, I was so sad to say goodbye to Mr Hosea and Miss Belle Russell. Hosea gave me a signed carte de visite of himself. It is still one of my most treasured mementos. Hosea was a gentleman. He had lived through a terrible period of America's history, and it was an honour to know him and work alongside him.

Chapter Seventeen – Touring with *The Cabin*

In November 1878, we went on tour with *The Cabin.*

All my children came along.

First stop was the Victoria Theatre in Newcastle, New South Wales. The audience was very enthusiastic. There was so much applause afforded so continuously throughout the performance. The pit and stalls were densely packed to the very doors. The dress circle was very fairly filled, which was wonderful considering that under ordinary circumstances this part of the theatre is rarely patronised. We all received wonderful reviews.

Mr Robert B Lewis played the role of Uncle Tom. The reviews noted his manner, voice, makeup and general acting realised all that the reader of Mrs Stowe's picture of slave life could well imagine. The review also noted that Topsy seems to have stepped bodily from Mrs Stowe's book onto the stage, which made me smile.

The critics went on to say, Miss Nellie Holmes, who played the role of Little Eva, was so realistic that at times there was scarcely a dry eye in the house. Especially in the dying scene, when a breathless silence proved that the feelings of the audience were wrought to the highest pitch.

The curtain had to be raised at the close of each act, and the principal performers were repeatedly applauded.

*

We returned to Melbourne to open the Christmas season with *The Cabin*. Opening night was on Monday, 23rd December 1878 at the New Princess Theatre.

The play was being reproduced for the 96th time.

I resumed the character of Topsy. Miss Nellie Holmes continued in her role as Eva, and Mr Robert B Lewis sustained the part of Uncle Tom. The Georgia Jubilee Singers furnished the choruses – they were different to the Original Georgia Minstrels, but they were equally as good. Dr LL Smith's bloodhounds, Leo and Juno, appeared again upon the stage.

It was said at the time, if you were from the country visiting the city, the visit would not be complete without seeing the play *Uncle Tom's Cabin*.

*

We continued touring again after the Christmas season and were in Mount Alexander in January 1879. Whilst we were in town, I'd overhead people talking about a young lad named Alfred Brown, from Peg-Leg. Alfred had saved a young girl from drowning. Miss Gray, who was only eight years old, had been crayfishing in the dam adjoining Mr Clark's farm, and by some means she fell into the water. Alfred Brown had passed the dam a short time previously and noticed the little girl fishing, and on his return, he missed her. He looked into the water, which was very clear, and saw her lying at the bottom of the dam, the depth being six feet.

Without any hesitation, Alfred immediately plunged in and brought the insensible child to the surface. Remedies were applied, and in a short time, Miss Gray was restored to consciousness and taken home, apparently very little the worse for her immersion.

There is no doubt that without the prompt action taken by young Alfred Brown, death would have resulted, as the child had sunk for the last time. Many of the townspeople were saying the brave deed deserved to be rewarded by the Humane Society. I agreed.

I remember Mr George Coppin talking about how he just didn't understand why more people didn't learn how to swim. He had taught his own children, and they had rescued many people as well.

Next stop was Echuca. We played in the Temperance Hall, which is a difficult place to perform in. If you pitch your voice high, you are heard to bawl; if low, you are often not heard at all.

The Riverine Herald newspaper, Thursday 9th January 1879, had a very good review of the play. The newspaper said:

> 'We come to speak of Miss Fanny Wiseman (Mrs South), and we might write a great deal in her praise, had we space to do so. We think it quite impossible that this character of Topsy could be better or more ably represented. It is not a burlesque, it is not a grotesque representation, but it is exactly played as we think the author intended it to be understood. And there is a great deal of real, genuine humour in it. Miss Wiseman has so identified herself with this part that she will always be remembered by it, if not by anything else she has ever played. No praise is too high for the thorough spirit she infuses into it.'

I was well pleased with that review.

Our last performance of *Uncle Tom's Cabin* in Echuca also marked Miss Nellie Holmes' first benefit. It was tendered to her by the management on the last performance night, as it was also her birthday. She turned six years old.

Then we went back to Melbourne to the New Princess Theatre for Wednesday, 22nd January 1879, another grand opening night. We had many of the actors who had been on tour with us. The Georgia Jubilee Singers, with 30 artists, also performed. Miss Nellie Holmes played Little Eva, Mr Robert B Lewis played the role of Uncle Tom, Mr GW Collier played the role of Simon Legree, and my husband played the role of Tom Locker. I again played the role of Topsy.

The orchestra was under the conductorship of Mr Leech, and William's uncle, Mr Thomas King, was the lead clarinet.

Prices at the time were: dress circle was four shillings; stalls were two shillings and sixpence; pit was one shilling; and children under 12 were half price. Tickets were sold for stalls and pit during the day at Nathan's tobacconist in Princes Street, Allen's Railway Cigar Divan in George Street, and Solomon Friedlich, the tobacconist at the theatre entrance. Doors opened at 7:15 pm, and the performance commenced at 8:00 pm.

After our Melbourne performances, we left for Sydney with a portion of the original dramatic cast and some of the Georgia Singers. We opened at the old Victoria Theatre, then under the direction of Mr John Bennett. It was wonderful seeing his familiar face again. He was, of course, the theatre manager from Back Creek and Lamplough.

While we were playing at the old Vic, the stock company were on half salaries.

Mr Bland Holt joined the show to play the character of Marks the Lawyer, and Miss Flora Ansteed played Eliza.

At the time, a rival company started up, also putting on *Uncle Tom's Cabin*, at the Queen's Theatre in Sydney. There were many versions of *Uncle Tom's Cabin*, some better than others, but all were popular. The copyright for the play was in the public domain, so theatre managers could alter the play to their own preferences, as long as it retained recognisable characters and plot. The rival production did not hurt us in any way.

Mr Bland Holt was the son of Mr Clarence and Marie Holt, whom I had the honour of working with years ago in Adelaide and in New Zealand. Mr Bland Holt would go on to great success as an actor and stage manager.

From Sydney we went to Newcastle, then back again to Sydney, then off to Wellington and Christchurch in New Zealand.

Around this time, a small company started making dolls based on the main characters of *Uncle Tom's Cabin*. I was honoured to have Topsy represented. It was a little black doll, frocked in hessian and complete with black curly hair tied with white rags. Fancy that! I had my own little doll. I could never have imagined that.

While we were in Christchurch, the politician Sir John Cracroft Wilson invited several of us to lunch. He told me I should meet some of my old friends. He would not tell me who they were, as it was to be a surprise.

Well, I almost fainted when I saw it was my dear old manager and friend, Mr William 'Billy' Hoskins and his second wife, the very pretty Miss Florence Colville, who was also an actress. I was so happy to see Billy. But I couldn't help thinking of poor Julia, Billy's first wife – she had died in 1872 of dropsy.

We were a very merry party that day, and Billy could not stop himself from telling the story of when we first met and my outlandish comment about his 'swinging' leg. He often told that story, and to my defence, I reminded him I was only 10 years old at the time. It was all in good fun.

Sir Wilson was very generous and looked after our entire group. He had been in India for a time, so we shared stories of our travels, the places we'd been and things we saw.

Later that night, Sir Wilson attended the theatre to see our show and he brought along several of his friends, including Billy and his wife, Miss Florence. It was another great performance, and the audience was very appreciative.

Billy came to see me backstage after the performance had ended. He said to me,

'I loved your performance Fanny, but I do wish you hadn't to blacken your face.'

I replied, 'Yes, I agree. But I cannot play Topsy with a white face. I've been told that there are no black actresses to take the part, so there's no question, it has to be done.'

'Ah, yes, I understand,' he said.

I then had the chance to ask about his health, and he said,

'I'm very well, my dear. You know, I was heartbroken when Julia died. Florence was a great support to me. Although I am much older than her, more than 30 years, we are very happy.' And I could see he was happy.

After Billy left, I proceeded to remove the greasepaint, all the while thinking about what he had said. Why weren't there any experienced black actresses to take the role? Or maybe there were but they weren't given the chance. I remembered meeting Mr Ira Aldridge when I was only four years old. He was a great actor who had left America to live in England, away from bigotry and prejudices. Some people just couldn't see past the colour of someone's skin to see the person. There were many male American black actors who were touring Australia with different companies, and a few Aboriginal male actors, but I couldn't think of any black female actresses. The thought didn't leave me.

I always felt so fortunate to have been able to follow my heart into the acting profession. It had afforded me many opportunities that most other women didn't have. I had travelled to many countries and across Australia and met people from every walk of life, from a Prince to gold fossickers. Most women were bound by societal expectations, and whilst I had many responsibilities, my acting gave me independence and freedom.

We were in New Zealand for about six months and visited all the larger towns. My children were good travellers, and they loved being on tour. There were the occasional upsets, but that was to be expected. For the most part, my children were part of the company, and my fellow actors helped me when I needed it.

At the beginning of May 1879, we left New Zealand and set our sights for Hobart, Tasmania.

We played at The Theatre Royal on Campbell Street for four weeks and stayed in the Theatre Royal Hotel next door. It was a fabulous time, and the Hobart audiences were raucous, loud and appreciative of our talents. The theatre held 700 people, and we packed it almost every night. The theatre had a luxurious red velvet carpet and chairs, and the most glorious domed ceiling. It was a large theatre, however, it was incredibly intimate – we could see every smile, frown, and tear on our audience's faces.

On one of our last days in Hobart, I can't remember who, but it was suggested we go down to Port Arthur Gaol. We needed a permit, which we obtained with the help of Detective Sincox. He was our official guide.

William and I decided to leave the children in the capable care of the hotel manageress, Mrs Davies – she was a very capable lady with a warm smile. We had heard of the horrors that had occurred in Port Arthur Gaol, and we didn't want the children to be frightened.

When we arrived, I had an overwhelming feeling of sadness. It was an eerie place. Only two years had passed since it had been closed. And now we could go and look, but there was no way I wanted to stay there.

Detective Sincox asked us if we would like to go into the condemned cell, and we all said 'yes.' While we were all talking and looking around, Detective Sincox quietly slipped out and locked us in. A practical joke that went bad, for while he was laughing and turning the key to let us out, the key broke in the lock. We were prisoners for over two hours. That little episode put an end to my curiosity as far as gaols were concerned!

From Hobart, we travelled to Launceston for two weeks, then back to Melbourne.

The company then disbanded.

We were all pleased with a very successful tour.

Uncle Tom's Cabin had unprecedented success, of which I had never seen or would ever see again. We performed 109 nights in Melbourne and 75 nights in adjacent colonies. The success of the play mirrored the success of the novel.

Chapter Eighteen – The Firm

After our long tour with *The Cabin,* it felt wonderful to return to Melbourne and settle back into our domestic routines. This, however, didn't last long.

William and I were approached by Mr Tom Scott Chantey, husband of Mrs Mary Scott-Siddons, to take a three-month tour. That was in August 1879. Among the company were Mr Herbert Flemming, Mr Charles Brown, Mr Nat Douglass, William's brother James South, Miss Meta Pelham and Miss Docy Mainwarring. Miss Meta was to become a very dear and close friend. Back in those days, in Scott-Siddons Company, we were expected to learn many parts in case anyone was unwell and couldn't perform. We were paid around £3 a week and had to find our own costumes.

Miss Meta's name became a word for the punning comedians to play with. Once, when the gas lighting failed in a scene from Mr Tom Taylor's play *The Ticket-of-Leave*

Man, the stage manager gagged and said, 'We'll soon have the lights going, there's plenty of gas in the *Meta*!' Well, that lightened the mood, and we could feel the audience settle back with good humour.

Mrs Scott-Siddons was a bright and radiant star. It was such an enjoyable engagement, I didn't want it to end. When we all parted, the regret was mutual among all of us.

✳

When Mr JC Williamson and his wife, Miss Maggie Moore, returned to Australia in 1879, they brought with them the rights to *HMS Pinafore,* a comic opera by Gilbert and Sullivan. They opened on 23rd August 1879 under Mr George Coppin's management at the Theatre Royal in Melbourne.

Mr Williamson obtained the Australasian rights to all the Gilbert and Sullivan pieces. It became the launching pad of his theatrical empire. Mr James Cassius Williamson founded JC Williamson Ltd., also called Williamson, Garner and Musgrove. But everyone in the theatre business just called the company, 'The Firm.'

Mr JC Williamson became the most successful theatre manager in the world, and he controlled a long chain of theatres in Australia and New Zealand.

I had met Mr JC Williamson many times. He had asked me if I would sign up to The Firm. He offered a great package to be part of his stock company. I was very tempted, and the thought of regular employment was attractive.

However, there was something that stopped me. I knew I did not want someone telling me where to go, what to do, or which part to play, not even my husband. Those decisions should be for me to decide, and I had been doing well up to then, surviving on my wits, my talent and my ambition.

I had seen how rich and powerful men controlled their surroundings and the people around them. I think I had developed a fierce independence over the years.

There were times when I did question my decision and thought my life might have been easier had I accepted the offer to join The Firm. I had always thought of my acting career as a vocation, not a lucrative trade. Ultimately, in life, we cannot look back; we must look forward.

*

In November 1879, William and I were finally able to buy a little house in Ballarat. It was something I had dreamt of when I was in India. The children loved it, and we felt we could relax a little.

William and I were engaged by Mr Keogh to open at the Academy of Music in Ballarat. We performed several pieces, including *Under the Gaslight* by Mr Augustin Daly, in which I played Peachblossom. In the scene where old Judas has to pull my hair and beat me, my two boys, Charlie and Tom, who were in the front of the house, thought I was being too roughly treated. Charlie, my eldest boy, who was nine at the time, sang out at the top of his voice, 'Kick her mother, kick her, don't you stand it!'

The applause and laughter that followed was almost deafening.

⁂

In February 1880, I appeared again at the Academy of Music, Ballarat, in Charles Dickens play *Bleak House*, as the character Joe. The version I played was one dramatised for me by Madame Anna King, my sister-in-law. She was a highly cultured and gifted woman.

If you're not familiar with the play *Bleak House*, my character Joe is an unfortunate street sweeper who was 'allus being moved on.' In the last act, Joe is 'moved on' for the last time in this world. My stage makeup showed a cadaverous face shaded by tangled black hair. I had to portray the weak weariness of a boy as he struggles from his bed to go and sweep the steps that led into the graveyard. The critics described my acting as 'well and faithfully portrayed'. However, they weren't as kind to my husband's portrayal of Inspector Bucket.

We had heard the gossip about Mr Joseph Aarons, who was managing the Academy of Music at the time. The theatre was losing money and had been for a while. Soon after *Bleak House* had ended, he staged a version of WS Gilbert and Gilbert A'Beckett's *The Happy Land*. The play focussed on ridiculing several recognisable politicians which included the premier of the colony Mr Graham Berry. Production of the play was then banned by political censorship and as they say, 'that was the last nail in the coffin'.

Soon after the political drama debacle, the lease held by Mr Joseph Aarons elapsed. Our old friends Miss Rose Edouin and Mr GBW Lewis were granted the lease and renamed the theatre the Lewis' Bijou Theatre. My sister Alice's husband, Henry Westley, helped with all the legal paperwork, as he was the Lewis' solicitor.

*

Everyone from my generation remembers where they were when they heard the news that the Kelly Gang had been captured. I was in Ballarat, rushing to the theatre for rehearsals. When I walked backstage, everyone was talking about it.

There could have only been two possible endings to the Kelly Gang story – escape or capture. On the 28th June 1880, Dan Kelly, Joseph Byrne and Steve Hart were killed in the siege at the Glenrowan Inn. Ned Kelly was shot multiple times by the police and taken into custody.

I was sure the authorities would make him suffer. I had seen occasions when the heavy hand of the law was used, but equally I'd seen justice and compassion. But in this circumstance, I felt like Ned Kelly had run circles around the authorities, and it was now their turn to be in control. Ned was no saint. However, I think many people in Victoria felt that he and his family had been discriminated against because they were Irish, and they had acted in self-defence.

Ned stood trial and was found guilty of murder and sentenced to execution by hanging. After his execution, his death mask was displayed at the Wax Museum in Bourke Street, Melbourne. What purpose did it serve? Was it a reminder to all of us of the power of the police? Was it morbid fascination or was it for scientific purposes? I'm not sure what the answer is, perhaps a combination of all I mentioned. For me, it was a ghastly practice.

Mr Ned Kelly and Mr Joseph Byrne's horses were also captured by the police, and they were auctioned by the Crown. My old friend Mr George Coppin secured Ned's mount Mirth, a reddish-brown mare, and Joseph Byrne's horse, a grey mare named Music, and decided to use them as an added attraction in a new drama in which he was involved. You might call it sensationalism, but Mr Coppin had a knack for knowing what the people wanted. The well-trained horses duly took to the boards and 'acted' as they were directed. After their performances were no longer needed, they were sold and their new owner used them to draw his phaeton carriage through the streets of Melbourne.

After all is said and done, the story of the Kelly Gang remains one for the ages. It has all the elements of a Shakespearean tragedy – love, death, revenge and a tragic hero.

*

On 13th August 1880, I had another baby boy. We named him Austin Holgate Theoden South. We were still living in Ballarat and had plenty of help from the rest of the family. William's parents lived in Skipton Street just around the corner from us.

Our house was very full now. We had five children, Charlie, Tom, Minnie, Laura and Austin. William and I had steady work, and when things were quiet, William would help his father in the saddle shop, and I would take care of the children.

Our association with Ballarat stretched back to the early 1850s. William's parents, James South and Sarah Ann King, like mine, had moved there and established their business. William's father, James, was the first saddler in Ballarat, and William's mother, Sarah Ann and her kin were all talented musicians. William's sister, Miss Eliza Anna South, or better known by her stage name, Madame Anna King, was a music and singing teacher in the town for many years.

Chapter Nineteen – Sydney, New South Wales

In early April 1881, William and I sold our home in Ballarat, and with our five children, we left for the colony of New South Wales. It was a great wrench for me to leave Ballarat; it was my home, a haven of rest.

We settled in Balmain, close to the harbour. We had only been in Sydney for a fortnight when a telegram arrived addressed to me. It was from my sister Laura.

I sat down, trying to prepare myself for whatever was contained within. All I could see when I opened it were the words,

'Emily... died.'

At that point, I must have fainted.

Thinking about this again, so many years later, is almost as heart-rending as when it happened. It was devastating. An enormous shock to all of us. I can hardly talk about it, for it takes me back to inconsolable grief. I had experienced that grief before with the loss of my children. Like a shadow returning to its owner, grief returned and attached itself to me. If it were not for William and my children, I would have been consumed entirely by overwhelming sadness.

They brought me out of the darkness and back into the light in many ways – flowers from the garden left on my bedroom dresser, little notes with love hearts drawn on them, and endless cups of tea. These little but thoughtful acts went a long way in my recovery.

My sister Laura had been living with Emily, Johnnie and their son John Jnr. Emily had been unwell for several weeks and was recuperating at her home in Botanic House, North Terrace, Adelaide. But then she had a sudden and severe attack of paralysis, and nothing could be done for her. She died on her birthday, the 26th April 1881. Her husband, Johnnie, was away in Queensland for business at the time.

My poor sister Emily was so beloved by her husband, her son, and by all who knew her. Johnnie wasn't able to get back in time for the funeral, and I was also too far away. Laura had to arrange the funeral, a very difficult task.

My dear sister Emily Louisa Ann Wiseman Wolloxhall was buried at West Terrace Cemetery, Adelaide. I hoped that her young son, John Jnr, would be alright; he was only 14 years old and ready to start making his way in the world. A world without Emily was a very sad place.

I missed her terribly.

✻

In August 1882, I had another baby, and we named him Sydney Anthony South. A beautiful, healthy baby. I felt blessed.

Two months later, William's brother James asked us to join his company, The South's Comedy and Opera Company. James had engaged Mr Whittington as our business manager – he was one of the best, and I knew we would be well taken care of. I certainly needed that reassurance.

Our tour was for eight months, but this was extended to nearly 12 due to its success. It was hard work, but I loved it. My children adapted to the touring lifestyle very quickly.

Charlie was 12 years old and helped with setting up stage equipment and distributing the playbills around the various towns we travelled to. Tom was nine years old and helped his older brother with all his responsibilities. Minnie was six years old, and Laura was only four, so they stayed with me or William or the other members of the company. Austin was two years old, and of course, Sydney was still a baby. So, you can imagine I had my hands full all the time.

James and his wife, Miss Edith, were the stars. William's sister, Madame Anna King, was part of the company, along with many other talented artists. Dear Mr J Rayner, a very old actor whom I had acted with when I was a child at the Queens Theatre in Melbourne, was also with us.

I was so glad that Madame King was on tour with us. She was the musical director of the company and a skilled soprano vocalist. She played the pianoforte for all the accompaniments and the choruses. She had also added acting to her repertoire. She was so energetic, she lifted all our spirits, especially when we became tired and irritable.

We had complete scenery and a magnificent wardrobe, and no pains were spared to ensure full public approval.

I must say that James' wife, Miss Edith Pender, was a conundrum. She was a very clever artist and possessed the sweetest voice, but on one night her singing would be perfect, the next it was like a cat calling. I thought she was careless with her abilities and wasn't disciplined enough. In contrast, my sister-in-law, Madame Anna King, honed her skills with disciplined practice, and the result was grace, elegance and consistency.

Our repertoire consisted of Lytton's play *Lady of Lyons*, Shakespeare's *Merchant of Venice*, Byron's comedy *Our Boys*, three of Boucicault's plays *Colleen Bawn*, *Arrah-na-Pogue*, and *Octoroon*, Dickens' *Bleak House* and Williamson's *Struck Oil*. We also presented several operas. All the Gilbert and Sullivan operas were by arrangement with Mr JC Williamson, for he held the rights to them.

I had plenty of work to do, as I played the roles of Arrah, Eily, Lizzie Stofel, Paul, Belinda, Jo, Maggie, Buttercup, Ruth, and Isabella. The tour was very successful. There was plenty of money made but spent just as quickly.

In March 1883, the company toured to Newcastle and then down the coast to Kiama and then Bega. As was the way back then, telegrams were sent to different towns when a show was on tour. Thankfully, the Kiama reporter had sent a telegram to Bega, saying, 'a grand treat was in store for your people.' So, when we opened in Bega, our reputation had preceded us.

While we were in Bega, we had to attend the local courthouse. Not as a defendant or witness but as a victim. A forgery had taken place by a mere lad of 12 years. I must admit I was very moved by the poor lad's plight. He had obtained admittance to one of our performances by means of a forged ticket. Information reached the police, and several similar tickets were found in the lad's pocket. Our tickets are green and have the word 'stall' printed on them. The young boy had secured pieces of card of similar colour, and on them had written the word 'stall' and successfully presented one of these at the door to gain admittance.

The lad's father had given him a good character reference and said his mother was then very ill. From their appearance, they didn't seem to have much money at all. James told the judge that he did not wish to proceed against the lad. The boy then confessed he had printed the tickets and given one to a little boy.

The Bench admonished the poor lad and told him he must thank Mr South for letting him off. If a charge had been pressed, 12 – 18 months' imprisonment might be the consequence. The boy promised never again to yield to temptation and was discharged. My heart ached for the boy's hardship and for the simple act of wanting to be entertained for a few short hours to take his mind off other things.

In July 1883, we were in Queanbeyan, playing at the Theatre Hall. The audience was very appreciative of our rendition of Shakespeare's *The Merchant of Venice*. We had the support of the district band. For an hour before the commencement of the play, the district band rendered a selection of excellent music. After their performance, a skilful pianist beguiled the audience for a few more minutes, till the rising of the curtain to reveal the courtly pageant of the trial scene from the play. Shylock was portrayed by my husband, William. The critics said he acted with a reality that held the audience in positive rapture.

On our last night in Queanbeyan, we played the drama *Struck Oil,* which was so well received wherever it was played. Mr JC Williamson and Miss Maggie Moore had brought this play to Australia and had great success with it. The audience was delighted.

The plot of this popular play is set in the oil regions of America and is said to be founded on facts. The story is about the Stofel family – John, a Dutchlander, his American wife, and his daughter (by a first marriage), Lizzie, a playful, restless, sensitive girl. John is a shoemaker and owns a small freehold, where he plies his craft. Through his wife's thriftiness as a needlewoman, they managed to survive.

The villain of the play is Deacon Skinner, a grovelling, cowardly hypocrite. He manages to convince John to take his place to serve in the American Civil War. The enticement involved a payment of $750 and the title deed of a farm. Before his departure, John places the precious title deed document under the bricks of the hearth in his cottage for safekeeping.

Meanwhile, the deacon discovers that the farm, though useless for agriculture, contains an oil well.

Before leaving home, Stofel exacts a promise from his wife that she will never sell the little homestead as long as a wall of it is standing or a brick of the chimney remains in its place. During his absence, the wily deacon tries unsuccessfully to ingratiate himself with Mrs Stofel and daughter Lizzie.

The war comes to an end, but sadly, it is believed that John Stofel has died in combat. Lizzie is married to Dr Brown, whom she has loved from her girlhood.

At this point, we see a man wandering in the neighbourhood. His fate would be the madhouse but for the attentions of Dr Brown. The man does not know who he is, not even his own name. Eventually, his memory returns, and he is John Stofel.

He remembers the secret location of the original deed, rushes to the spot, removes a brick from the hearth, and brings to light the document. During the previous few days, the deacon had forged John Stofel's signature on the title deeds, and he was thus caught out as a forger, a perjurer, and a hypocritical knave.

John Stofel's return not only raised his wife from the desolation of widowhood but placed her with him in a position of wealth.

I played the part of Lizzie Stofel.

At the close of the performance, my brother-in-law James came before the curtain and, in the name of the company, thanked the people of Queanbeyan for the hearty reception we had received there. He said the company would carry away pleasant memories of the people and the place and cherish the hope of visiting the district again before long.

We left Queanbeyan in a Pooley and Malone special horse-drawn coach and headed for Goulburn, where we advertised to perform for three successive nights.

By September 1883, we were in Burrangong, New South Wales. Opening night at the Mechanic's Institute was on Saturday, 1st September. Our opening piece was the dramatisation of some of the incidents in Dickens *Bleak House*. I again played the character of Jo, the poor street sweeper. The critics mentioned my impersonation was excellent and procured several calls before the curtain.

The characters of Lady Deadlock and Hortense were both taken by Madame King. Mr James South played the character of Guffy; his droll portrayal of the character served to break the lengthy emotional portions of the play. William played Inspector Bucket. The full company were all good in their respective parts.

The play was watched with the greatest interest by the audience; the silent attention being only broken by the applause which followed any particularly telling incident.

The tour had been very much a family affair. William, his brother James and his wife Miss Edith Pender, and his sister Madame King. Our boys, Charlie and Tom, had worked side-by-side with us, and I could see on their faces how proud they were of the success of the tour.

We finally returned to Balmain, on beautiful Sydney Harbour. From our terrace house, we could see down to the water. I never tired of looking out the window to see the glinting sun dancing across the water.

On the 21st June 1884, I gave birth to a beautiful baby girl and named her Mary Lillian South. She was my third daughter. The children quickly decided she was more a Lilly than a Mary, so from that early time, she became known as Lilly.

Chapter Twenty – Wedding anniversary

On 7th January 1885, William and I celebrated our 20th wedding anniversary. He bought me the most beautiful Royal Doulton teacup and saucer – valuable and fragile, much like our marriage. I'd spent more than half my life with William. We had had 11 children, seven beautiful children that were still with us, and four that had sadly died. I loved William deeply. Yet at times, old arguments would resurface, and he would be vehement in his emotions and words. But we did our best, as you do.

*

From February to May 1886, William and I were engaged in Sydney with the Hiscocks Federal Minstrels at the Academy of Music. We played good old *Uncle Tom's Cabin*. The hall was crowded every night.

Then we were in the Olympic Theatre (the Old Masonic Hall), in York Street, with Boucicault's play *Octoroon*. We were under the management of Mr D'Arcy Read and Mr

John Peel. It was hailed as a 'good evening's entertainment, given at exceedingly popular prices.' It was another successful venture.

⁕

I loved living in Sydney and would, when I had the chance, take the ferry across to Manly. The whole family decided to take a special trip in December 1886, as we had heard of the recent opening of the Manly Aquarium. Mr Griffin and Mr Evans were the proprietors, and they had spared no expense in completing the aquarium in every detail. Thousands of people had already visited the aquarium, and everyone had been saying how extraordinary it was.

We boarded the ferry at Circular Quay. The ferry ride across Sydney Harbour was very rough, as the winds were up, and the ferry was riding the waves. The young deckhand was checking on everyone, making sure we were all safe inside the ferry. He came over to me and the family, and said,

'Good day, Miss Wiseman. Is this your family?'

I was a little surprised by his familiarity. But I quickly realised that the deckhands knew everything that happened in Sydney. They saw the comings and goings and were expected to answer all the questions the passengers might ask. That included what was showing at the theatres, what was good to see and what should be missed.

'Oh, how do you do, young man, yes, this is my family. We're heading to Manly to visit the Aquarium.'

He gave us a big smile and said, 'I think you'll enjoy it. Everyone who comes back from the aquarium talks about all the fish and how colourful they are. I haven't been there yet, but I hope to go soon.'

Then there was a big wave, and everyone held onto their seats. Not the deckhand, though. He didn't need to hold on to anything; he seemed to move with the boat.

He laughed and said, 'Good thing the piano is fastened tightly. Wouldn't do to have that rolling around.' There were a few laughs as people could see this decky was well used to the big waves and he wasn't the least worried.

I asked what his name was, and he answered,

'Darcy Cameron,' and then he said, 'Miss Wiseman, I must tell you I saw you in *Uncle Tom's Cabin*. You were really good. It was all anyone could talk about on the ferries for months.'

I was so touched when he said that.

We were approaching Manly Wharf, so he quickly left to throw the ropes to tie up. As we were walking across the gangway, Mr Darcy was there making sure we all left safely. We all waved, and he gave us a whistle goodbye.

When we arrived at the aquarium and walked through the main doors, we could see all the wonderful fish. The highlight for the children was seeing the two baby seals from Seal Rocks.

*

Throughout 1887, I continued to be engaged in several performances, but things were a little quieter for William.

The family had grown substantially, and it was to continue to grow. On the 10th October 1887, I gave birth to a beautiful baby girl and named her Emily Elizabeth. I was 41 years old. I now had eight children, ranging in ages from Charles, the eldest, at 17, to my newborn. Emily's name was quickly changed by all her siblings to Emmie. She was to be my last child. Whenever I held any of my babies, I would remember my four little boys who had died. It was always bittersweet.

We were still living in Balmain, which had become a very comfortable and full home.

I wrote to my parents in New Zealand with the wonderful news of Emmie's birth, and soon after received a letter back. The letter was full of love and congratulations on the new baby, but there was also a note from my mother informing me that my father had started to suffer from poor eyesight. It was the beginning of an illness that would eventually result in blindness.

⁂

The following year, in September 1888, I had the good fortune to appear in *Uncle Tom's Cabin* in the role of Topsy again. Mr George Rignold had asked me to take the role, and I jumped at the opportunity. Mr Rignold was the lessee, manager and also a performer in the play.

I had never worked with Mr Rignold, but I'd read plenty of reviews about him in the newspapers and the *Lorgnette* theatre magazine. I must admit I was a little apprehensive. The critics had described him as being fiery with an explosive temper. He was also well known to be a very exacting director.

At the first rehearsal of the play, I met all my fellow actors and, of course, Mr Rignold. He was very tall and broad-shouldered. I could see why he had been dubbed in the newspapers as 'Gorgeous George.' He was quite handsome.

Mr JR Greville, my dear old manager, was playing the role of Van Tromp. I will never forget my first encounter with Mr Greville, and our time in Adelaide back in the 1860s and his lucky escape from his fishing encounter.

Opening night at Her Majesty's Theatre in Sydney was Saturday, 8th September 1888. It would have been hard to pack any more people into any part of the theatre without very serious inconvenience. Every seat in the house was taken by the time the curtain rose on the first act at 7:30 pm.

The play had a good run for about two months.

Mr Rignold's version of *Uncle Tom's Cabin* was totally different to any I had ever played in, but from a dramatic and spectacular point of view, superior to any I have seen.

I liked Mr Rignold's version because the closing act ends on a high note instead of a low one. Instead of following the plot of the story as Mrs Harriet Beecher Stowe wrote it, Mr Rignold recognised that the audience wanted a final triumph of the hero. The playgoer likes to see vice punished and virtue rewarded.

Mr Rignold ensured that there were realistic sensations, produced without regard to expense or labour. He took every opportunity for effective scenery and striking stage pictures.

The last act showed a skating scene on the frozen waters of the St Lawrence River. Some skilful performances were given by women on roller-skates. When Eliza is escaping, she is floating on the treacherous ice and tossed here and there by the troubled waters. We could see the excitement plainly visible on every face in the audience. After Eliza's safety was assured, there was spontaneous and continued cheering.

With all these effects, there were a few delays; however, the audience knew the great labour and expense required to present something in a realistic drama at Her Majesty's. These unavoidable delays were taken by the audience with excellent good humour, and the few words of explanation which Mr Rignold courteously offered were greeted with a good deal of encouraging applause. Although the performance lasted a little after midnight, the bulk of the audience watched its progress with sustained interest to the very last.

After opening night, the critics said,

> 'The figure that seemed to command the most attention was that of Topsy, played by Miss Fanny Wiseman, the only lady in these colonies who can play that difficult character. The mischievous tricks and pranks and clever little ways of Topsy, as represented at her hands, gave full satisfaction on Saturday night.'

I certainly appreciated the critic's review.

One night after the performance, Mr Rignold sent word to me to come to him immediately. Having seen his temper flare several times during rehearsals and when things didn't go to plan backstage, I was a little worried I'd done something wrong. I was still in full costume, but I did not delay. When I knocked on his door, he said,

'I have a surprise in store for you, Miss Wiseman.'

He opened his door and who should I see but the wonderful Mr George Coppin. My makeup prevented an embrace, but our mutual excitement to see each other was visible. The dear old soul was so glad to see me, and I can assure you the feeling was mutual. He looked wonderfully well at that time and was full of fun. He told me all about the work he was doing in the establishment of the Victorian Humane Society and the St John Ambulance in Melbourne. He also updated me on the Dramatic and Musical Society that he helped form in 1871. He was truly a remarkable man, and many in the theatre world referred to him as 'The father of Australian Theatre.' That was to be the last time I saw George.

✳

On Sunday, 14th October 1888, I woke up early with a terrible feeling, an uneasiness. I couldn't quite understand why. I found out a few days later from a friend that my dear brother-in-law Johnnie Hall had passed away in Melbourne on that very day. He was only 51 years old. For the past few years, he had suffered from a pulmonary complaint which had developed into consumption.

His last performance was in May 1888, as a grave digger in Shakespeare's *Hamlet*, at the Melbourne Princess Theatre. It gave me shivers thinking about it.

I was still performing in *Uncle Tom's Cabin* in Sydney and was unable to travel to Melbourne in time to attend the funeral.

I felt so incredibly sad thinking about his son, John Jnr, now without his loving father and his mother, my sister Emily. I remember when Emily and I met Johnnie in the early 1860s. It was love at first sight for my sister. Now they are together again with their beautiful son Asa, who passed away in 1866 when he was only ten months old.

✳

My brother-in-law, James, and his friend, Mr D'Arcy Stanfield, had started the Stanfield and South Burlesque Company and had been touring up north in Brisbane. In

April 1889, they asked William and me to join them in the play *Dick Whittington and his Cat* at The Academy of Music, Sydney. I was playing the character Dick, and James was Mrs Fitzwarren.

Easter was always a popular time for people to attend the theatre. Many people enjoyed time off work and didn't mind spending a little extra money going out. I remember Easter Monday, 22nd April 1889, was an exceptionally good night, packed to the rafters and great applause at the end of the play.

The next day, all the actors were assembled at the theatre getting ready for our next performance when someone stormed in with the news that the Bijou Theatre, in Little Collins Street in Melbourne, had been destroyed by fire. We all had friends in Melbourne and hoped that no one had been hurt.

We read later in the newspaper that people had seen a column of smoke rising above the theatre, which increased dramatically in the space of only a few minutes. They yelled 'fire, fire' a cry that was speedily taken up by others until the fire brigade was alerted.

Thousands of gallons of water were thrown upon the fire from every available spot that could be reached. But for a long time, it appeared that the fire was out of control, and several of the adjoining buildings would be destroyed. One of the adjoining buildings was the premises of Mr William Marshall, the well-known printer who produced the weekly

Lorgnette theatrical magazine. The fire completely gutted his building. The Palace Hotel was also feared destroyed, but it was saved.

Crazy as it sounds, there were spectators lining the roadway, making it nearly impossible for the firemen to secure good positions from which to battle the flames. It was not until 6:00 pm that the firemen had at last obtained thorough control of the fire. Sadly, all that remained of the Bijou Theatre were charred walls.

Two people had been killed in the fire, and many others were injured. Captain Parsons, of the East Melbourne Fire Brigade, was struck on the head by a piece of falling brickwork and died three hours afterwards. Mr Charles Williams, a young fellow who was the hall-keeper, employed by the Victorian Racing Club, fell through a skylight while assisting some of the firemen, and he died soon after.

The newspaper reported there were seven firefighters who had been injured. Their injuries ranged from lacerations to concussions and burns. I remember reading about Constable Patrick Coffey, who had a fracture to the bone of the leg, received while ejecting a larrikin from the burning building. It was one thing to be fighting a fire, but another to be dealing with the idiocy of people!

The injured men were placed in fire-reel carts, and others were put in hansom cabs, the two-wheeled horse-drawn carriages, and driven to the hospital. Many people at the time questioned why the city didn't have ambulance wagons with cots or hammocks. It was common knowledge that in other parts of the world, like San Francisco in America, there were ambulance wagons on duty day and night, to pick up street accidents and to attend to fires.

Many people started to demand the same service for Melbourne, and my old friend Mr George Coppin was very vocal in his support of this service. He'd been to America and had seen how successful their ambulance service operated.

It was estimated that the loss to the managers of the Bijou Theatre, Mr Robert Brough and Mr Dion Boucicault Jnr, was £35,000. They had a large amount of theatrical property stored in the theatre. Individual members of their company suffered a big financial loss too, as their costumes were also destroyed.

Mr Brough and Mr Boucicault found one silver streak of luck in the dark cloud of misfortune. All the manuscripts of the various comedies, burlesques, and dramas of which they held the exclusive Australian rights had been recovered intact. This was of more importance to them than the public was aware. Those manuscripts could not have been replaced without considerable delay and expense. Without them, the work of the company could not have been resumed. In addition to this, they saved all their office books, except their letter book – the ledger with outgoing correspondence. The takings at the theatre on Good Friday and Saturday nights were also found to be safe. This sum was, however, much smaller than is generally supposed, as Saturday morning was treasury day, and all the salaries were paid out of the receipts.

Mr Brough and Mr Boucicault regarded the result of the disaster as really the destruction of their three and a half years' work. However, Mr Walter Brookes Sprong, the artist, is the one to be commiserated with. Before he arrived in Australia, he had visited various parts of the Old World, and wherever he went, he took sketches of the scenery, buildings and dresses to serve him in his work of scene painting. In addition, he had several large photographs which were of incalculable value to him for reference. All these were destroyed, and no amount of money could replace them. We heard that some insurance would assist Mr Brough, Mr Boucicault and Mr Sprong, but poor Mr Marshall, the *Lorgnette* printer, had nothing.

With these types of disasters, the theatre community came together, and it wasn't long until a benefit performance was held to assist Mr Marshall, which raised £582. My old friends Mr George Coppin, the Majeroni's, Mr JC Williamson and Mr Bland Holt were some of those actors who stepped forward to help.

The benefit helped Mr Marshall re-establish his printing business. Sometime later that year, several issues of the *Lorgnette* featured biographies of prominent artists along with their photo-engraved portraits. I was honoured to be included in this list. However, my husband was not included in these special editions. I knew his ego would have been bruised.

⁂

After our engagement with the Stanfield and South Burlesque Company came to an end, William became the director of the Haymarket Theatre in Sydney.

Soon after this, in August 1889, Mr JF Sheridan contacted me and asked if I would join his company and perform in his play *Fun on the Bristol* at the old Opera House in Melbourne.

If I accepted, it would mean relocating the family to Melbourne. William agreed I should take the opportunity, as it was steady work. But he wanted to stay in Sydney. He had only recently taken the director position and wanted to make it work. So, it was decided that the children would stay with me and travel to Melbourne. Only Charles, our eldest, had left home.

⁂

It was wonderful to see Mr Sheridan again. We had spent so much time together only two years before with *Uncle Tom's Cabin*.

Mr Sheridan had an excellent company with one of the principals being the sweet and dainty Miss Gracie Whiteford.

We played *The Bristol* for six weeks to crowded houses. Mr Sheridan played the role of Widow O'Brien. He became extremely popular in this role and had the audience roaring with laughter at his impersonation of the elderly Irish widow Mrs O'Brien. He would exaggerate the Widow's eccentricities and had so much fun with the absurd and funny interactions with all the other characters. Miss Whiteford took the soubrette or flirtatious role and played the role of Miss Nora O'Brien, one of the Widow's daughters.

We had to break the season owing to The Firm having the theatre and staging *Paul Jones*. In the meantime, we went to Ballarat, Bendigo, Castlemaine and Geelong, then back once more to the old Opera House in Melbourne with *The Bristol*. We played to packed houses for every performance. We finished up in late January 1890. Mr Sheridan wanted to extend my engagement and keep the company together for another production. I agreed.

I saw my sister Alice regularly. She was a very close friend of Miss Rose Edouin. Alice and her husband Henry had attended Miss Rose Edouin and Mr GBW Lewis' silver wedding anniversary, which was also Mr Lewis' 71st birthday. The event was held on 19th November 1889 at their house in St Kilda. I had also been invited, but was touring at the time. Alice said the garden was magical and illuminated by hundreds of Chinese lanterns. She told me of the magnificent and sweeping view from the upstairs drawing-room where the ball was held. She could see out across to Port Phillip Bay.

Alice described the warm sea breezes floating through the gardens and the house. Rose wore a trained gown of white and the palest shade of green brocade, the design outlined in gold and blue, with side panels of amber satin, and clusters of ostrich plumes. Diamond and ruby ornaments and a bridal bouquet completed the outfit. Mr Henry Harwood, the actor-manager who had been their friend for so many years, proposed the toast.

Alice missed being on the stage, but she was friends with many actors and actresses. Her husband, Henry, represented many in the industry as their legal advisor. Alice was, probably not surprisingly, very knowledgeable with all the gossip, intrigue and shenanigans that went on 'behind the scenes'.

Chapter Twenty-One – Changing times

In February 1890, I started the next production with Mr Sheridan, with good old *Uncle Tom's Cabin*, another revival. This production was another adaptation of the original. The company was augmented through the courtesy of The Firm, lending Miss Edith Bland, who played the role of Eliza. Mr Sheridan played the role of Marks, and I again had the pleasure of playing the role of Topsy.

Our costumes for this production were slightly different from other *Cabin* productions. Miss Edith Bland departed from the traditional gown worn by Eliza and dressed more becoming to her figure, in a plain grey material made in robe fashion, with a scarf of pink silk falling in loose knots down the front of the dress. Striped cottons of all the hues of the rainbow formed the staple material of the slaves' dresses. My extraordinary costume in the last act won continual applause.

The critics said of my acting,

> 'Miss Wiseman invested in the role of Topsy with so much humour, grim gnome-like diablerie "black magic" and withal pathos.'

The business was again enormous.

After two weeks, in late February, the company left for a tour to Adelaide.

My children travelled with me, all except Charles and Tom. Minnie was 14 years old and the eldest of my children on that tour. I relied on her heavily; there is no doubt. But they all chipped in where they could, as did the rest of the company.

We sailed to Adelaide on the *Parramatta*, a very reliable frigate. And thank goodness she was reliable and was well accustomed to rough seas, because that's what we had.

We arrived at Semaphore, and as the seas were so rough, we had to be lowered by a chair into the tender (a small boat), which then took us to the jetty. We were met by the Theatre Royal manager, Mr W McMahon.

We were all drenched to the bone, and there was no time for small talk. We went straight off to our lodgings to get dry.

We played in Adelaide for four weeks, where the business was the same as in Melbourne, very popular. Then we were off to Broken Hill. A very bumpy carriage ride overland.

I loved Broken Hill and the expansive skies and desert plains. But one night, during the second act of the *Bristol*, one of those dust storms that the said 'Hill' is famous for, started. The wind was so strong that stones were flying around, smashing the windows of the hall. We were enveloped in clouds of red dust. Dust in our eyes, nose and throats. Oh, it was terrible. We all struggled on till the end of the piece, but we and the audience were all very glad when the curtain fell at last.

Our next trouble was how we were going to get to our hotel. Miss Edith Bland and I were staying at the same hotel. We put a bold face on and sallied bravely forth. But it was no good. We had to come back and seek the assistance of one of the firemen stationed at the hall. We each held him by an arm, but even then, we could not face the wind and pebbles flying about, so we walked home backwards.

When we reached the hotel, I was a dirty cream colour – a combination of my greasepaint and the red dust. I was in desperate need to wash it all off me. But when I asked the hotel staff for extra water, it was like asking for their lives. Water was very scarce at the time.

The business was immense at Broken Hill, but those dust storms were awful. We finally left, headed for Adelaide again, for a fortnight, then returned to Melbourne.

At the conclusion of the Melbourne season, we took *Uncle Tom's Cabin* to Geelong, Ballarat, Bendigo, and then all the large towns overland to Sydney.

In Sydney, we opened at the Criterion Theatre for six weeks, then off to Brisbane's Opera House in April 1890.

We travelled via train from Sydney to Brisbane and crossed the new Brooklyn Bridge over the Hawkesbury River. The construction of the bridge was completed in 1889 and filled the missing link in the railway network between Adelaide and Brisbane. The bridge was a marvel of civil engineering due to the depths of its piles – over 279 feet – the deepest in the world at the time!

Mr JF Sheridan appeared as Marks the lawyer, Miss Gracie Whiteford as Eva, my old friend Mr Hosea Easton joined us in the role of Uncle Tom, and I played Topsy.

It was wonderful to see Mr Easton again. We spent a lot of time catching up on each other's lives. He was an extraordinary man.

Our Queensland performances were attended with the same good fortune that favoured us in Melbourne and all the other towns we had visited.

It was around this time that we met a traveller who had been working on the rabbit-proof fence. He'd put in a tender to undertake the work and had started fastening wire netting to the rabbit fence already erected or in course of erection, east from Hungerford. His name was John Joseph Malone, but he told us to call him John-Joe.

He had travelled from Westport, County Mayo, 'I'm from the west of Ireland,' he said. The allure of adventure and a new life had brought him to Rockhampton in 1883. His accent was delightful, soft and lilting, yet there was a sadness to him. He missed his family back in Ireland.

He told us about his brothers Michael and James, and his sisters Mary, Margaret and Bridget. He was raised to work hard and had learnt the art of farrier and blacksmith. He was trying to make a new life for himself and said he hoped that his family could join him in Australia, one day. He knew his family would love the colony of Queensland as much as he did, but he did admit that acclimatising to the heat had taken a while. Most of his warm clothes were still in his bag; they were of little use to him. I remembered travelling to Dublin back in 1870, and also how I felt when I first arrived in Melbourne. The two countries were worlds apart in their climates.

⁕

I received a telegram from my father in August 1890. I was always nervous when opening a telegram. It meant either wonderful news or devastating news; there was nothing in between. My father wrote that my mother had died on the 16th August 1890. She died at their home on Brown Street early in the morning. She had had a short illness and then had an attack of paralysis, which ended her life. She was buried in Thames, Waikato, New Zealand. She was 70 years old. I missed her so much. She was the kindest and most loving person. The inscription on her headstone said,

> 'Sacred to the memory of Mary Ann
> The beloved wife of Richard Wiseman,
> Mother of the late Mrs JL Hall.
> Died 16th August 1890.

Good, true and self-denying.'

Soon after my mother's death, my father moved from New Zealand to Melbourne, where he lived with my sister Alice and her husband Henry. He, like my brother Richard, had failing eyesight and without my mother, he could no longer run the boarding house.

*

After our Queensland tour, we travelled back to Newcastle for two weeks, then left for Tasmania. We had four weeks in Hobart and two weeks in Launceston.

Then we travelled over to New Zealand, opening on Boxing Night, 26th December 1890, in Dunedin with *Uncle Tom's Cabin*. It was a wonderful reception, and at 7:30 pm, the placard at the front of the House said, 'House Full.'

At the end of January 1891, we went to Christchurch, where we met a great reception, then on to Wellington, then to Auckland. It really was one big boom from the first night we opened until the last.

I had to relinquish my engagement with Mr Sheridan and return to Sydney in March 1891. It had been one of the most pleasant engagements I had ever had. Mr Sheridan, during the time I was a member of his company, had been a most considerate and just manager in every respect. I shall always look back with pleasure on that period of my life.

I returned to Sydney because my brother Richard had become almost totally blind.

⁕

During this time, my relationship with my husband had become very tenuous. The last few years had been difficult as we'd spent little time together. Working long hours and going on tour put pressure on both of us.

When William and I did have time to talk, almost every second conversation would end in an argument about some long-ago trifle or upset.

One of my last happy memories of being with William was when we travelled to Brooklyn, on the Hawkesbury River, to meet up with his cousin, Captain James Hodder South. Captain South had sent William a message a week before Easter and had invited us to luncheon with him. He said that he was sailing the *Lucinda* from Queensland to New South Wales for an important government meeting for the Easter weekend, 27th to 29th March 1891, but he would be free for a few days after that.

William and I, along with six of our children, Minnie, Laura, Austin, Sydney, Lilly and Emmie, travelled by train from Central Station to Hawkesbury Station. The *Lucinda* was anchored next to the Brooklyn Wharf. It was the loveliest steam yacht I have ever seen.

When we boarded, I felt like royalty. No expense had been spared in the design and construction of the yacht. It had luxurious teak and ornate furniture, and electric lighting.

Captain South was a dapper man with clear blue eyes and was very charming.

After Captain South had shown us around the *Lucinda* and we were sitting down for lunch, he told us the details of the government meeting. He had brought the Queensland Premier, Sir Samuel Griffith, to New South Wales to meet up with Mr Charles Kingston and Sir Edmund Barton. They were finalising the draft constitution for the proposed Commonwealth of Australia and didn't want to be constrained by minders. Three lawyers were also present as advisers, Mr Bernard Wise, a young barrister from New South Wales, Mr AJ Thynne from Queensland and Sir Henry Wrixon from Victoria. They worked from early in the morning to late in the evening, drafting the constitution. But it wasn't all hard work. They had sailed up the Hawkesbury River and spent some time in Refuge Bay, where many of the crew and government men had a shower under the well-known waterfall.

Captain South regaled us with stories of when he ran away to sea at an early age. Stories of the old sailing ship days. On more than one occasion, he said, the ships he was onboard had remarkably close 'shaves', but it was 'all in the game' in those days. William told me later that his cousin had nerves of steel.

It had been one of those lovely warm Autumn days and spending it on the *Lucinda* cruising along the Hawkesbury River was one of my fondest memories. When it was time to go, we farewelled Captain South and boarded the train back to Central.

✳

William was also by my side when the generous managers, belonging to the theatres that were then open in Sydney, wanted to host a benefit matinee for my brother. Richard had been unable to work due to his poor eyesight.

It took some time to organise, but eventually the benefit took place at Her Majesty's Theatre in Sydney on Wednesday 2nd September 1891 at 1:45 pm.

My old manager, Mr George Rignold, held the lease and gave the use of the theatre and the entire staff free of charge. He was truly a generous man. You know he never had any children, and when he died a few years ago, in December 1912, he left his entire estate, valued at £11,000, to the Royal General Theatrical Fund.

Over £200 was raised from the performances, and all of this was given to my brother. It saved him and his family from becoming destitute.

✳

Many of us in the theatre business had heard of the demise of the marriage between Mr JC Williamson and Miss Maggie Moore. The theatrical community were a close-knit group. We all knew each other or had heard of each other. But none of us would ever go to the press with personal information or gossip about any of our fellow actors. Many of us had worked with Mr JC Williamson, and he was a very powerful and influential man. We had a deep respect for him and for Maggie.

I would never cast aspersions on who was to blame for the breakup. Like most relationships, it can be very complex, and no one truly knows what happens behind closed doors. But the final 'nail in the coffin' was when Maggie went off with her young man, New Zealander Mr Harry Roberts. He was, of course, an actor. He was young, handsome and tall, with a very impressive voice. He was actually 15 years Maggie's junior. But perhaps Miss Maggie Moore and Mr JC Williamson had a fractured relationship well before this. It was known that Mr JC Williamson had an eye for the young chorus girls.

In 1892, Maggie toured throughout Australia with her own company. The next year, she took *Struck Oil* to New Zealand. The company openly billed her 'new' love as her leading man. Mr Roberts took the leading role of John Stofel in *Struck Oil.* I heard through the grapevine that this set Mr Williamson off into a rage. The role of John Stofel had been his role, and I think he took that insult as the final twist of the knife.

He condemned Maggie's conduct as legally and morally inappropriate.

The failed marriage was finally in the public arena when Mr Williamson took the matter to court. The magistrate expressed surprise that Mr Williamson could not 'control his wife.' Under Australian law at the time, all marital property belonged to the husband, so it was impossible for Mr Williamson to win a case against Maggie based on property rights, as he already owned everything!

It was the time of the suffragettes, and times were changing. But you can see from the magistrate's comments that some attitudes were deeply entrenched.

Chapter Twenty-Two – Skating on thin ice

My father had been blind for several years and had been living in Melbourne with my sister Alice. He wanted to return to New Zealand, so in July 1892, I travelled with him and my children to Wellington. We decided to settle there for a while.

William decided to stay in Sydney, but he wished us well.

My father was not in the best of health. We opened another boarding house, and my father enjoyed being the host, although in a somewhat limited capacity. He was very amiable and a well-liked person.

I was giving elocution lessons and picked up some acting work. I played Topsy in *Uncle Tom's Cabin* in Wellington in August 1893, with Mr Newton Griffith's Company.

It was an exciting time to be in New Zealand. I was proud to be living there when on 19th September 1893, Governor Lord Glasgow signed a new Electoral Act, making New Zealand the first self-governing country in the world to enshrine in law the right for *all* women to vote in parliamentary elections.

The government could not ignore the overwhelming support to give women the vote, which was shown by the 31,872 signatures collected during a seven-year campaign. This was the largest petition ever gathered in Australasia. This petition was presented to Parliament and led to all adult women obtaining the right to vote. Two months later, 109,461 women enrolled to vote in the New Zealand 1893 election!

When the Act was passed, suffragettes celebrated throughout the world.

Only a year later, South Australia followed New Zealand with the government passing the Constitutional Amendment (Adult Suffrage) Act on 18th December 1894. It would take all the other colonies several years to fall into step, but eventually, all white women in Australia had the right to vote. But Aboriginal women and men are still waiting for that right in Australia.

To think, for so many years, women were denied so much that was granted to men. Women could not own property or manage their own finances, wages were typically lower than men, and job opportunities were significantly worse for women. Whilst that wasn't always the case, and I may have been an exception in terms of work, my wages were always lower than William's, even though I played more prominent roles. This was sometimes a sore point for William and me, but for different reasons.

*

I stayed with my father in New Zealand for two years. We had talked often about returning to Sydney or Melbourne. But he wanted to stay in New Zealand. He said he felt closest to my mother there.

His health was failing, so he decided to enter the Mount View Asylum in Wellington. It catered to his needs, which were for therapeutic care. It also looked after terminally ill and people who needed support for their mental health ailments. Although I wasn't happy leaving him, the institution was well set up, and he wanted to stay there.

It was a difficult farewell. My children were very upset about leaving their grandfather, as was I.

When I returned to Sydney in June 1894, I had plans to visit my father regularly. But life was very busy, and whenever work came along, I had to take it. 'Make hay while the sun shines', an apt phrase in terms of the acting profession, for you never knew when your next engagement would be and for how long. With a family to look after, I had to keep working. I wasn't able to visit my father as regularly as I'd wanted.

I must admit, it felt good to be back in Sydney. I had missed my husband, and the children had missed their father. But things had changed between William and me.

He was living in a small one-bedroom apartment in The Rocks.

I found a place for me and the children in Balmain, just around the corner from where we had previously lived.

⁂

At the end of June and throughout July 1894, I was engaged to play *The Ticket-of-Leave Man* at the Government Printing Office Dramatic Society in Sydney. The Government Printing Office usually give performances in aid of other people, but they had to give a benefit for themselves, which they did at the Royal Standard Theatre. Their performances were put on with a healthy desire to replenish the funds of the society, which, due to being a charity, had become somewhat depleted. The play was well received. There were large audiences, and the performances were a success in all respects.

Next was a run for four weeks at the Criterion Theatre in Sydney with Mr Tom Taylor's *An Unequal Match*. It was a bright little comedy in three acts. It is an old play originally produced in 1857, although it had not been seen in Sydney for some years. Miss Hilda Spong played the role of Hester Grazebrook, the village girl who married a title and became a polished lady. I played the part of Bessie Hobblethwaite.

Then I was back with the Government Printing Office Dramatic Society for another five-week run performing with Sydney Grundy's farcical comedy, *The Snowball*, at the Royal Standard Theatre in Sydney. There was a very good house, and the piece was thoroughly enjoyed. As a curtain raiser, we performed a piece from Buckstone's well-known farce *A Kiss in the Dark*, which elicited a great deal of laughter.

*

My eldest son, Charlie, had been living in Grafton for a while, where he was managing an ice-skating rink. That was around 1894-95. He was 24 years old and making his own way in life. You know we have to thank my old friend Mr George Coppin for the ice-skating craze that swept throughout the colonies. He was the person who brought ice-skating to Australia.

When George was in America, he had seen an old man of 80 years of age skating with his young granddaughter. George had a vision and decided to risk a lot of money on a hunch, and it paid off.

Back in 1868, George converted the Apollo Music Hall in Melbourne into the first ice-skating rink in Australia. He brought out Mr Fuller, who was a champion skater who gave performances and tuition. The popularity of ice-skating took off like a bushfire. Plimpton's skates were the skates to have, and with every pair sold, a royalty was paid to George!

Chapter Twenty-Three – Old love, new love

I felt like my life had taken lots of twists and turns, and I was now at a point that felt unfamiliar and strange.

My husband was living in The Rocks, still managing the Haymarket Theatre, and I was living in Balmain with the children. Minnie was 18 years old, Laura was 15, Austin was 13, Sydney was 12, Lilly was 10, and Emmie was seven years old. Charlie and Tom were working with different theatre companies, so they were often travelling.

I felt like William had decided that our marriage was over. We had not lived together for several years. I was still holding on to what we had, but the final emotional break for me came in March 1895.

William's brother James and his business partner, Mr Edmund Duggan, had formed the Duggan and South Dramatic Company. They had organised a regional tour of Goulburn at Her Majesty's Theatre and Dubbo's Protestant Hall. They asked me to join them on the tour. My daughter

Minnie was extremely capable, and we all agreed that this time I'd go on my own and the younger children would stay in Balmain under Minnie's care.

I had all the details of the tour and all the names of the actors that James had engaged, many I knew and a few I did not know. I had told James that I would meet him in Goulburn for rehearsals about two weeks before the first performance.

I can still remember entering Her Majesty's Theatre in Goulburn by the stage door and walking confidently through the corridor towards the back of the stage. It was not the first time I'd been there.

I could hear the familiar voices of James and Edmund. They were arguing with another man who had a deep baritone voice. As soon as I entered the stage, they all stopped talking and turned in my direction. I felt a flush of heat radiate from my body as I saw who owned the baritone voice. Someone I'd never met before but instantly felt an attraction to.

My brother-in-law rushed over to me and embraced me. He was thrilled I had arrived and exclaimed,

'Now here's my sister, and she'll bring some calm and clarity to the problems we are facing.'

He turned me quickly towards Edmund and away from the other man. But then I heard the baritone voice say clearly,

'Mr South, I believe you are forgetting your manners. I have not been introduced to the lady.'

James twirled me around and said with a flourish, 'Mr Valentine, I'd like to introduce my sister-in-law, Frances Jane Wiseman.'

I extended my hand in greeting, and he took it firmly, pulling me a little towards him. I lost my balance slightly and stumbled. His strong arms balanced me while my face turned red with embarrassment.

His stage name was Valentine, and his real name was Walter St Valentine Lambert. He was to turn my world upside down, and he would continue to unbalance me in the most delightful and unexpected ways.

Before I left the theatre, James called out to me and said he'd accompany me to my hotel accommodation. We walked out together and down the road. I had the greatest respect for James; he was a very dear friend and brother-in-law. He stopped for a moment and said nervously,

'Fanny, I don't want to speak out of turn, and I don't want to say anything that would upset you.' I looked at him with love and urged him to continue.

Then he said, 'Valentine has an eye for the ladies, so please be cautious.'

I wasn't expecting that, and I think I blushed, for the second time that day!

'Oh James, you don't need to worry about me, but I thank you for being so frank. I know you have my best interests at heart.'

He smiled and seemed satisfied he'd discharged his brotherly duties and had voiced his concerns.

One of the first plays we performed was *All for Gold,* by Mr FRC Hopkins. Mr Edmund Duggan portrayed the part of a falsely accused officer who had escaped from Afghanistan after being sentenced to death. My brother-in-law supplied the comic element, his role being a relief to the sombre surroundings. One of the main characters is the wicked and relentless villain, the part taken by the young and dashing Mr Walter St Valentine Lambert.

Mr Lambert was tall and had an impressive black moustache and could play the role of the villain extremely well.

As I got to know Valentine, as that's the name he liked to be called, I felt like I knew less about him. He was an enigma. He hailed from Nottingham, England, from wealthy parents, yet he lived a gypsy's life. He said he was a widower and did not wear a wedding ring, but wasn't very forthcoming with any other information. He said he was 41 years old, so only seven years younger than me.

We travelled to several towns over the next few weeks, usually by train and horse-drawn carriages. I slowly became more comfortable in his presence.

One day, Edmund and James arrived a little late for rehearsals. They were very excited. They announced they had procured an old paddle steamer to convey us to the various settlements along the banks of the Darling River. The plan was for us to come ashore and give our shows and then return to the boat to continue our journey.

It was quite thrilling and romantic travelling on the paddle steamer. At dusk, we would cast the anchor and go to sleep with the gentle movement of the water.

We arrived in Bourke and planned to stay a few nights to provide the evening entertainment. The heat was stifling. I suggested our shows be given onboard the paddle steamer, while the vessel was in motion, and thereby achieving a cooling breeze. The idea was tried and was a success. The venture continued, where practicable, for some considerable time. I believe this was the first showboat in Australia!

We returned to Sydney, all feeling happy and content that things had gone so well.

During that tour, three things became very obvious to me. One, I was inextricably attracted to Valentine. Two, it was time to file for divorce from my husband. And three, life would never be the same.

*

A year later, in March 1896, Valentine told me he'd formed a company with Mr Hawthorne. He asked me to join him in the Hawthorne and Lambert's Criterion Comedy Company for a very short tour. My daughter, Minnie, again looked after the younger children while I worked. The company opened at the Theatre Royal in Grafton, New South Wales, for three nights, then went downriver to Richmond and played another three nights. It was a whirlwind tour for many reasons. We then returned to Sydney – Valentine to Woolloomooloo and me to Balmain.

Although the Hawthorne and Lambert's Criterion Comedy Company was comprised of some fine actors, the business didn't go as well as we all hoped. I found out later that on the 18th May 1896, Valentine had filed for bankruptcy. I think he was too proud to tell me at the time that the tour had not paid well, and he couldn't pay the bills.

*

Later in the year, I was engaged by the Cosgrove Musical Comedy Company for the play *Fun on the Bristol.* Opening night was 19th September 1896 at Her Majesty's Theatre, Sydney.

We knew there was another show opening the same night. But the other show wasn't a theatrical show; it was a 'cinematograph' show opening at the Tivoli. It was something we knew nothing about, but something that changed history and almost destroyed the theatre industry.

The cinematograph was the beginning of the cinema or film industry.

Opening night for *Fun on the Bristol* was a great success, and the show ran for two weeks. The play had always been a popular piece. The eccentric development of the many-sided character of the Widow, her aspirations for the Count, her encounters with her daughters, and the comical experiences on the sea trip afford scope for unlimited displays of broad Irish humour.

The character of the Widow found a capable representative in Mr William Cosgrove, who played the part with sympathy and discretion. The house enjoyed the performance immensely and testified its appreciation with unquestionable force. Mr Wilfred Shine met the requirements of the character of the Count. His interviews with the Widow, his incidental songs, were all excellent. Mr John F Forde was the bibulous Captain Cranberry, and I played the part of Bella Thompson.

The newspapers were extremely complimentary of our show and said:

> 'Miss Fanny Wiseman as Bella is simply immense. An amusing dance by Miss Fanny Wiseman brought the deck concert to a close. The doll dance is nightly encored. The performance altogether was an exceedingly good one, and the house was more than satisfied. *Fun on the Bristol* should have, as doubtless it will, a successful run.'

While the newspapers gave us compliments, they were in *raptures* about the competing entertainment – the cinematograph. After our play finished its run, Valentine asked me if I'd accompany him to see the cinematograph show. I was intrigued to see this new invention and to see Valentine.

We agreed to meet at the Tivoli. I wasn't quite ready to have him call at the house.

When we were seated, and the lights were dimmed, the show began. It was like a magic lantern, throwing photo-like and life-sized views onto a screen. The figures moved and acted as in real life. Nearly a dozen pictures were shown.

There were scenes from London streets, the sea breaking on rocks and beach, and an opera. Westminster Bridge was the most popular scene. The pedestrians, horses and vehicles are clearly delineated, and the fact that an elderly man turned his head round proved a source of great merriment. Several members of the audience, who'd been to see the show before, whistled immediately before the elderly man looked round. This resulted in a roar of laughter from the crowd.

Another scene was the hugging of a young lady by a soldier. While the couple are cooing on a seat, a burly elderly woman squats on the seat next to the soldier. The young girl reaches behind the soldier and shoves the interloper off the seat. Everyone in the audience applauded and laughed.

All the scenes were shown without any glitches. It was extraordinary. We'd never seen anything like this before.

*

After *Fun on the Bristol*, the company started *A Trip to Chicago* on Friday 2nd October. It ran until 10th October 1896 at Her Majesty's Theatre. *A Trip to Chicago* is the next chapter or sequel in Widow O'Brien's life. We were the first company to show it in Australia. Indeed, we were the first company to show it anywhere in the world.

In the play, Widow O'Brien discards her original name of Bridget for the high falutin' name of Gwendoline. She discards her skirts in favour of rational or 'bloomer' costume. The vision of the Widow in a bright green cycling suit with pink stockings and buckle shoes was a sight to convince the most sceptical of the many advantages of the man-woman costume. I knew this myself of course, having worn breeches for many roles. I knew of the comfort and ease of movement these clothes afforded.

Then on Monday, 12th October 1896, we started *Foiled.* We were still performing at Her Majesty's Theatre in Sydney. Mr Harry Overton and Mr John F Forde were the serious and comic villains respectively, and both were highly successful. Miss Maud Lita had bestowed careful study on the part of Magdalen, the repentant adventuress. Her artistic dying scene was a change from the gasping and twisting to which many actresses had resorted to under similar circumstances.

Valentine and I played supporting roles. Unfortunately, attendance was low even though we had the show at popular prices.

We were competing against Mr Bland Holt who was showing *For England* at the Theatre Royal, Sydney. It had opened on Friday 2nd October 1896, and was doing very well, as expected. Mr Holt was one of the best stage managers there was. In the performance he had a typical English hunting seen, with huntsmen, hounds and deer. This realistic scene extended back into the street where the hunters, hounds and quarry entered in a race which took them up near the footlights! Stage realism and scenic magnificence was Mr Holt's forte.

*

The saddest of days occurred on the 14th October 1896.

My father died.

He was 75 years old. I loved him dearly and couldn't imagine not seeing him again. He was my biggest supporter and had always encouraged me to work hard, enjoy my work and be honest and fair.

He had been living at the Mount View Asylum in Wellington, New Zealand for a few years. He had, up to the end, maintained his humour, even though his blindness gave him such despair. He loved the theatre, loved the costumes, loved the excitement. His passion transcended through the generations to his children and grandchildren. Alice's husband Henry made the necessary arrangements and organised the funeral. It was heart-wrenching not to be at the funeral. In those days funerals took place very quickly making it near impossible for family to attend if they lived in a different colony or country.

My brother Richard and I were both living in Sydney. My sister Laura was in Tasmania, and my sister Alice was in Victoria. Richard and I met and commiserated. Our father had a long and happy life. He brought us to a new country so many years ago and I think he felt he'd given us a good start in life.

After seeing my brother, I was very worried about him. He was almost totally blind.

*

We were still performing at Her Majesty's Theatre in Sydney, and *Foiled* was replaced by *The Serpent's Coil,* making its first appearance in Australia. Opening night was on Saturday, 24th October and it ran until 28th October 1896.

The Serpent's Coil was produced under Mr William Cox. The new play, which was in five acts, has a Scotland Yard detective as the hero, and the action takes place in many lands, including London, Naples, and Peking. An attack on the heroine by a boa constrictor and a mutiny amongst the Chinese workers at a plantation form the subjects of the various acts. Mr Vaughan and Mr Ricketts painted wonderful new scenery.

Mr William Cosgrove played the character of Gordon Swindale of Scotland Yard, Mr Wilfred Shine played the role of Charles Ford, the hero. I played the role of No-Ce, a Chinese Lady's maid.

Included in the programme were a number of Chinese men and women who helped to make the scenes in China of a realistic character. The theatre was crowded by an audience which appeared, by every outward token, to be thoroughly pleased.

The villainy of the character Gordon Swindale is absolutely colossal. He stops at nothing. His favourite weapon to clear the pathway of rivals is an electric desk, the touching of which by both hands electrocutes his victims. Finally, this finishes him off, but not before he attempts such trifles as handing his wife over to the tender mercies of a boa constrictor. My character, No-Ce, had the honour of beheading the serpent! The villain is of the deepest dye, and there were shouts of laughter and uproarious applause for his downfall and the triumph of the hero.

People liked plenty for their money, and they were very happy with the play. It was an extravagant melodrama.

Our final play at Her Majesty's Theatre, was the sensational melodrama *Face to Face*. Mr Cosgrove staged it for the first time in Australia. Opening night was on the 14th November 1896. The play commences in the garden of the Hotel de Londres, Paris, where we are introduced to the usual set of gamblers and to the murder which is necessary to the development of your true melodrama.

The third act takes us to Rats Dive, in which I played the character of Old Moll, the thieves' housekeeper. The character suited me down to the ground, as I'm particularly happy in character parts. The scenery reflected great credit on Mr Kinchela and Mr Ricketts, and the front of the house was well looked after by Mr Ernie Blackstone.

After more than two months of non-stop performing with the Cosgrove Musical Comedy Company I finally had the chance to stop and breathe. To be honest being busy had kept my mind off many other troubles. The loss of my father had hit me hard. But then something more unexpected happened.

My first love and father to my children, William Thomas King South, died in Melbourne on the 5th December 1896 from cancer of the oesophagus.

William and I had divorced only the year before. I still loved him. He had been my 'other half' for so many years and had shared all my joys and all my sadness. My children grieved the loss of their father, and I grieved the loss of my soul-mate.

Valentine gave me great support during that time.

*

In mid-December 1896, I was offered an engagement with Henry's Dramatic Company. I accepted the engagement, perhaps as a distraction, perhaps to pay the bills. The engagement involved showing a series of plays, not in the full versions, but pared back. We opened on Tuesday, 22nd

December 1896 at Leichhardt Town Hall, Sydney with my favourite play *Uncle Tom's Cabin*. I played the role of Topsy, of course. The piece was well performed, and the artists were called before the curtain at the end of each act.

And then, to top off the most tumultuous year, Valentine proposed to me just before Christmas.

He asked me to join him for a walk through the Botanic Gardens. The Gardens were always beautiful no matter what time of year it was. While we were walking under a beautiful flower archway, he took my hand in his and said,

'Fanny, I love you with all my heart. I can't think of a greater happiness than to spend the rest of my life with you. I promise to love you for all eternity. Will you do me the greatest honour and marry me?'

Of course, I accepted. There was no hesitation.

We were married on Thursday, 24th December 1896 at the Baptist Church on Elizabeth Street in Haymarket, Sydney. Not all my children could attend the ceremony, but my sons Charles, Austin and Sydney, and daughters Lilly and Emmie were there to witness the happy event. And I was happy that day.

But nothing lasts forever, does it?

When I saw Valentine write his age on the marriage certificate, I was a little shocked. When I first met him in March 1895, he had told me he was 41 years old, only seven years younger than myself. But he wrote 35 years old on the marriage certificate. I wrote my correct age which was 50.

This was the first of several misunderstandings that we would have.

We spent two nights away in the Blue Mountains. We took the train and stayed at the Springwood Hotel.

When we returned, Valentine moved from Woolloomooloo, and me and the children moved from Balmain, and we started our new life together in Darlinghurst.

✳

In January 1897, Henry's Dramatic Company had another successful run in the Leichhardt Town Hall with *Living or Dead.* I played alongside my daughter Emmie, who was nine years old.

From February through to March, the Company continued in the Leichhardt Town Hall and produced *Ten Nights in a Bar Room.* My husband, Valentine, played the character of Mr Romaine, my son Charles played Tom Peters, and I played the role of Mehitable Cartwright.

We then moved on to the Royal Standard Theatre with the same production of *Ten Nights in a Bar Room.* We had our last performance on Saturday 6th March 1897.

Life settled into a new pattern. I only had four of my children living with me – Austin, Sydney, Lilly and Emmie. They were still grieving the loss of their father; however, they accepted Valentine unconditionally and gave him respect and love.

You might think that life was a lot simpler; however, Valentine was not an easy person to live with.

Interlude

Sister Kitty had discreetly provided Mr Robinson and me with lunch and countless cups of tea throughout the day. We had been totally absorbed – Mr Robinson listening and writing attentively, and me remembering my life and talking about all that had happened.

'Excuse me, Mr Robinson, Miss Wiseman, it's getting a little late in the day. It's close to dinner time and I think Miss Wiseman you should be taking a break.'

All of a sudden, the tiredness came over me.

'Yes, thank you Sister Kitty, you are quite right.' She really was a gem and took such good care of me.

'Mr Robinson, can you return tomorrow?'

'Of course Miss Wiseman. It will be my pleasure.'

*

After I had retired to bed, I fell into a deep sleep.

I dreamt of William and Valentine.

Love gained and love lost.

Chapter Twenty-Four – The courthouse

I had risen early, excited to see Mr Robinson again. I felt like this would be the last day that we would spend together. I had told him so much of what had happened in my life. I felt comfortable with him, and I trusted that he was recording the information as I gave it.

I made my way down to the parlour just before 9:00 am. He was already there, waiting for me.

'Good morning Mr Robinson.'

'Good morning Miss Wiseman, you're looking lovely today.'

I had decided to wear my favourite light blue dress with yellow daisy flowers and a dark blue merino cardigan. Mr Robinson was a good-looking young man, and I wondered if he had a sweetheart. It may have been a little presumptuous of me to ask, but then again, he already knew so much about me.

'Thank you Mr Robinson. I hope you don't mind me asking, as you already know so much about me, do you have someone special in your life?'

He blushed and responded, 'Well, kind of, but I don't think she knows I exist.'

'Oh, I think she probably has noticed you.' I smiled.

He smiled too and then said, 'Shall we pick up from where we left it yesterday?'

'Yes. My new life with Valentine.'

And so, I began telling Mr Robinson about my life, again.

⁕

My brother-in-law, James South, Valentine and I had been talking about taking *The Cabin* on tour. So, we formed the South and Lambert Dramatic Company, and we started doing the circuit in April 1897.

All the business and creative decisions were made by me and James, and it was a partnership where we both agreed the profits would be shared equally. Valentine begrudgingly agreed to the arrangements and had admitted to me by this stage that he was no businessman and had filed for bankruptcy the previous year.

I was excited to be on tour and to be performing side by side with my son Charlie, who was playing Uncle Tom, and my daughter Emmie, who was playing the part of Little Eva. My other children, Austin, Sydney and Lilly came too and helped with the numerous jobs that had to be done. James played the role of Lawyer Marks, and Valentine played three characters – George Harris, Mr St Clare and the Auctioneer.

We had been performing in Wellington, New South Wales, for a few nights. All was going well until one night, after the performance had ended, James asked me to help him with some of the costumes. I told Valentine not to wait for me, as I knew James would walk me back to the hotel. Charlie and the other children also left, knowing I wouldn't be long.

James and I started to walk towards the costume room, but when we got there, he pulled out the accounts book from under his jacket.

He said, 'Fanny, some of the accounts don't look right.'

I didn't know what to say.

'Val is the only other person with access to the funds to pay for incidentals,' he said.

I knew everything was supposed to be written down in the accounts book.

James disliked dishonest people with a vengeance. His grandfather, Thomas King, had been a chief watchman back in Bristol, England. He had taught all his children and grandchildren right from wrong and to always act in an honourable way, regardless of whether you were a nobleman or a street sweeper.

James took my hand in his. He knew the last few years had been very tumultuous for me. But he said these things had to be aired.

He said that in the morning, he would come and see Valentine and me in the hotel dining area. I nodded and agreed.

I just hoped there was a reason for the mismatch of funds.

The next morning, Valentine and I were in the dining area waiting for our tea to be served. James arrived and sat down opposite us. I could sense Valentine's disapproval of James's familiar nature. James said in a convivial manner,

'Good morning Val, good morning Fanny.' Valentine just nodded and huffed under his breath.

James took a deep breath and said,

'Now, Val, I have noticed something amiss with the accounts, and I need an explanation from you.'

Valentine stood up abruptly and said,

'That is no way to speak to me. We can discuss this later.'

James remained seated. Valentine became irate, and he again said,

'We can discuss this later. Now leave us, and if anyone questions my character, they will have blood on their hands.'

At that point, James stood up calmly and said,

'Now you have thrown down the gauntlet, I will make it warm for you.'

Valentine's anger turned into rage. He pushed James violently, but thankfully, it didn't come to blows. After that, they both stormed off in opposite directions.

It was very uncomfortable after that exchange of words and actions. I spoke separately to James and to Valentine. They had both calmed down, but neither was backing down.

Valentine told me the inconsistency with the accounts was due to his borrowing some money to pay for the extra scenery that was needed, and he had simply forgotten to write it up in the accounts book. A mistake anyone could have made.

We had a huge argument about it.

Our next performance was in Dubbo, New South Wales.

We had all our costumes packed in tin trunks, which were tied with cord and transported via train from Wellington to the train station in Dubbo.

I asked Valentine to have nothing to do with the management from 1st to 5th May while we were in Dubbo, just to let things cool down.

The only thing I asked Valentine to arrange was for our luggage to be collected from the station. He proceeded to engage Mr Richard Jamieson, a carrier, to retrieve our trunks.

While we were performing in Dubbo, Valentine was dogmatic and would not stay away. He was behind the stage every night and dictating to members of the company. He was trying to take over the management of my company. He kept interfering.

Although he was a good actor, he didn't know the business like James and me. We had grown up on the stage and knew everything that was involved in running a successful company.

Soon after the last night's performance, a policeman found Valentine and me at our hotel. He told us that Valentine was accused of larceny, stealing a tin trunk belonging to Mr Edmund Tipper and his wife, Isabella.

The matter was to be heard in court on Friday 4th June 1897, before Judge Mr LS Donaldson.

Valentine wanted to defend himself, he said,

'Of course I didn't steal anything, it has simply been a mix-up. I just need to explain what has happened to the judge. He will believe me. I have a good name, and I have served in the British army.'

With that statement, he stood there, as if at attention, his nostrils flaring. I just looked at him. I could not believe he could be so foolish. He was not only jeopardising his good name, but he was also jeopardising the good name of my company.

I took a deep breath and stood to my full height, which, as you know, is not very tall, and as clear as a bell I said,

'You will attend court, and we will engage a solicitor to represent you.' And then, without thinking, I said,

'And you had better not be guilty of this charge.'

I then walked out of the room.

We engaged Mr EJJ Ryan to appear for Valentine. Mr Ryan was ordinary in appearance, medium height, brown hair, unremarkable oval face, but when he spoke, he commanded respect. His knowledge of the law was top-rate. Mr Ryan wanted to call me as a witness, but I refused. I said,

'You should call on my brother-in-law, James South. There will be no love lost between Valentine and James. James will tell it as it is, and his truth will speak volumes. The Judge will weigh James's words with greater credibility than mine. It is the way with some men who have power, they sometimes think very little of the words of women.'

Of course, I didn't know anything about Judge Donaldson, but I had met men in those types of positions, and their wives had told me some interesting stories.

We arrived at the courthouse at the allocated time, 9:00 am. I had told my children to stay at the hotel. Our solicitor, Mr Ryan, was waiting for us and ushered us in. I sat at the back of the court. The wooden pews were well-worn; countless people had sat where I sat. I wanted to be in court to hear what was said, but I did not want to be too close to the front.

Judge Donaldson entered the room, and we all rose. The similarity of the courthouse and the theatre did not escape my attention. All eyes were on the 'performers' – the judge, the accused, the witnesses, and the lawyers. They all had their parts to play. But the 'play' was unwritten and unfinished, and only time would tell how it would end. I held my breath for a minute in anticipation. And then the proceedings began.

The court stated that 'Mr and Mrs Tipper had come from Wellington to Dubbo. They had several tin trunks that were transported on the train. When collecting these trunks from Dubbo train station, they noticed that one was missing. It contained articles of clothing, including Mr Tipper's dress coat.'

The court was shown a tin trunk that had been found. Mr and Mrs Tipper were asked to examine the trunk. They agreed it was their trunk, but there were some items missing; some dresses and underclothing. The flounce had been taken off one dress and left in the box. Two dresses in the box had been worn. Mr Tipper's clothing, including his dress coat, had also been worn.

The court then called Mr James Anthony South. It was stated that he was a comedian, with no fixed home, travelling from place to place. This was accurate, but I didn't like the inferences made. James was a very honourable and respectable man.

The court asked him, 'Do you know the accused Mr Lambert?'

James answered 'Yes, I know him. He's married to my sister-in-law, Fanny Wiseman. We are in the same acting company, and we have toured with several plays.'

He was asked to provide some details on his whereabouts during the time the trunk went missing.

James said 'On 30th April, I arrived in Dubbo with part of the company. The next day, Mr Lambert arrived. The company remained in Dubbo for about a week, and then we travelled to Narromine, Warren, Nevertire, Nyngan, and then to Cobar. We all went to Cobar, including Mr Lambert.'

I could see that James was uncomfortable in the courtroom; it was an unsettling place. I was hoping he could imagine the courtroom was like being on the stage. I could see he gathered himself, and with a deep breath, he continued.

'When we were at Cobar, we were giving a Saturday evening concert. I didn't have a dress coat, and when we were in the dressing rooms, I asked if anyone could loan me something suitable for the concert. Members of the company were supposed to find their own clothing for acting in, but we lent clothes to one another all the time. Mr Lambert spoke up quickly and said he had seen something that might do. He then gave me a very fine dress coat. I must admit I was a little surprised as I hadn't seen the coat before, but I was thrilled at the same time. It fit me perfectly. I asked if I could borrow the coat for a few days, and Mr Lambert said I could.'

James continued with his story, 'As I said, I never saw the coat before and I did think it was odd that Mr Lambert had produced the coat "out of thin air". But having said that, there were lots of costumes and clothing that we all borrowed.

I did have some quarrels with Mr Lambert, and he had upset my sister-in-law. She told Mr Lambert not to interfere with the management while we were in Dubbo last month. There had been a dispute about the disbursement of monies. I'd asked Mr Lambert what had been done with the money. We did argue about this.'

The court then showed James the tin trunk and dress coat. They asked him if he had ever seen the items before. He said, 'I have never seen the trunk before, but I know that coat. That is the coat that Mr Lambert gave me. When I heard that a tin trunk with clothing had gone missing from the train station, I went to see Sergeant Nies in Cobar. I handed in the dress coat to the Sergeant.'

Our solicitor, Mr Ryan, asked James if luggage and trunks had gone missing in the past. James said,

'During my career, I've known occasions in which people's luggage got amongst that belonging to the company, and it had always been returned. Although there are times when things have been stolen from us. It's well known that Miss Avonia Jones had costumes and jewellery stolen from a coach when she was travelling to Bendigo in 1861, and Lady Don had a box of jewellery go missing.'

Mr Ryan asked how the company kept track of their luggage. James said,

'The company has many property boxes and tin trunks, and they are usually tied together when they are being transported on the train or on coaches. The property boxes contain all types of costumes, and they are open to any member of the company to get things out of.'

The accused, my husband, was then sworn in.

Our solicitor, Mr Ryan, stated to the court that Mr James South had borrowed a coat for two or three days. He then stated that Mr Lambert never looked after the luggage, so he could not have pilfered the coat and other items. Mr Lambert knew nothing about a lost trunk until the policeman told him at Cobar. Mr Lambert agreed that at Cobar, he had spoken to Mr James South about a dress coat. Mr Lambert said several dress coats were hanging in the dressing room at the hall. When Mr South asked if anyone had a coat he could borrow, Mr Lambert took the coat off the peg and tried it on Mr South to see if it would fit him. It fit him perfectly. Mr Lambert then hung it back on the peg. Two or three other dress coats were hanging on the pegs. The next morning, he found his coat hanging on the peg, and he still had it.

Mr Ryan said the accused had a conversation with Mr South about a dress coat, but he did not know whether Mr South took the coat from the peg and wore it. The coat produced might have been one of the dress coats hanging up in the dressing room.

Mr Ryan then stated to the court that Mr Lambert concurs that he had some words with Mr South about the settlement of funds.

Mr Ryan then asked Valentine to address the court. Valentine said,

'The company left Wellington on 30th April, bound for Dubbo; some travelled by train and some by horse-drawn coach. I came the next day. The company had left me stranded. There had been a dispute between me and members of the company. At Dubbo, my wife asked me to arrange the collection of the luggage, which I did. I engaged Mr Jamieson to go to the train station and collect the luggage. He went at about 2:00 pm. He told me all the luggage was in the booking office. There were about five or six trunks. When Mr Jamieson asked for his payment, I told him to see "the boss", that's my wife, of course.'

I could see the Judge smirk, and a few of the court staff stifled their laughter.

'I never looked after the luggage, I only arranged for it to be collected. I knew nothing about an extra trunk until the policeman told me at Cobar. Mr Henry Douglas looks after our costumes when we are performing. He would know if the dress coat we are talking about belongs to the company or not.' With that statement, Valentine sat down.

Mr Ryan stated for the court, 'The next morning, Mr Lambert found his coat hanging on the peg, and he has it still. The accused never lent the coat to Mr South; he never had it in his possession. He did not know whether Mr South took the coat from the peg and wore it. Mr Lambert does, however, admit that he had some words with Mr South about the settlement of the accounts.'

Mr Ryan made his final statement to the court and said that Mr Lambert owned his own dress coat. He did not know how Mr Tipper's dress coat had got into the dressing room. It would be reasonable to assume that the Tipper's tin trunk had been accidentally collected from the train station. The trunk did not have the Tipper's name on it. The trunk did resemble all the other trunks that belonged to the theatrical company.

The Judge said the evidence given by the accused gave such a reasonable explanation of the whole matter that it justified him in discharging Valentine from the court.

When we all walked out of the courthouse, we collectively felt the anxiety fall away. But other emotions would not fall away as easily.

Valentine decided to leave straight away and went back to Sydney ahead of the rest of the company. He gave me a hurried farewell and then was gone.

We finished the tour. I felt forlorn. I had the distraction of travelling with the rest of the company and my children. They knew I was upset, and they did their best to cheer me up.

*

Things did not improve very much when we returned to Sydney. I tried to talk to Valentine and smooth things over, which worked for a few days, and then something else would happen, and his temper would flare up. The accusations and the angry outbursts would start again. He accused me of siding with James. He accused me of being too friendly with James. Valentine was a jealous man.

We were still working and had plenty of offers coming in. We had a successful run with *All for Gold*, with the Cosmopolitan Dramatic Company at the Manly Aquarium Hall. Opening night was on Wednesday, 16th March 1898. It was a full house. The piece was played with remarkable smoothness, and the principal parts were undertaken by me, my daughter Emmie, Valentine, and James. James and Valentine had to put their differences aside when it came to work.

I didn't know it at the time, but this would be the last time I would act alongside Valentine.

⁂

In May 1898, I was engaged by Signora De Baraty Ferrari's Company at the Opera House, York Street, Sydney. We presented new dramatic performances on Mondays and Saturdays. It was another great run, and everyone was pleased, except Valentine, who was sulking and complaining that not much work had come his way.

He sometimes accused me of 'taking the light' away from him, or of 'being a primidone.' I honestly couldn't think of anything more ridiculous. The simple fact of the matter was I worked hard, and I was a good actress. I had to be. I had to make sure there was food on the table for my family. I had learnt that you can only rely on yourself, and you can't blame others for your own shortcomings.

With all this going on, I did have some happy moments. My daughter, Minnie, had fallen in love with Mr George Atkins. They married in Subiaco, Western Australia, on 31st August 1898.

Chapter Twenty-Five – Two more daughters

My relationship with Valentine was so different to the relationship I had with William. William and I never had any secrets. We knew, even from a slight eyebrow lift, what the other was thinking. But Valentine was like a dark cave, and I couldn't see in.

One day in early September 1899, he just blurted out to me that he had two little girls. They had been living in England, and they were preparing to travel to Australia. Thelma was eight and Eva was six years old. I knew Valentine was a widower when I met him. He told me about his first wife, Emma Chapman, and said she died quite young, but he failed to tell me that she had two children with him.

He announced,

'My daughters and their governess, Miss Peel, will be arriving soon. I expect you will take care of them as your own, as you are their stepmother.'

'Of course, Val, I'll love them as my own. But why did you not say anything about them before? Why am I hearing about them almost on the eve of their arrival?'

He did not answer me.

Valentine's daughters would be arriving in Melbourne, and he said he was going to travel there to prepare things for them. He decided it would be better if he spent some time with them before introducing me and my children to them. He said it might come as a shock to them to learn that their stepmother already had eight children of her own.

Yes, I had eight children, all mostly grown and leading their own lives. Emmie, who was 11 years old, was the only one of my children living with me. She was the sweetest child and would have welcomed two new sisters into the family.

When it was time for Valentine to leave, he gave me a heartfelt embrace and kissed me passionately. It felt like he was kissing me for the last time. He told me he would send for me and Emmie when he had settled his daughters in Melbourne.

November arrived, and I was still waiting for Valentine's letter and details on where to join him. I was getting anxious and worried that something had happened. Sometimes, news travelled slowly from colony to colony. I was constantly thinking of him. I was very distracted with my thoughts.

I finally received a letter, if you could call it that. It was very brief. I remember reading the words on the paper and not quite understanding what they meant. A strange feeling, when my whole life has been about interpreting the meaning of words.

The letter said, 'I have arrived safely in Melbourne. My girls are well.'

I read it over and over. There was no return address. What did this mean? I was angry and hurt. I just didn't understand this man.

I threw myself into work. Now that was something I did understand.

✻

Mr Johnson Weir and Mr Douglas Ancelon formed a new company. They asked me to perform in the play *Buried Alive,* which had its opening night on 15th November 1899 in Sydney. The company included many experienced actors. Among the stirring scenes is a balloon ascent, something none of us had ever seen.

New Year's celebrations were always something I looked forward to. I love the finality of a year ending and the excitement of a new year beginning. It could also be some time off to enjoy other entertainments in the city. But not for me, that year anyway.

On New Year's Day, the 1st January 1900, I had been engaged by Mr E Lewis Scott for the play *A Tale of the Transvaal* at the Criterion Theatre. I was playing alongside

Mr Weir, Mr Russell, and Mr Ancelon. I played the role of an African boy.

There was stiff competition amongst all the entertainment in Sydney during the Christmas and New Year period.

Mr JC Williamson had two shows playing in Sydney. He had the Christmas panto *Little Red Riding Hood* at Her Majesty's Theatre, and at the Theatre Royal, he was showing an adaptation of *A Tale of Two Cities.*

The annual Highland Gathering was held at the Sydney Cricket Ground on New Year's Day, and a huge programme of sports and competitions was on offer. The events included military contests, Highland piping and costumes, Highland dancing, wrestling and Scottish games. The committee devoted 25% of the profits to the widows and orphans of the Scottish regiments who fell in South Africa.

Emmie was invited by her best friend, Jemma, to spend the day at 'The Brighton of Australia,' as Manly was universally referred to. There was a flotilla of steamers that the Port Jackson Cooperative Steamship Company ran throughout the day.

Jemma and Emmie had a lovely friendship. Jemma had a smile that would light up a room and bring joy to everyone she met. They had a thrilling and enjoyable day, and I was very happy for Emmie.

A week later, my son Charles and I were engaged by Mr Walter Bentley for a short season at the Criterion Theatre,

Sydney. Mr Ancelon and Mr Weir were the managers, and I enjoyed working with them again. Opening night was Saturday, 6th January 1900.

Then my daughter Lilly and I played opposite each other in Mr Charles Darrell's new play *Defender of the Faith*, which opened on Saturday, 3rd March 1900 at the Lyceum Theatre, Sydney. The new melodrama dealt with the period of Queen Elizabeth and was richly staged with beautiful new costumes.

I thought of Valentine often. I wondered what could have happened to him and his little girls. Had I done something terribly wrong? My imagination conjured up the worst possible scenarios.

*

In late March, my brother's wife, Sarah Ann, wrote to me and mentioned that Richard had caught a severe cold, and his lungs had been badly affected. He bore his misfortune with great fortitude and worked bravely for his family as far as possible.

He had been going blind for about 12 years and was now totally blind. There had been great sympathy from the theatre folk for his terrible misfortune. From the benefit he received back in 1891, Richard had invested the money in a small business, and he and his family lived on the profits generated from the business.

Sarah Ann told me that the business had declined, and the family had become very poor. I sent what little money I had to help them.

Then two months later, Sarah Ann contacted me and told me the terrible news that my brother had died on 1st June. He was only 52 years old.

I helped Sarah Ann make the necessary funeral arrangements. My brother was buried at Waverley Cemetery. Many people from the theatre business attended the funeral. Richard had been well known on the stage in the 1860s – 1870s. He had for many years worked as a theatrical agent and travelled with different companies throughout the colonies of Australia and New Zealand.

It broke my heart seeing Richard's five young children, Emily, Richard, Alice, Dorothy and Cyril, trailing behind their mother, with their heads hung low. Grief and loss marked their little faces. I hugged them all so tight. While I was living in Sydney, I did as much as I could for them. Things were tough for all of us.

*

Work engagements were always irregular. I was never sure what was around the corner. So, with courage and conviction, I decided to form my own company, this time without the support of my brother-in-law.

I called the company, The Miss Fanny Wiseman's Dramatic and Comedy Company. I took my future into my own hands.

It felt incredible, but at the same time, daunting.

Two of my daughters, Minnie and Laura, lived in Cue, Western Australia, so I decided to start a tour with my new company there.

I was looking forward to seeing Minnie and her husband, George Atkins. They had two children now. George Jnr, was two years old, and James was a newborn baby.

Laura and her husband, William Archibald MacPhail Johnstone, also had two children. Esther 'Essie' was two years old, and Archibald 'Archie' was only one. I simply adored babies and could not wait to hold them.

Before my daughter Emmie and I left Sydney and not knowing when we would return, we visited The Zoological Gardens in Moore Park. The lions, tigers, leopards, and pumas were fed at 4:00 pm every afternoon. These majestic creatures were a sight to behold, but I think even more impressive were the elephants. Emmie even rode one of them. I remembered the last time I'd seen elephants was in Calcutta in 1869, when the Prince was visiting.

After arriving in Western Australia in September 1900, my company put on many shows and often my daughters Laura, Lilly and Emmie and my son Austin, or as he was known, Gus Deno, were onstage with me. The Miners' Institute in Cue was a great venue. We performed *Uncle Tom's Cabin, Soldiers of the Queen*, and the burlesque *Aladdin* by Byron.

My son and daughters received great reviews, which made my heart sing. The greatest joy as a mother is to see your children enjoying their work and being recognised for their efforts and talents. My son Austin was a clever comedian, and the audiences just loved him.

Another telegram bearing its sad news arrived at the end of November 1900. My lovely nephew John Laurence Samuel Wiseman Woolloxall had joined 'the great majority' the previous month. He was only 34 years old. He died in Brunswick, Victoria. He had a turbulent time since his mother, my sister Emily, had passed away on her 37th birthday. John was a talented actor and had travelled the countryside, going to Richmond River with a theatrical company and then to Thursday Island and India. He'd married Miss Henrietta Lambrette Allen, also an actress, but things didn't work out for them.

While we were in Western Australia, Mr Henry Aston Betteridge joined the company and played the role of Simon Legree, the heartless and brutal slave dealer in *Uncle Tom's Cabin*. He played the part so well. He would receive applause for his hard looks, which often culminated in a hiss from the audience. He had fine enunciation. Mr Betteridge, who became known as 'Betty', was my right-hand man in Cue. He quickly became part of my theatrical family, and before long, he became part of my real family.

My daughter Lilly had fallen in love with Betty, and they married a year later.

Lilly was only 17 years old, but when love takes hold, nothing can stop it.

Chapter Twenty-Six – A new century

On the 1st January 1901, a new century began. Such a strange feeling knowing you've crossed over from the 19th century to the 20th century. Saying the words even felt strange. The new century started with optimism as Australia's six colonies joined to become one nation – Australia was now a Federation.

It gave me a deep sense of pride knowing that William's cousin, Captain James Hodder South, had played a small part in forming the Federation. He had brought together the important political and government officials onboard the *Lucinda* to draft the Constitution, back in Easter 1891.

The feeling of optimism quickly changed when Queen Victoria died on 22nd January 1901. It was truly the end of an era. Queen Victoria's reign had lasted 63 years.

I was busy with my small company. We played in many towns but didn't travel too far from Cue. I was paying my actors £10 a week – it was the best I could do at the time.

The annual meeting of the Murchison Goldfields Racing Club was held in November in Cue. Large numbers of visitors from outlying parts of the district were in town, and hotel accommodation was considerably taxed. The town was full of excitement and gaiety. There were three days of racing and one day devoted to a pigeon match for a prize of £40. I had been so hopeful of a full 'purse' as I expected a lot of people to come and see our play; however, I was to learn that race week is not the best time to present plays.

*

Emmie and I were living with my daughter Lilly and her husband, Henry. We were thrilled when we received news from my son, Tom, that he had married Miss Alice Mary Law in Sydney in 1901. The celebrations kept coming as Lilly gave birth to a daughter, Phyllis Frances Betteridge, in 1902, and then a son, Eric Aston Betteridge, in 1903.

My son, Charles, wrote to tell me he had met the most wonderful woman, Miss Mary Emma Daly. She was an actress of great ability. He'd fallen head over heels in love. They married on the 12th May 1903 at St George's Church in Paddington, Sydney. I was thrilled for them.

Soon after that, Charles picked up some work with Mr Bland Holt in Melbourne, in August 1903, with the drama *Going the Pace* at the Theatre Royal. In his letters, he described the circus ring scene. Mr Holt had installed on the stage a 40-foot ring with a background of tiers of seats for an audience. The scene was true in every detail and made thrilling with stunts by real circus performers and their well-trained animals.

Mr Holt used to draw on the works of Mr Henry Lawson when he required bush atmospheres for his plays. He would pay the author well for his services. Apparently, Mr Lawson was required to present himself backstage on opening night to receive his payment and the thanks of the producer.

✳

I loved the autonomy of managing my own company, but at times the responsibility was overwhelming. I had to make all the decisions and never second-guess myself. I experienced chauvinistic attitudes from some men who just didn't believe I was capable of making business decisions or managing money, and so they weren't willing to lease their theatres to me. Some were polite, whilst some were hostile and rude. Those who knew me from previous work engagements gave me support. I'll always be grateful to those gentlemen who saw past the dress I was wearing and saw my abilities.

I decided that if other work opportunities arose, I would take them if they were more advantageous than managing my own company.

The Brandon-Cremer Comedy Company approached me and offered Emmie and myself a position in their company. From May through to September 1904, we went on tour with them to Kalgoorlie, Boulder, and Perth. We presented *Uncle Tom's Cabin* and many other plays. Once again, I played the role of Topsy, and thankfully, the critics were complimentary, saying:

> 'The vivacity, the deviltry - if that be not too strong a term of Topsy (Miss Fanny Wiseman), once seen, is not likely to be forgotten.'

And to finish off the year, in December, I was in the play *Outlaw Kelly,* in the Theatre Royal, Perth. Miss Kate Howarde's Company presented the exploits of the notorious Kelly Gang, with much explosion of cartridges. The story of the Kelly bushrangers is known to all Australians. Some of the critics thought it was improper glorification of 'robbers and murderers' and they were made to 'appear like noble heroes.' But many of us prefer to think that they stood up for the oppressed and challenged the corrupt authority of the time.

The play was well-staged and well-acted. The scenery was good, and the burning of the Glenrowan Inn, in the last act was splendidly shown. The cast of characters was a long one, and several actors had more than one part, and the programme honoured them with a different name for each character. Mr Walter Dagleish was well suited to the part of Ned Kelly, and his efforts were rewarded with copious applause. Kate Kelly, the devoted sister, was played by Miss Kate Howarde. I played a breeches part, that of Daft Dick, a ragged outcast and a confederate of the Kelly's.

*

It had been a very busy few years, both professionally and personally. My children were living their own lives, marrying their sweethearts and having families of their own. It was wonderful to see from a mother's perspective. Yet, now and then, the sorrow of my first husband's death would hit me. The disappointment of my second marriage to Valentine was also a deep sadness.

It was at the end of 1904 that I finally heard what had happened to Valentine. My friend Miss Lizzy Naylor, who had been married to Mr Charles Edouin, wrote to me in Cue. She told me that she'd been travelling through Echuca, Victoria, earlier in the year.

At the mere mention of Echuca, my mind instantly saw the streets and the Temperance Hall in Echuca, where we'd played *The Cabin* back in January 1879.

Lizzie told me that she'd been talking with some of the local shopkeepers, and the conversations turned to recent events with actors who had toured through the town. They mentioned how sad they were about Valentine Lambert. They showed her Valentine's obituary in the local newspaper. I almost fainted. I wasn't expecting that news.

She told me the obituary said that Valentine had died on the 20th December 1902 from consumption, and it referred to his wife and two daughters. But the surprise came when she said that Valentine had remarried and his wife's name was Jane Anne Peers! There was no denying he was a charmer, but I would never have thought him a bigamist as well!

I felt a great sadness, even after all the pain and anger, the longing and the wondering about where he'd gone and what he was doing. I was happy he didn't die alone, which I think is a fate not wished on anyone.

*

A wonderful benefit was given to me on Monday, 4th June 1906. It was a wintry evening, but thankfully, it did not deter a large number of people from being present at the King's Theatre in Fremantle, Western Australia.

I had been acting since I was eight years old and had toured many parts of Australia. I had worked with many of the greats, Mr GV Brooke, Mr George Coppin, Miss Rose Edouin, and Mrs Mary Scott-Siddons, a career which few artists at the time could match.

My daughters, Lilly and Emmie, and my son, Austin, were part of the benefit and played their parts well. The performances concluded with the production of the second act of *Uncle Tom's Cabin*, in which I appeared as Topsy. The benefit was met with liberal patronage.

I was still performing quite regularly, but I was also enjoying my time with my family. I had several grandchildren in Western Australia. My son Tom and his wife Alice, who were in Sydney, had three children: Tom, Roy, and Alice, whom I hadn't met yet.

My youngest daughter, Emmie, was 19 years old and had grown into a beautiful young lady.

I had a lot to be grateful for, and I was grateful. But at times, the sadness crept in, and I would take myself away from whatever was happening. I would take long walks and think through the dark and sad thoughts until I arrived at a happier place.

*

In July 1906, my sister Alice wrote to me with the sad news of the death of Mr GBW Lewis. He was 87 years old and had suffered from cystitis. His wife, my dear friend Rose, was, of course, devastated, and I knew the pain and suffering she would be going through. I hadn't heard from Rose for some time, but my sister Alice was still very close with her. I wrote to her and offered my sympathies.

*

I left Western Australia in 1907 and went touring again. I was engaged by the Grattan Coughlan Dramatic Company, and we played in the newly built Theatre Royal in Broken Hill. We produced *Uncle Tom's Cabin* and *Fun on the Bristol*, two of my favourite plays.

In 1908, my son Austin and daughter Emmie joined me for a South Australian tour. We performed *A Sailor's Sweetheart* and *Struck Oil.* Austin was making a name for himself as an acrobat and dancer. He had always been quick-witted and a great comedian. But there was one time when he was not so quick – he was working with some camels and one of them bit half his finger off!

We celebrated another wedding when my daughter Emmie married Mr John Lawrence Lewis in New Zealand in 1908. John was a talented photographer and an excellent actor.

*

I had loved living in Western Australia, and Sydney was a beautiful city, but I was definitely my happiest when I was in Melbourne. I knew a lot of people through the theatre business, and there was always an opening night of a play or an art exhibition to go to.

I returned to Melbourne at the end of 1908. I was once again engaged to play Topsy in *Uncle Tom's Cabin,* this time with The William Anderson's Company. The production was at the King's Theatre in Melbourne.

I settled into my old part, and the critics called it 'perfection.' I had first performed this role when I was 13 years old, and I was now 62! My old friend, Mr Edmund Duggan, played the role of Simon Legree. Seeing Edmund again brought memories of travelling in the paddle steamer down the Darling River with him, my brother-in-law James and Valentine. Bittersweet memories.

Mr Ernest Fitts played the role of Uncle Tom. Mr Bert Bailey, Miss Vivian Edwards, Baby Watson, and Miss May Granville were also in the play, and all deserved much credit. Each evening, we were encored.

Mr William Anderson, the manager, spared no expense in staging the play, and the scenic studies by Mr Rege Robins were beautiful. The play was very popular once again.

The company then toured to Sydney in September 1910. We presented Mr Nat Gould's sporting play, *The Change of a Lifetime,* at the Criterion Theatre. Then we went to Brisbane, Newcastle and then back to Melbourne in November to play *The Worst Woman in London* at the King's Theatre. It has a powerful plot and sensational scenes, one of which represents the heroine sliding along a telephone wire from a burning house. It was the greatest of all Walter Melville's dramatic successes.

*

In January 1911, my youngest daughter, Emmie, had a baby boy, and they named him John Arnold Lewis. I remember seeing her husband, John, holding the baby for the first time. He cried tears of joy, and after carefully handing the baby back to Emmie, he proceeded to dance around the room.

They were living in Carlton, and I was living just around the corner in Gertrude Street and then in Moor Street in Fitzroy, Melbourne. I was very close to them and could easily walk between the houses to help them. My son Austin was living with me at the time. He'd recently returned from touring with Vincent M Beebe in vaudeville shows across

Australia. Austin had been billed as the Indian Rubber Man!

Life was never dull when Austin was around. He was a born entertainer.

Emmie took to motherhood easily, but she told me her understanding of life and the responsibilities of being a mother had been overwhelming. She realised how hard I had worked to raise a family and continue working professionally as an actress.

She told me I was her role model and said that I had been instrumental in female emancipation and the suffragette movement. She said that I had helped lead the way forward for female equality. I didn't feel like I had done that, but I suppose I lived outside the usual Victorian societal restrictions placed on women.

Emmie had seen me start my own business, procure engagements and form working relationships with male managers, staff and actors at numerous theatres. I had undertaken years of arduous touring, endured chauvinism on and off the stage. I often took the roles of strong and independent women. These roles had inspired many women to want and expect more in life.

I also had role models of my own, whom I modelled myself on. Lady Don was not only a great actress, but she was also a theatre manageress of great repute. She was not afraid of adventure or challenging men when they put barriers in her way. I had seen her do it often.

Mrs Mary Scott-Siddons was another role model. She was a very public example of a working mother often working up to the 8th month of pregnancy, like I had done many times. My dear friend Rose Edouin was another great woman. She had been a directress and worked alongside her husband, making business decisions for many years.

However, when I really thought about it, it was my mother who was my greatest role model. She had been courageous and kind, and uncompromising in her love for her husband and her children. She challenged unfair and discriminatory behaviours and taught me to accept people for who they were.

My home state of Victoria gave white women the right to vote in elections in 1908. However, Aboriginal men and women were not given this right. Based on the colour of their skin, they were cruelly discriminated against. There were many people who saw the injustice of this and worked tirelessly to right this wrong.

*

In March 1912, the New Hippodrome in Wirth's Park, Melbourne, staged *Uncle Tom's Cabin*. However, I was not asked to play Topsy; my clever daughter, Miss Lilly Wiseman, did the honours. And she certainly did the part justice.

But it seemed that the tide was turning on this great American story penned by Mrs Harriet Beecher Stowe back in 1852. Mrs Stowe had been opposed to slavery, and she wrote the novel before the American Civil War to rally abolitionists and swing individuals against the South's slavery practices. When the novel was published, white southerners were outraged by its content, fearing it might cause slave rebellions. It was actually banned in the southern states in 1852. And yet, even though it was banned, it was the second best-selling book of the 19th century – number one was the Bible, of course. Mrs Stowe had shone the light on the cruel and brutal practice of slavery. People realised how abhorrent slavery was.

You know it is said that when President Abraham Lincoln met Mrs Harriet Beecher Stowe in the White House in 1862 during the American Civil War, he said,

'Why, Mrs Stowe, right glad to see you. So, you're the little woman who wrote the book that made this great war!'

But looking at the play now, I can see how many stereotypes are in it. When I had to 'blacken' my face, I didn't think I was being disrespectful. For me, it was a costume, like all the other costumes I had to wear onstage.

The passage of time often brings new knowledge and wisdom, and sometimes a change in attitude, hopefully for the better. Nowadays, some folks use the term 'Uncle Tom' as a derogatory term for a black person who behaves in a subservient manner to a white person. In the original text, the character Uncle Tom dies from being whipped to death by his white 'owner.' He is whipped because he refused to denounce his faith or betray the hiding place of two fugitive slaves. The actions of Uncle Tom in these final scenes of the play, and in the novel, were definitely not subservient actions, and he paid the ultimate price for standing up for his religion and his morals.

At the end of the day, having been part of the play for over 50 years, there were many admirable sentiments within the play. And I felt that the novel and the play had shifted society's understanding of prejudice, racism and the wrongful practice of slavery.

*

In April 1912, the *RMS Titanic* was on its maiden voyage, and the excitement was incomparable. Everyone had been talking about it. It was reported there was a swimming pool, gymnasium and squash courts aboard the ship. There was an immense first-class dining saloon and four elevators. The *Titanic*'s grandeur and opulence had not been seen before. It was claimed that the ship was unsinkable because of its construction and safety controls. Many wealthy and influential people clamoured to be passengers on the maiden voyage and to be part of history. And they did make history, but for all the wrong reasons.

I, like many of my friends, had travelled across the Atlantic Ocean and had feared being in a shipwreck. Such a vast ocean to travel across. My mind goes back to Mr GV Brooke, who died, along with 250 other passengers, in 1866 aboard the *SS London* when it sank off the coast of Spain in the Bay of Biscay.

The *Titanic* hit an iceberg, which tore a hole in the starboard side and opened six compartments to the sea. When the ship sank on 15th April 1912, it felt like the whole world stopped to mourn the enormous loss of life, as well as the loss of a dream. It seemed that everyone knew someone who had either helped in the construction of the ship in Belfast, Ireland, or who had been a crew member, entertainer or a passenger. More than 1,500 people died, and many of these were third-class passengers and crew.

My heart went out to all the families who had lost loved ones.

Many of the survivors were interviewed afterwards. Their stories helped put together all the pieces of the puzzle.

People at the time just could not believe it had sunk. They were angry that there were not enough lifeboats, angry about lax regulations and angry about the unequal treatment of third-class passengers.

Many of my musician friends knew the bandmaster, Mr Wallace Hartley, and they openly wept when they heard that the musicians onboard played the hymn *Nearer My God to Thee* as the ship sank. We were told that it was protocol for the ships band to play music in any emergency to help calm the passengers.

I hope someday the wreck of the *Titanic* will be found. It lies somewhere on the bottom of the ocean floor. A watery grave and resting place for more than a thousand souls.

*

Another loss, this time more personal for me. My brother-in-law, James Anthony South, passed away on 25th October 1912 in Toowong Hospital. He had spent a lot of time in Queensland, touring and performing, and I hadn't seen him for many years.

He was a kind person and would have given his shirt off his back to anyone needing help. I felt blessed that I had known him. He helped me when William died and gave me a shoulder to cry on when Valentine left me.

He was only 68 years old.

Chapter Twenty-Seven – The war to end all wars

We all know what happened in 1914. An event that changed the course of history and affected so many lives across the world. The assassination of Austrian Archduke Franz Ferdinand set off a chain of events that led to The Great War. When the United Kingdom declared war on Germany, it meant that Australia also joined the war. Australians were, after all, British subjects.

'No country was ever saved by the other fellow; it must be done by you, by a hundred million you's, or it will not be done at all.' This quote was very popular at the time, but I can't quite remember who the author was. It certainly struck a chord with the nation.

My youngest son, Sydney, was working as a butcher, and he was the first in the family to join the Australian army. He enlisted in Liverpool, New South Wales, on 23rd April 1915 in the 2nd Battalion. He was 32 years old.

I still remember the day I said good-bye to him. I had travelled to Sydney to see him. I hugged him so tight. I didn't want to let him go.

The Australian and New Zealand troops had landed at the Gallipoli Peninsula. They were hoping to capture the peninsula and open up the Dardanelles Strait and allow the Allied troops to take Constantinople. Over 50,000 Australians were sent to Gallipoli, and over 8,700 were killed, never to return home. My son was one of those who did not come home. He died at Lone Pine, Gallipoli, on the 6th August 1915.

I was living in a small cottage on Hotham Street, Collingwood, in Melbourne when I received that telegram. My knees buckled, and I collapsed. I couldn't open the telegram. I already knew what it said. The shock of having this news delivered in such a way was unbearable. Even now, so many years later, I can hardly talk about it. The sadness and the despair. It is such a private and personal emotion, and yet it is an emotion I share with so many other mothers and families. The country grieved for our lost sons and daughters.

Then, my eldest son, Charles, enlisted in the army on 24th September 1915 in West Maitland, New South Wales. His training was at Broadmeadows Camp. I knew he would be next to enlist as his marriage to lovely Mary had fallen apart.

They had three children at the time, Kathleen, Constance and Charles Edward. It breaks my heart to tell you, but my other son, Austin, had fallen in love with Mary, and she felt the same way about him. It is something that can break a family in half, and for a long time, it did just that. My sons, Charles and Austin, had fallen in love with the same woman, and their relationship was irrevocably broken.

Mary and Austin moved to Cessnock with the three little children. They then had four children of their own: Austin, Frances, Jack and Esther. I felt honoured they had named their little girl after me. I learnt many years later that Frances and Esther became skilled dancers and acrobats, and they would go on tour with their father, Austin.

During the war, we were all trying to do our bit and bring an end to the war.

I was never sure where the army sent Charles. I think he was in Egypt for a time, then went to France in early 1916 to fight at the Western Front.

Later in 1916, Charles returned home as an injured soldier. I felt so thankful that he was coming home to us. But the war had changed him.

My daughter Laura actively worked for the men at the front and helped form a branch of the Red Cross Society at Queen's Park in Perth, Western Australia. She was the honorary secretary and worked tirelessly. Her eldest son Archie enlisted in June 1916; he was only 16 years old. I couldn't bear to think what he was going to face. But there was no stopping him, and his parents, Laura and William, had agreed to let him go. He was assigned to the 38th Battery of the 10th Field Artillery Brigade, as a driver.

Only a few months before Archie enlisted, his cousin, and my nephew Alfred Arthur Anderson, enlisted. He was a little older than Archie, at the grand age of 21! Such young men, sent off to fight a brutal war. Alfred was my sister Laura's youngest son. He joined the 3rd Infantry Battalion.

The war was dragging on, and it was in its third year. Britain wanted more men on the front, but fewer men were enlisting to fight. No wonder, with massive casualties and deaths.

In mid-1916, the Australian Government under Prime Minister Billy Hughes called for a plebiscite on the issue of conscription for war service. Actually, there were two plebiscites on the issue. The second one was held in December 1917. Billy and his government wanted to make military service compulsory. There was a lot of debate about the issue with flyers circulating around in support and in opposition. I heard a song that resonated with me. It was called *I Didn't Raise My Son To Be a Soldier*. The chorus goes like this,

> I didn't raise my son to be a soldier
> I brought him up to be my pride and joy.
> Who dares to put a musket on his shoulder,
> To kill some other mother's darling boy?
> The nations ought to arbitrate their quarrels

It's time to put the sword and gun away.
There'd be no war today,
If mothers all would say –
I didn't raise my son to be a soldier.[x]

The Australian people told Billy twice what they thought of conscription. The answer to both plebiscites was a definite 'No.' The vast majority did *not* want military conscription!

I was living in Albert Park in Melbourne with my daughter Emmie and her husband John, and their little boy John Arnold, who was seven years old.

When the war was finally declared over at 11:00 am on the 11th November 1918, everyone took to the streets to celebrate – to embrace each other, to cry and to laugh.

The war had raged for four years, and more than 16 million people across the world, soldiers and civilians, had been killed.

We all tried to resume our lives as they had been before the war, but this was never to happen. The men and women who came home were irrevocably changed. The horrors of war were to stay with them until they joined their fallen brothers and sisters.

Archie, my grandson, returned to Western Australia in February 1919, three months after the war ended. He had been in hospital suffering from shell shock. He was only 19 years old.

My nephew Alfred Anderson went to England, and I haven't seen him since.

They survived the worst war in history, and they had to live with the memories.

We put on our brave faces and did our best.

*

On the 5th August 1920, I attended a special ceremony with the Mayor and other dignitaries at the Fitzroy Town Hall, Melbourne. I was presented with the 1915 Star, which had been 'won' by my dear son Sydney. The medal was awarded to those who served in The Great War between 1914 and 1915. It was a four-pointed star made of bronze and topped with a crown. The newspapers wrote about the ceremony, and described me as being,

'A proud mother, prouder than at any other time during her long stage career.'

I can tell you I was always proud of Sydney – proud the first day he walked, proud of the first word he spoke, and proud of the man that he became. I would have given anything to have my son back.

On the day of the 1915 Star ceremony, it had been five years and one day since Sydney had died. We marked the date by putting a notice in the Family Section in Melbourne's *The Age* newspaper.

The special section was called 'For our ANZAC Heroes.' Our notice read,

SOUTH – In loving and proud memory of Private Sydney A South, 2207, 2nd Battalion, AIF, who was killed in action at Lone Pine on the 6th August 1915, the dearly loved youngest son of Frances J South (Fanny Wiseman) and the late William South, affectionate brother of Charles E South, (late AIF), TA South, Minnie and Laura (WA), Lillian (QLD), Emmie (WA).
My boy was loved by all who knew him.
Never to be forgotten.
He died the noblest death a man may die,
Fighting for God and King and liberty,
And such a death is immortality.

SOUTH – In fond and proud memory of my dear brother, Private SA South, 2207, 2nd Battalion, AIF, who sleeps at Lone Pine since 6th August 1915.
And the world knows many heroes,
But my heart holds but one.
Emmie.

SOUTH – In fond and proud memory of my dear brother, Private Sydney A South, 2207, 2nd Battalion, AIF, who made the supreme sacrifice at Lone Pine on the 6th August 1915. He was loved in life, honoured in death, treasured in memory.
Lillian.

✳

My health had declined since Sydney's death. I knew it was due to grief and sadness. And then, as if the gods had seen and heard my despair, they lifted my spirits with the offer of a new acting engagement. Work had always been my panacea, a remedy, giving me purpose.

In August 1920, Mr Allan Wilkie asked me to play the third witch in *Macbeth*. I only hesitated for a moment, and then I accepted the engagement. I was 75 years old, and the thought of being in another Shakespearean production was thrilling.

The rehearsals were wonderful, and my energy levels and spirits were increasing every day. Being around fellow actors was uplifting.

One afternoon, when Mr Wilkie and I were taking a break, he asked me about my time in Calcutta. My mind went back to India, and I could see all the places that William and I had been. I told Mr Wilkie about the excitement of travelling across the country on the trains, the heat, the cyclones, and the crowds of people. It was an exotic place that had welcomed us and given us so much, but it had also taken a lot.

Then Mr Wilkie told me about his time in Calcutta in 1911. He'd taken his Shakespearean company on a three-year Asian tour to Ceylon, Singapore, British Malaya, Hong Kong, China, Japan and the Philippines. When he was in Calcutta, he said there were crowds of Bengalis when he performed at the Kohinoor Theatre on Beadon Street. He said the audience would openly weep during the more moving scenes of *Othello*[xi].

In *Macbeth,* the realistic combat between Macbeth and Macduff aroused the Bengali audience to such a frenzy of excitement and panic that many of them dived under their seats and others made a mad rush for the doors.

He said, 'Of course Fanny, you will remember how many monkeys there were, mostly living on the outskirts of town, and sometimes in town.'

He smiled as he remembered his own experiences.

'At one of our shows at the Grand Opera House in Calcutta, one of my actors had to be taken off stage for he'd been struck on the head by a piece of wood. It wasn't a disgruntled audience member throwing something at the actor, but one of the monkeys in the theatre roof!'

At this point, I couldn't help myself, I started to laugh. The more I tried to stop, the more I laughed. To be honest, this was the first time I'd smiled or laughed since my son had died. But my laughter turned into tears. The floodgates had been opened, and torrents of tears came forth.

Mr Wilkie knew why I was crying. Memories, happy and sad, come to us in moments when we allow ourselves to just feel emotion. He was a very kind man and held my hand. I was 30 years older than Mr Wilkie, probably a similar age as his mother, and I felt he paid me the same respect he'd pay his own mother.

He kept holding my hand and asked me gently if I'd travelled to Bangalore. I nodded.

He said,

'When we were in Bangalore, we were showing *Hamlet*, and half a dozen students from a remote village walked for 60 miles through the jungle to the closest train station, then travelled 300 miles on the train, to see the play. I met these young men after the play. They were extremely polite and kept thanking me. But really, I was the grateful one. Seeing their commitment just cemented my resolve to keep presenting Shakespeare. When the young boys were heading off home, they said it would take them a week. I could only imagine the cost involved. But for those boys, it was a once-in-a-lifetime opportunity to see the play.

You know, there were times when I felt truly tested. Bouts of sickness often left productions short of actors and in one performance of *Romeo and Juliet*, I played the roles of Friar Lawrence, Mercutio and Prince Escalus!'

Mr Wilkie had worked his magic on me; he allowed me to be vulnerable and to feel safe at the same time. I had stopped crying and felt like a huge weight had been lifted from me. He was a wonderful person, and I'll never forget his kindness.

*

Macbeth's opening night at the Princess's Theatre in Melbourne was in September 1920. There were 40 cast members, along with an augmented orchestra under the direction of Mr Lou Weichard.

Before the curtain rose, Mr Wilkie called us all together. He was excited and said, 'I'm so proud of all of you. Tonight's going to be amazing and I wish everyone chookas!'

Mr Allan Wilkie played the part of Macbeth and was commanding and powerful. His voice and physique were perfect for heavy Shakespearean parts. My fellow witches were Mr Arthur Goodsall and Mr Edward Landor. Arthur was a skilled artisan and designed the costumes and colour effects, which were greatly admired.

There were 23 scenes in *Macbeth*, and in order to present them all without incurring prohibitive expense, Mr Wilkie had introduced a scheme of effective stage hangings. He used just a square of scenery in the background to suggest a setting.

With the overwhelming success of cinematograph or silent films, as they were known, where scene changes are immediate, audiences expected the same onstage.

Miss Hunter-Watts took the part of Lady Macbeth. She was exceptional, and her acting in the sleepwalking scene was physically applauded by the audience and literarily applauded by the critics.

My fellow actors were all superb, and I was having the time of my life. Mr Guy Hastings played Macduff, and in the big fight with Macbeth, he looked completely stressed with the effort, which deprived them both of breath. Another actor in the play was Mr Griffiths, who played an old man; he was 82 years old, so he really was an old man! He had been in the profession for many years.

The theatre was crowded, and at the conclusion of the play there was a remarkable outburst of enthusiasm from the audience. Amid the din of cheering and handclapping, someone called out, 'Good old Shakespeare,' a remark which seemed to epitomise everyone's feelings.

Mr Wilkie had a passion and drive that I had only seen in one other man, my old friend Mr George Coppin. Mr Wilkie felt that Shakespeare was for all time and for all people. He established Australia's first permanent touring Shakespeare company in 1920, and his ambition is to present all 37 of the Bard's plays in towns and cities around the country.

My last paid acting engagements were with Mr Allan Wilkie in 1922. After *Macbeth,* I played the Nurse in *Romeo and Juliet*, and Dame Quickly in *Merry Wives*. I have always enjoyed performing in Shakespeare's plays and was grateful that there were a few interesting roles for older actresses.

*

I appeared at Her Majesty's Theatre in Melbourne, in early April 1922, to raise funds for the Old Actors Appeal. My youngest daughter, Emmie, had written a poem[xii] which I recited from memory.

It was called *The Actor*,

We have laughed and danced for your pleasure
Maybe with an aching heart!
For the actor has little leisure
To grieve when playing his part

We have striven and fought for your favour
We have laughed for you, we have cried
We have given to you the best we know
But now we are laid aside

We have kept our faith with you ever
That you might your gladness take
We have hidden our woes and our troubles
Because of the public's sake

We have struggled 'gainst odds overwhelming
That only the actor knows
But in spite of all that o'er could befall
We were there when the curtain rose

We have spent our lives in your service
And at times you were hard to please
And there's something gone at each curtain fall
That no audience ever sees

We have given our youth and our brightness
And the best of our life's fair day

But the night has come, and life's busy hum
Comes now from the far away

We have laughed and danced for your pleasure
But now that our day is through
And the whirl of the world has passed us by
We are turning again to you

To ask if in truth we succeeded
To smooth the care from your brow
If we pleased you at all in the days past recall
Will you remember us now?

Now that our charm has faded
And the gifts that pleased you have fled
If we helped you then in those days gone by
Will you help now our youth has sped?

Will you brighten the path we are treading?
Someday it will be your own
And you take your last call alone!

It seemed the only way to raise funds for worthy causes was to put on benefits, so that's exactly what we did.

I was involved in another matinee benefit, again at Her Majesty's Theatre in Melbourne. It was held for the Distressed Diggers and their families on Friday 12th May 1922.

The long arm of war still touched so many of us – those who had lost family and those who had their loved ones returned. Many of our sons and daughters had returned with injuries, some you could see, like burns or lost limbs, and others you couldn't see which could be more debilitating. The horrors of war changed people; how could it not. And the change didn't just affect the soldiers, it affected their wives and their children. I had two sons, one grandson, and one nephew in the war. Everyone had someone who'd been affected.

The Distressed Diggers' matinee organised by Mrs JL Stein and Mrs Hector Tanse was a great success. No less than £900 was raised from the entertainment. There was not a vacant seat to be seen at Her Majesty's that afternoon. The audience responded warmly to the wiles of Miss Ada Reeves, who made such a fascinating auctioneer that money flowed in. One of Melbourne's favourites, Miss Maggie Moore, proved how popular she was when her autographed photo brought over £30.

I was warmly greeted by the audience when I recited my daughter Emmie's poems *Stick to your Mates* and *Diggers All.*

The best artists from all the theatres combined to make the matinee one of the most enjoyable that was held in Melbourne. The theatre was beautifully presented and there were many helpers selling sweets, flowers and novelties.

Melbournians are usually generous in their support for good causes, and this matinee once again proved this characteristic.

After the matinee, I was contacted by several ladies asking if I could assist their daughters with elocution and stagecraft. I had given elocution classes when I was in New Zealand many years ago, so I once more rose to the challenge.

In August 1922, I advertised my availability as an elocution and acting teacher. I had several young ladies attend my home at 8 Alston Grove, off Orrong Road, in St Kilda. It was a delight to share my skills with attentive young ladies.

Chapter Twenty-Eight – The last act

In April 1924, my son Charlie and I went across to Western Australia to visit my daughters, Minnie and Laura, and their families. Minnie and her husband, George Atkins, had been living in Western Australia for many years, and they were well settled there. They had their four children living with them: Richard, Frances, Esther and Edward.

Laura was a widow. Sadly, her husband William Archibald MacPhail Johnstone had died in 1918. Laura's son Archie lived with her, as well as her daughters Minnie and Olive. Laura's eldest daughter Essie was married to her second husband Mr John Flowers, her childhood sweetheart. They had been separated by The Great War and Essie thought her sweetheart dead, so married another man, Mr Bill O'Reilly. But as fate would have it, Bill was already married and was charged with bigamy, so releasing Essie. When John Flowers returned from the war, none were more excited and thrilled than Essie. They were reunited at long last. I was looking forward to seeing all the family and finding out what was happening in their lives.

I had last been in Western Australia in 1907.

When we arrived in Perth, we found a very comfortable house to rent in 65 Newcastle Street, East Perth. Charlie and I had planned a purely non-professional trip, however after a while, I was asked and agreed to recite two monologues at the Theatre Royal in November 1924. I was slowing down by this stage. I had some rheumatoid arthritis which was giving me some grief. But the show must go on!

After about 12 months, I started to feel very homesick for Melbourne. My finances were low, and God bless my daughter Laura, because she wrote to the editor of the *West Australian* newspaper on the 16th September 1925 and asked if a benefit could be put on for me. She told the editor,

> 'Although we are a large family (myself a widow) there are families to maintain and lately my mother, Miss Wiseman, has wished to return to Melbourne to be near her husband's remains, the late WTK South.'

The theatre folk rallied and came to my aid. A big benefit concert was organised and held in the Theatre Royal on Sunday evening, 6th December 1925. It was a bumper programme, as it was the combined talents of three theatrical companies: the Prince of Wales, Midnight Frolics, and the Luxor Theatre. The Theatre Royal had been kindly loaned by Sir Benjamin Fuller, and his brother John and all services were voluntary. It was a packed house.

I made my entry about halfway through the programme. I was welcomed onto the stage and invited to speak. I delivered a short recitation about an actor's farewell to the stage. I felt young again, alive and full of energy; however, my appearance, with grey hair and small stature, betrayed my actual age. Floral tributes were handed to me. I expressed my great thanks to the audience, the management, the artists of the three theatres, all the musicians and the staff.

Twenty-five items were performed onstage. The programme was representative of the best the city had in amusement and fully deserved the volume of applause which greeted every item. The success of the evening was added to in no small degree by the excellent music performed by the combined orchestras from Perth.

Over 30 performers took part in the entertainment, which was extremely well done, from curtain rise to fall, and which realised £137. I was humbled by the generosity of the Perth audience and all the people involved in putting on the benefit.

It never ceases to amaze me how progress occurs. Can you believe, as a result of my benefit, many of the young actors and actresses met up and unanimously decided to form an Actor's Benevolent Fund. They asked me to attend a meeting on Thursday 10th December at the Theatre Royal to discuss how they were going to go about it.

I was not feeling my best, and decided the young ones were best placed to make the plans. They told me later the main objective was to assist any actor or actress, who may be temporarily in distress through ill-health, bad luck, or other causes. To raise the necessary funds, they decided to give a series of Sunday night concerts throughout Australia. The first concert was given in Perth on Sunday 27th December 1925 and several more followed.

With the money raised through my benefit concert I was able to return to my beloved Melbourne last year, in 1926.

When I returned, I can honestly say the call of the footlights was raising no response in my heart. My acting days were irretrievably over, and with that realisation came a feeling of sorrow that it should be so.

It is gratifying to know that I haven't been forgotten, and only last month, some lovely young performers from Madame Pompadour's Company came to visit me when I celebrated my 81st birthday. They were such sweet little children, bringing me lovely gifts and armfuls of flowers, which brightened my room like sunshine.

I have had a long and successful career as an actress. I have 'trod the boards' for 71 years, and I have travelled to many parts of the world. I had my own company, and I've had the pleasure of teaching elocution and stagecraft to the up-and-coming young actresses. I have a large family and was able to provide for all of them. I had 12 children, but sadly, five of them have died. Of all the roles I have played, from Little Buttercup, Lizzie Stofel, Topsy and the Nurse in *Macbeth*, I think being a mother has been my most challenging and rewarding role.

Interlude

'That is the end of my story Mr Robinson.'

I could hear the tiredness in my voice.

With a slight laugh, I said,

'I think I have given you enough details for several articles in your newspaper.'

Mr Robinson looked up, his pen still poised in his hand, ready to take more notes. He seemed a little startled, like he wasn't quite ready to finish. Then he took a deep breath and slowly exhaled. He straightened his jacket and shifted his position in the chair.

I could see he had been paying attention and had taken careful notes on all that I had told him. Had I touched his heart with my story, and of the wonderful people who had been in my life? I think so. I trusted that the story he would write for the newspaper would be true and just.

'Thank you Miss Wiseman. I must admit your story has taken me by surprise. I am in awe of your experiences and the people you've worked with. I've never even left the shores of Australia!'

I nodded my head and smiled, 'You know Mr Robinson, all the actors and actresses I worked with were professionals. We all took our responsibilities with great seriousness. Oftentimes, we presented plays that were socially challenging and made people think about right and wrong, but often we provided light-hearted entertainment. We all need to laugh, especially when times are difficult. When I was onstage, my fellow thespians were my family. Sometimes there were silly quarrels and sometimes fierce competition, but at the end of the day, we all delighted in each other's company and talents. Much like any family.'

Talking about and remembering my family and friends, many of whom were no longer alive, had brought a sad smile to my face. My memories were like shadows from the past, come to stay with me for a while, but now I needed to say goodbye to them.

'Mr Robinson, alas I'm feeling quite weary now. I must say farewell and I wish you safe travels. But before you leave me, at the risk of being considered old-fashioned, I must have a good 'tag' for you to finish this interview. It's from Miss Ella Wheeler Wilcox, and here it is,

Be worthy of your work, if you love it
The king should be fit for his crown
Stand high as your art or above it
And make us look up and not down.'

Epilogue

After my interview with Miss Wiseman, I wrote up my notes. It took me a few days to summarise the story and submit it to my editor. I knew only a fraction of the information would make it into the newspaper. Three articles appeared in *The Herald* during October 1927.

I received a letter from Miss Wiseman two days after the last story was published. When I opened the envelope, a well-folded white note was inside. The note contained the most elegant handwriting and said,

'Mr Robinson, I write to you with a heartfelt thank you. You have made an old lady smile. You have given me a great gift. To be remembered and celebrated for one's lifelong work is a wonderful honour. Thank you. Yours sincerely, Miss Wiseman.'

I was enamoured by this petite yet powerful lady.

I found myself scanning the daily newspapers, looking for her name. I read in many of the society pages that she continued to support the arts, but also that her health was failing.

Miss Wiseman's daughter, Emmie, was receiving glowing reviews for her performances. She had recently joined the Betty Ross Clark Company and toured with them to Western Australia for a period of time. I knew Miss Wiseman would have been enormously proud.

I read with interest in *The Argus* on Sunday, 10th June 1928, that Miss Fanny Wiseman was the guest of honour at the opera *Norma* by the Fuller-Gonsalez Grand Opera Company playing at the Princess Theatre, Melbourne. Sir Benjamin Fuller had turned his hand to operatic management and was doing very well. He would have remembered Miss Wiseman from her benefit that he supported in Western Australia in December 1925.

Miss Wiseman had been in the same production of *Norma,* 72 years ago, when it played at Mr George Coppin's Olympic Theatre. She had told me that her sister Emily and her, were the lead child actors, and they simply loved the production. When she had recalled the time when she had appeared in *Norma,* she said the music came back to her 'as fresh in my memory as though I had been fortunate enough to hear it only last night.'

The Argus newspaper article said that Mr Cecil Beveridge, the manager of the Princess Theatre, had sent a car to Miss Wiseman's nursing home to pick her up for the Saturday matinee performance of *Norma* on 9th June 1928.

Miss Wiseman was dressed in a pink bonnet and party frock.

Signorina Rosita Silvestri and the two little girls who played the child parts in *Norma* visited the stage box where Miss Wiseman was sitting, and they laid tributes of flowers at her feet. One of the children was Miss Shirley Beveridge, only three years old, and the daughter of the manager. The public recognised Miss Wiseman, the great Australian actress and gave her an enthusiastic ovation.

The article went on to say that Miss Fanny Wiseman stood up and briefly told the audience how she had, as a child, performed in the first production of *Norma*. When she ended her speech with, 'And now the young ones take our places,' the packed house shouted, 'Never! Never!' till the rafters rang.

With great sadness, I read on the 30th January 1929 in *The Herald*, that the great Ms Gladys Moncrieff was asking to start a fund for Miss Fanny Wiseman. Ms Moncrieff said that Fanny only had enough money to pay the nursing home fees but had nothing left to pay for medicine or any little comforts. Ms Moncrieff, rightly so, reminded the public that Miss Wiseman had given so much amusement and pleasure to Melburnians, and now is the time to help cheer her up.

I believe many people supported the worthy request.

I wondered what Miss Wiseman thought of the 'talkies' that had captured the public's interest and resulted in the theatre world's downward spiral. I read an article in *The*

Mail, Adelaide, South Australia on Saturday 19th April 1930, entitled 'From Stage Glamour to Humdrum Toil.' It described how Miss Fanny Wiseman's daughter, Lilly Wiseman, and her second husband, Mr Crosley Ward, have a cosy greengrocer store. They threw in the theatre business for the more certain pay packet of selling vegetables. Miss Wiseman was a pragmatic woman, but I think her love of the theatre and performing onstage would have been unshakeable.

By 1932, I felt lucky to still be working at *The Herald*. Unemployment in Australia had reached 32%, with more than 60,000 men, women and children dependent on the Government sustenance payment, or 'the susso' as most people called it. It only enabled families to buy the bare minimum of food – just enough to keep alive.

I read in the *Melbourne Daily Telegraph* newspaper, on the 21st September 1932, that Miss Wiseman had just celebrated her 86th birthday. I knew her daughter, Emmie, would be right by her side.

And then, as I had expected and feared, I read that Miss Fanny Wiseman had died on 25th April 1933. She had still been living in the Ivy Grange Rest Home on Princess Street, Kew, Melbourne, where I had visited her five and a half years ago. She was buried at the new Melbourne General Cemetery at Fawkner. The newspaper said the chief mourners were her daughter Emmie and her husband John

Lawrence Lewis, and John Arnold Lewis, grandson of the deceased.

She left behind seven children, 19 grandchildren and 12 great-grandchildren.

I often thought of Miss Fanny Wiseman when I attended the opening night of a Melbourne play. The theatre business had given her so much, and in return, she had given all of herself.

Rest well, Miss Frances Jane Wiseman.

You will not be forgotten.

Author's note

Miss Fanny Wiseman is my great-great-grandmother-in-law. I was first 'introduced' to her when my husband took me to visit his grandmother, Frances Ausmar Cameron (née South), whom we affectionately called Grandy.

Grandy had photographs of her grandmother, Fanny Wiseman, proudly hanging on her walls, along with all the other members of the family.

The photos of Fanny Wiseman showed her in theatrical costume as The Nurse from *Romeo and Juliet*, and the Third Witch from *Macbeth,* two of Shakespeare's most famous plays.

At the time, I only had a passing interest in this family member, who looked back at me from the old-style sepia photographs. She had obviously lived a long time ago, but I had no clue at the time how inspirational she was.

My interest in Fanny Wiseman grew over the years, as I started to learn more about her.

Fanny Wiseman had a significant public profile during her lifetime. During the 19th and 20th centuries, her name was well-known, especially by Australian and New Zealand audiences. She was prolific in her acting career, and she travelled regularly and extensively throughout Australia. However, like so many other notable actresses of her time, for example, Rose Edouin, she has not been remembered. Although during my research I was heartened to find a book written by Mimi Colligan, which shone a great deal of light on the life and work of Rose Edouin and her husband, Mr George Benjamin William Lewis.

I started to wonder why the pages of history only mentioned Miss Fanny Wiseman in passing. Sometimes her name appeared in biographies of other theatrical greats, but usually as a footnote. There was minimal information on the main websites, yet I found hundreds of newspaper articles from the Trove (the Australian online library database) that advertised the performances of Miss Fanny Wiseman and The Wiseman Family.

Miss Fanny Wiseman was not rich, nor powerful; she hadn't married into an influential family and hadn't attached herself to influential theatrical companies like The Firm. Having wealth and power *can* put you in the history books even if you weren't talented. But Fanny Wiseman was talented, independent, and uncompromising in her professionalism. She played an influential part in developing the Australian theatre industry.

Her first performance was when she was eight years old. Her last paid performance was when she was 75, and her last appearance on stage was when she was 79 years old.

She was married twice, had 12 children and had the hardest role in life, that of balancing the responsibilities of raising a family and working. There is no doubt Fanny Wiseman struggled with this balancing act; how could she not. She was a professional actress who held herself to high standards, *and* she was a loving mother, which she also took pride in.

Fanny was a woman who forged her own future in a male-dominated world. It was a time when women fought for the right to vote and to be treated equally. She held on to her maiden name, which remained her stage name until she died in 1933.

She survived many hardships, travelled the world and forged a career that sustained herself and her family. She gave everything she had to her profession, her audience and her family.

My Aunty-in-law Nicola 'Nicki' Cameron is the family historian. She shared a lot of information about Fanny Wiseman with me. Nicki encouraged me to start writing this book, as did all my family. I think they could see I had become intrigued and needed to tell Fanny Wiseman's story.

Whilst this story is written in the style of historical fiction, it is closely based on Fanny's life, her performances, her travels, her sorrows and joys.

I hope you've enjoyed meeting Miss Fanny Wiseman, a truly remarkable woman.

***

Timeline of events

20 September 1846	Frances Jane Wiseman born in London, England
18 March 1854	The Wiseman family emigrate to Australia and arrive in Melbourne on 16th June 1854
December 1854	Fanny and sister Emily's first appearance onstage in *Cherry and Fairstar,* Queen's Theatre Royal, Melbourne
June 1855	George Selth Coppin opens the Olympic Theatre Fanny and sister Emily appear in the opera *Norma*
7 January 1865	Fanny marries William Thomas King South in New Zealand
November 1866	William Wiseman South born in Ballarat, Victoria
20 July 1867	Fanny and William South travel to Calcutta, India, aboard the *SS Underley*
17 September 1867	Opening night Lewis' Royal Lyceum Theatre, India
Date unknown	Richard South is born
Date unknown	James South is born
Date unknown	Richard South is born (editor's note: Fanny Wiseman's Death Certificate notes two sons with the name Richard South)
7 October 1870	Charles Ernest South born in Umbala, India
18 April 1871	William Wiseman South dies in Ballarat, NSW
4 November 1873	Tom Llewellyn South born in Middlesex, England
13 January 1876	Minnie Frances Alice South born in Liverpool, England
7 October 1876	Fanny and family board the *SS Northumberland* in England
23 November 1876	Fanny and family arrive in Melbourne, Victoria
5 May 1878	Laura Charlotte Ann South born in South Melbourne
8 June 1878	Opening night *Uncle Tom's Cabin,* New Princess Theatre, Melbourne
13 August 1880	Austin Holgate Theodin South born in Ballarat, Victoria
26 April 1881	Emily Louisa Ann Wolloxhall dies in South Australia
August 1882	Sydney Anthony South born in Balmain, NSW
21 June 1884	Mary Lillian 'Lilly' South born in Balmain, NSW
7 January 1885	Fanny and William celebrate 20-year wedding anniversary
10 October 1887	Emily 'Emmie' Elizabeth South born in Balmain, NSW
16 August 1890	Fanny's mother Mary Ann Wiseman dies in New Zealand
1895	Fanny files for divorce from William Thomas King South
14 October 1896	Fanny's father Richard Wiseman dies in New Zealand
5 December 1896	William Thomas King South dies in Melbourne
24 December 1896	Fanny marries Walter St Valentine Lambert in Sydney
1 June 1900	Fanny's brother Richard Wiseman dies in Sydney
20 December 1902	Walter St Valentine Lambert dies in Victoria
6 August 1915	Sydney Anthony South killed in action in Gallipoli, Turkey
25 April 1933	Fanny Wiseman dies in Ivy Grange Rest Home, Kew, Melbourne, Australia

Family tree

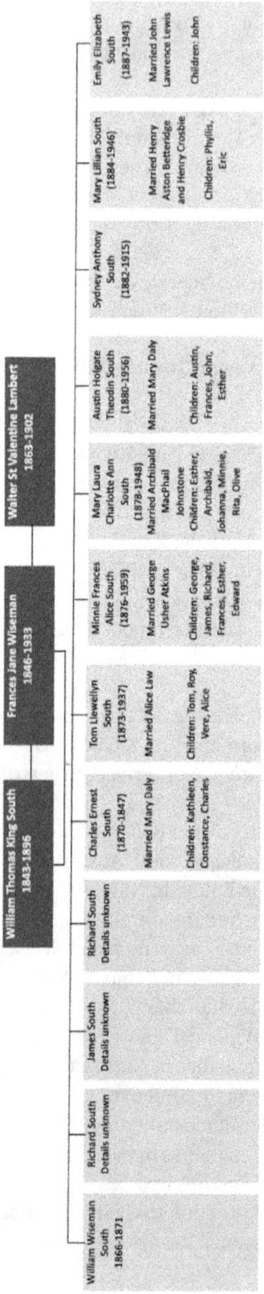
William Thomas King South 1843-1896
Frances Jane Wiseman 1846-1933
Walter St Valentine Lambert 1863-1902
William Wiseman South 1866-1871
Richard South Details unknown
James South Details unknown
Richard South Details unknown
Charles Ernest South (1870-1847)
Married Mary Daly
Children: Kathleen, Constance, Charles
Tom Llewellyn South (1873-1937)
Married Alice Law
Children: Tom, Roy, Vere, Alice
Minnie Frances Alice South (1876-1959)
Married George Usher Atkins
Children: George, James, Richard, Frances, Esther, Edward
Mary Laura Charlotte Ann South (1878-1948)
Married Archibald MacPhail Johnstone
Children: Esther, Archibald, Johanna, Minnie, Rita, Olive
Austin Holgate Theodin South (1880-1956)
Married Mary Daly
Children: Austin, Frances, John, Esther
Sydney Anthony South (1882-1915)
Mary Lillian South (1884-1946)
Married Henry Aston Betteridge and Henry Crosbie
Children: Phyllis, Eric
Emily Elizabeth South (1887-1943)
Married John Lawrence Lewis
Children: John

Photographs

Fanny Wiseman in costume, circa 1860s
Photograph courtesy of Australian Performing Arts Collection, Arts Centre Melbourne.

Fanny Wiseman as The Nurse, *Romeo and Juliet*, circa April 1922[xiii]
Inscription says, 'From your loving mother.'
Photograph courtesy of The Cameron Family Archive.

Endnote

---

[i] *Coppin the Great, Father of Australian Theatre*, Alec Bagot, 1965, page 176

[ii] *Coppin the Great, Father of Australian Theatre*, Alec Bagot, 1965, page 91

[iii] *The Land O' Cakes*, The Advertiser, Adelaide South Australia, Monday 1 December 1913, page 18
https://trove.nla.gov.au/newspaper/article/5388591

[iv] 'Charlie Napier Theatre', The Star, 16 July 1857, page 3
https://trove.nla.gov.au/newspaper/article/66043197?searchTerm=Fanny%20Wiseman

[v] *Charlie Napier Theatre*, The Star, Ballarat, Victoria, Thursday 16 July 1857, page 3
https://trove.nla.gov.au/newspaper/article/66043197?searchTerm=Fanny%20Wiseman

[vi] *Pleasant Memories*, Illustrated Sporting and Dramatic News, Melbourne, 1906 – 1907

[vii] *Circus and Stage, The Theatrical Adventures of Rose Edouin and GBW Lewis*, Mimi Colligan, 2013, page 82

[viii] *Circus and Stage, The Theatrical Adventures of Rose Edouin and GBW Lewis*, Mimi Colligan, 2013, page 86

[ix] *The Englishman*, Calcutta, India, 2 April 1870

[x] *National Archives of Australia*: BP4/1, 66/4/605. Papers regarding Miss Adela Pankhurst and Miss Celia Johns - Women's Peace Army Brisbane Branch, and Anti-Conscription League [Newspaper cuttings regarding meetings of Anti-Conscription League] - [Newspaper 'The Woman Voter', Edition No. 176 dated November 11, 1915] - [contains verse - *I Didn't Raise My Son to be a Soldier]*

[xi] *Allan Wilkie, All the Worlds My Stage,*
https://liveperformance.com.au/hof-profile/allan-wilkie-cbe-1878-1970/

[xii] *The Old Actors' Appeal*, The Herald, 30 March 1922, Page 6
https://trove.nla.gov.au/newspaper/article/243632659?searchTerm=Fanny%20Wiseman%20Romeo%20and%20Juliet

[xiii] *Fanny Wiseman as The Nurse in Romeo and Juliet*, The Argus, 25 February 1922, Page 11 https://trove.nla.gov.au/newspaper/article/4696789?searchTerm=Fanny%20Wiseman%20Romeo%20and%20Juliet

www.ingramcontent.com/pod-product-compliance
Lightning Source LLC
Chambersburg PA
CBHW050918030726
47503CB00007BB/2361
9781763578623